C000138065

Blood on the
Book 1
in the
New World Series
By
Griff Hosker

Blood on the Blade

Published by Sword Books Ltd 2018

Copyright © Griff Hosker First Edition 2018

A CIP catalogue record for this title is available from the British Library.

Cover by Design for Writers

Prologue

My name is Erik. My father was called, by some, Lars the Luckless. It was an ironic nickname. It was not his luck which was bad, it was his temper. However, as his temper normally resulted in dire consequences for him perhaps it was an appropriate name. He never had a bad temper at home. In fact, he was always smiling and cracking jokes. It was when he was with his oar brothers that he lost his temper. We learned this through the words of those close to him. He did not suffer fools gladly. We did not see him that often. More times than enough he would be away, raiding. Sometimes he might be away for a year or more. His arrival home normally coincided with another child which would, inevitably, be born when he was away.

In those days it was my mother, Maeve, who held the family together. We lived on a small farm on Orkneyjar. Orkneyjar was the name we gave to the islands off the Pictish coast. Our home was on the island of Hrólfsey. My uncle, Snorri, and his family had their farm within sight of ours. The Viking after whom the island was named had left long ago. We heard that he had gone to the land of the Saxons. We had a few sheep and a couple of goats. We fished the bay and collected shellfish from the rich waters. When we were old enough, we fished but my tale begins when we had no boat. I grew up with my older brother, Arne. I had no sisters. Many men thought that made Lars lucky. My mother did not think so. When I was little, I wondered if she had named him luckless. Each of those who would have been my sisters had died before they were a month old. She had two boys and both survived. My mother was a Saxon and a Christian. She managed to hide her religion from all for my father had a deep hatred of the White Christ. I know she had a wooden cross but she kept it hidden when my father was at home. She had been a slave. My father had taken her from Hwitebi in the land of Northumbria. She had been taken along with an old Saxon, Edmund. He was our thrall. Now that land was Danish but my father had taken her when he had followed Bacgsecg and Healfdene, the two Viking leaders who had ravaged through Mercia, Wessex and the Saxon kingdoms. He had not been luckless then for he had returned with mail, a wife and a chest of coins. More, he was not there when the Saxons inflicted the final defeat on the Danes and Norse. That was the year he brought my mother to his farm and my brother was born.

He took my mother because she was pretty and also because she was hardy. She fought him. Others who were taken threw themselves from the drekar on the way back to Orkneyjar. My father also brought a slave. He had hamstrung Edmund so that he could not run. He came from the same village as my mother and they knew each other. Edmund was much older than my mother. His wife had been taken by another Viking who lived on Bjarnarøy. Edmund was a Christian. He prayed openly that he and his wife would be reunited. If my father caught him doing so then he would beat him. Luckily for Edmund my father was away more than he was at home.

Our nearest neighbours were my uncle's family. Snorri Long Fingers was my father's younger brother. His wife, Gytha, was Norse. She was a volva and they had two children: Helga, and Siggi. We all lived on the north of the island. It was not a safe beach and scavenging for shellfish was a hazardous experience. The two families would join together to do so. My uncle and my father got on well and so there was never a dispute over ownership of animals. Even so, they kept their homes a good thousand paces from each other. The brothers were oar brothers. They spent every day at sea sharing an oar. It was natural that when they came home, they would wish to spend the time with their families.

When I was born my father and his brother were at their most successful. They had returned with the other warriors from Orkneyjar. All of them had so much treasure that he spent a whole year at home. I was a babe and knew nothing at the time but when I was older I was told this.

I was barely four summers old when I had my first adventure on the sea. It was rather in the sea than on it. My brother, Arne, and I had been sent by my mother to collect shellfish. Although dangerous it was how Viking boys learned to face and overcome adversity. I soon bored of it especially when I found a broken piece of wood in the rock pool. It was from a ship. The waters to the north and west of us were empty. Ships sailed there but, in the winter, there was ice which took many ships. We were used to finding wood. This one was slightly different. It looked to be from the keel of a ship. It had been in the water a long time. I turned it over in the water and saw something carved upon it. It was a name written in runes.

ᛒᛏᚱᛁᚱ

I did not know the name but I felt a shiver down my spine. This was the name of the man who had built the ship. My father longed for a ship. We had the keel of one, the snekke we were building, on the beach but it was a skeleton only. A snekke was the smallest warship our people used. My father and his brother Snorri had carved their names in the keel. None of their runes looked like these. I ran my fingers over the letters. They had been well carved. The builder had taken time over them and now his ship was sunk. The wood still floated. I had a sudden thought. I would sail as though I was on a ship. I pulled myself up and sat astride the piece of wreckage. In those days I was small. It was later that I grew. I used my hands to paddle and kicked with my feet. I felt the wind in my face. I moved easily yet I could feel the water tugging at my feet; the tide was ebbing. I played with the wreckage. I used my hands and feet to turn it. I let the tide pull me out and then the wind push me back. I was not afraid of the sea. Arne and I could swim. I had dived to the bottom to collect stones for my sling. Then I heard Arne as he shouted me. His words made me start and a wave, or perhaps the Norns, threw me into the water. I did not panic. The beach was just thirty paces from me. As I broke the surface, I saw the wood drifting out to sea. It was heading west beyond the seas sailed by men. It was going towards the unknown. Arne's voice called me back. Reluctantly I swam. The wood had been sent for a reason. The threads of the shipbuilder and of me had touched and now they were joined. The Norns had spun. That moment drew me to the sea and what lay beyond the horizon.

My father spent his time ashore making a better shield and building a snekke. He did not farm! A snekke was a mixture of a drekar and a knarr. It was as long as a knarr but narrower and could not accommodate as much cargo. It was like a drekar, fast and used oars. Unlike a drekar it did not have a high prow. If a snekke met a drekar then its only hope was flight.

My father and his brother thought to go trading and raiding. A snekke would allow them to do that with a small crew. Most snekke could be crewed by just a handful of men. I was much bigger by the time they had finished it. They raided a few more times but each time that my father returned he was unhappier with the leadership of the clan.

When I was old enough to help around the farm and fish with my brother the Jarl, Eystein Rognvaldson, called upon the men of the island for a raid. This was not a raid for treasure. They were heading to the mainland to make war on the Picts. Some Picts had raided one of the smaller islands and stolen sheep and cattle. Their King, Óengusa mac Eóganan, had refused to hand over those who had stolen the animals and the raid was to punish them. My father was less than happy to go. As he told us before he left, there was little treasure to be had from such poor people. Nor did he believe that the raid would deter the Picts. But he was a loyal member of the clan and he obeyed the jarl. That was when the name, Luckless, began to be applied to him. That was when he became more bad tempered on the raid than he had been. We learned this, not from my father, but from his brother. He was away for half a year and when he returned, that was when I grew up.

Chapter 1

When I had seen more than twelve summers my father took me and Arne with him on a raid. Siggi, my cousin, was just four moons older than I was and he would be going on his first raid too. We had lost another baby girl the previous year and my mother was with child again. My cousin Helga came to stay with her while we raided. Gytha was a volva and she could manage without her daughter. My mother needed help. I knew that Edmund would protect her but Helga was a girl. As my mother was with child again, it made sense.

At the time I did not care. I was young and become used to baby sisters dying young. I hoped that this one would be a boy. Selfishly I thought of myself; I was going on a raid. To a Viking boy that was all that was important. Now that I am older I see the world differently. Then I looked at it through a boy's eyes. I would tread the deck of a drekar. *'Moon Dragon'* was the warship of Eystein Rognvaldson. My father had described her to me. She had fifteen oars on each side and her prow had a black dragon head. The teeth were painted alternately red and white. The carver had made them look as though they were snapping. I could not wait to see her and I was excited to be sailing on such a fine ship.

It was as we neared the ship that my father began to change. The jokes he had cracked as we tramped to Westerness where we would join the jarl stopped and his face showed a frown rather than a smile. It was later I knew why. He did not like to serve the jarl. He did not respect the jarl. We spied the mast as we crested the rise. He and his brother laid the chest they were carrying on the ground. He turned to Arne and me, "Now, you two, you must not let me down. I have no time to watch over you pair. I do not want the jarl or any of the other warriors complaining about you. Neither your uncle nor I have any time to wipe your nose. This is your first step on your journey to becoming a warrior. You sleep on the deck and you will eat when we have been fed. The ship master will be the one who tells you what to do! There will be other boys aboard and they will have sailed before. If you wish to ask questions, then ask them."

The three of us looked at each other. Arne said, "Where do we raid? The land of the Picts?"

Snorri stroked Arne's head with his famously long fingers, "The Picts have nothing worth stealing. We sail to raid the Walhaz. They are the people who live close to Mercia. The Mercians have lost much to the Walhaz. I know not why for the Walhaz do not wear mail and their weapons are poor. It is only their arrows we fear and your father and I wear mail. We will be safe and when we raid them then we will be rich!" I saw my father nodding. "You need to watch and learn for when you are older, we shall have our own ship and then we will be as rich as the jarl!"

"Richer, for we are better warriors."

Snorri shook his head, "Brother, it is saying things like that which gets you into trouble. We have had to be farmers because you insulted the jarl last time we raided."

"A warrior must speak what is on his mind. If he did not like it then he could have challenged me."

"And he would have lost. There are none who can best you. The clan all know that you are the best warrior." He shook his head, "Come we have a ship to board and you are filling the boys' heads. They will need all of their wits about them if they are to survive. This will not be an easy voyage."

"You are right we have talked enough. Pick up the chest and let us board."

There was a jetty which led from the land to the drekar. I saw other men from the island as they carried their chests down the jetty to the drekar. Most carried them singly. My father and his brother had a larger chest than most and it contained all that they owned. They were close. There were other warriors with whom they would share the title oar brothers but Snorri and Lars were closer than any oar brother. They were brothers of the blood. All that we three had we carried on our backs. Apart from the kyrtle and breeks we wore we had a seal skin cape, a blanket, a sling, a bone knife tucked into a leather belt, a carved wooden bowl, a horn for beer and Thor's hammer also carved in wood and tied by a thong around our neck. Arne had spoken to other boys who had sailed on drekar and he was confident that we would come back with more than we left. We hoped for a dagger or a seax at the very least. The next time we sailed we would not have so little and we would also be bigger.

As we wound down the path to the sea I wondered at my uncle's comments. My father was a warrior, I knew that already, but I did not know he was such a good one. He never spoke of his raids. Mother and Edmund were also tight lipped about my father. I was excited that I would see my father fight and I would judge for myself.

The two brothers were bareheaded, their helmets were with their war gear in the chest. Their swords and short mail byrnie were also with their war gear. They carried their shields upon their backs and had their daggers in their belts. They both had sealskin boots and capes. There might be few trees on our island but there were seals aplenty. Their leather jerkins were studded with metal. My uncle had told me that they were arrows which had been used by our enemies. After a battle or a raid nothing was wasted. I thought it was clever to use something which might have wounded a warrior to protect himself in the future. I would have to wait until I was a warrior before I could have my own shield.

As we neared the jetty, I was able to study the other warriors who were boarding the drekar. My uncle and father looked bigger than they did. It looked to me as though everyone had done as my father and uncle had done. Their war gear was in their chests. According to my father, we had up to twenty days of sailing before their war gear would be needed. The sea could be cruel to swords, mail and helmets. They would be wrapped in grease and sheepskins. Men might have to endure the elements but not their weapons.

I saw that we would be almost the last to board. I had never met the jarl but I knew who he would be. He was the warrior greeting the crew as they came aboard. He had plaited hair, beard and moustaches. He had warrior bands about his arms and neck. My father did not hold with such adornments. He believed that a warrior was a fighter. He did not need to pose. The jarl had his sword strapped to his belt. It was a richly adorned belt and the scabbard had a dragon running down it. The chape was its tail and the head looked to be forming the hilt of the sword. Unlike my father and uncle's swords, his had a detailed pommel and there were silvered threads in the grip. His jerkin had regular studs of metal which were in neat lines and I saw, hanging from his neck, a silver Thor's hammer. He wore his helmet. It, too, had greatly detailed engraving upon it. It was a half mask helmet. My father and uncle wore a simple one with a nasal. Finally, his fingers had two rings on each hand. One was a dragon. It was studded with stones. The jarl was rich. I wondered why my father did not wear such things. I was impressed by the jarl.

The smile with which he had greeted the other crew members was replaced by a serious face. "Welcome, Lars and Snorri. You have brought your sons?"

"It is time they learned what it is to be a warrior. This raid will show them. They will serve as ship's boys until they are big enough to row."

The jarl nodded, "You three, go to the steering board. The steersman is Ulf North Star. He will tell you your duties." He looked down at me, I was the smallest. "Can you swim?"

I nodded, "Aye, jarl."

"Good. If you fall from the ship, we do not come back for you. You will have to swim home!"

I was unsure if he was joking and I ran after Arne to speak with the man who would get us where we needed to go. Ulf North Star was the colour of an oak barrel. He looked like one too. I almost giggled but feared a smack for my trouble. A better name would have been Ulf the Barrel. He wore a leather jerkin and had scuffed seal skin boots on his feet. At his waist he had a long, rounded dagger, which looked like a long bodkin needle and a wicked looking seax. He put his hands on his hips. "I have three boys who have been on a voyage with me before. One is my grandson. They know how to make this drekar fly. You three know nothing. The best you can do is to keep out of the way of those who know what they are doing!" He pointed to the mast. "That is where you will be needed. If I shout for the sail to be reefed then you get to the top as soon as you can. You spread out and when my grandson, Olaf Olafsson, tells you then you pull up the sail and secure it. He will show you the knot you use. If I say lower the sail then you do the opposite."

Arne said, "Is that it?"

Ulf smacked him so hard on the side of the head that I thought he would fall over. "Did I tell you to speak?" Holding back the tears Arne shook his head. I bunched my fists. If he hit me, I would hit him back. "Of course not! Olaf will tell you all of your duties but know this, on the last voyage two of the boys who set out with us did not return!" He seemed to take pleasure in that. I did not like the master mariner. "Olaf, here are the boys."

Olaf looked to be older than us. He looked much bigger than we were and I wondered when he would take an oar. He gestured for us to go to the prow. There was a small piece of canvas rigged over it. When we got there, he said, "This is your home. The little time you have for rest you will spend here. This is my last voyage on *'Moon Dragon'* as a ship's boy. I take an oar next time we raid. You will be the last boys I train."

I looked up at him. He had a seax in his belt. His leather jerkin was well made. He wore no boots but his breeks were made from sealskin. I was going to ask him a question and then thought better of it. I would not risk a clip.

He took three pieces of old rope. "These are for you three. Once we are at sea and there is time, I will show you how to tie ropes. The knots we use each have a purpose. I will tell you the purpose. Leif Ragnarson and Karl the Climber are the other boys. They will also tell you what to do. Most of the time you three will take ale and food to the men at the oars. If it is quiet and you have mastery of knots then you will run lines to catch fish. You will work harder than you have ever worked. If you survive and have done well then the jarl may reward you." He pulled out his seax. "He gave me this after we raided Saxons. He gave me coin too. Now go and climb the stays and see if you can reach the masthead. I would have you sit on the crosspiece."

Siggi said, hesitantly, "Stays?"

Instead of a clip Olaf smiled, "The ropes which secure the mast to the hull. There are four of them. The other way up is to climb the mast but the stays are quicker. Now go. We leave as soon as the last oarsmen are aboard."

We ran to the ropes. There were four of them and I picked one close to my father. I saw him and my uncle watch us as they secured their chest. I grabbed the rope and swung my legs up. It was slippery and salty. This would not be an easy climb. I had an

advantage over my brother and my cousin. I used to climb the
cliffs close to our home and steal seabirds' eggs. I was not afraid of
heights and I was stronger in the arms than Siggi. Even so by the
time I reached half way I was tiring. I had to carry my weight too. I
wondered if it might be easier climbing above the rope. Even
though I was tiring I reached the yard first. After the climb I found
it easy to swing myself up and sit across the spar. I noticed that the
hemp cord which secured the sail was like the bowstring my father
used. I saw the knot. I had used one before. It was secure but it
could be released by a simple pull.

Arne joined me and then Siggi huffed and puffed his way up.
We all grinned. We had succeeded in our first task.

Ulf North Star shouted, "Now get down! We wish to sail!"

I knew there would be a quick way to get down but I chose to
use the safer method. I came down slowly with my feet wrapped
around the rope. Arne just used his hands and Siggi made the
mistake of trying to slide down the rope. He made it half way and
then the burning was so severe that he had to let go and crashed to
the deck. Men laughed. Of the three older ships' boys it was only
Karl who thought it was hilarious. Olaf and Leif looked concerned.
I saw my uncle go to him and help him to his feet. We landed on
the deck and went to him. The palms of his hands were red raw.
His father shook his head, "Watch your cousins! They have more
sense. How is your leg?"

Siggi was more embarrassed than anything else. He shook his
head, "It is fine."

My uncle went to the mast fish to fetch his oar. Olaf shook his
head as he approached, "You did well, Erik Larsson. I have hopes
for you. As for you Siggi Snorrisson I hope your father has another
son for I fear that you will be feeding the fishes. Arne and Erik, get
to the ropes and prepare to untie them. Wait for my grandfather's
command. Untie them and throw them aboard and then leap."

Arne said, "Leap?"

He laughed, "Aye leap, for the oars will be pushing us off."

There were just two ropes securing us. Arne said, "I will take
the bow."

I nodded and went to the steerboard rope. I saw that it was held
by the end which was tucked inside the coils. I took a chance and
began to loosen it.

I heard the jarl shout, "Up oars!" The oars rose.

Then Ulf shouted, "Let loose the ropes!"

In one tug the end came loose and I unwound it as fast as I could. I know not why I did it but I coiled the rope in my hand as I did so. I managed to release it before Arne. I threw the coiled rope aboard and then leapt. The drekar was just a pace away from the jetty. I easily caught the gunwale and I slipped my leg over. I saw my father nod and smile at me. Arne had been just a little slower and the drekar was two paces and more from the jetty. Arne barely made the gunwale and he hung there. Siggi went to him and helped to pull him aboard. No one else helped. I saw then that we would have to help each other if we were to survive our first voyage.

We had no time to even begin to think. Olaf shouted, "Ship's boys to the mast fish."

Meanwhile, the oars were run out and we were pushed out from the land. The jarl held a staff. The top had been carved into a dragon head. He began to stamp on the deck to give the rowers the beat. My father had told me that when they were at sea they would sometimes sing. We began to move.

Olaf pointed to the spar. "We climb up! Siggi and Arne you come with and we will be on the steerboard side. You three take the other."

I took that as a compliment. Karl went to the mast and he began to climb there. He cast a superior look at Siggi. I used the same rope and I hauled myself up. I reached the yard at the same time as Leif who nodded, "You did well!" Karl joined us and just scowled. He did not like me. I saw that poor Siggi was struggling. He had not had time to apply the salve his mother had given him. He had had a poor start and he could not afford another disaster.

Karl was the closest to the mast head. I was in the middle and Leif was over the sea. He saw my look and shrugged, "The sea is softer than the deck!"

Karl laughed, "But as your head is soft and as addled as a bad egg it makes little difference. You will never be Viking warriors!"

I saw the look of horror on poor Siggi's face. When my cousin finally made it to the spar Olaf shouted, "This will be the only time we can do this at our leisure. It will take some time to reach the sea." He pointed to the pennant. It was red. "The wind is from the north and east. The gods favour us. The blót was a good one. When we are nearer to the land of the Walhaz it will be harder for there the winds come from the west."

I was able to look out and saw the largest island, Orkneyjar, to the south and west of us. We were sailing north and west up the channel. I saw the smoke from the many longhouses there. There were few trees now anywhere. Often our raids would be to places where we could get some wood. When our snekke was finished properly and seaworthy then we were going to sail it to the land of the Picts. My father wanted a drekar. It would not be a large one but he wanted to be a leader. He had had enough of following. I knew, from talking to my uncle, that a drekar could move very quickly. We were using oars at the moment but once we reached the sea and turned then we could lower the sail and we would fly. I was enjoying the experience, although as the sail was furled and we were protected by the land there was not as much movement as there might have been. I glanced down and saw that Siggi was clinging to the spar. The burning hands and the crash to the deck had unnerved him.

I saw ahead, the open sea. I took hold of the end of the hemp cord which bound the sail. I had six to untie. I knew that Ulf North Star would be highly critical of us. He would be looking for errors. I saw the jarl as he glanced up. He might have been looking at the pennant but he would have seen us. My father and uncle were just toiling at the oar they shared. We had a big crew. There were sixty men on board. We were stronger because of that but we would need to find a sizeable target to make it worth our while.

Olaf shouted, "Ready to loose the sail."

I looked down and saw that we had almost cleared the land. His grandfather must have given him a signal. Ulf shouted, "Loose sails!" I untied the first cord and quickly did the same to the others. The three of us on my side of the mast were fast for our half of the sail dropped quickly. Siggi, perhaps because of his hands, was a little slower. We moved faster as Ulf put the steering board over and shouted, "In oars!" I could tell that we had disappointed him for he glared up at the sail. Eventually, Siggi managed to untie the last one and the sail filled.

Olaf shouted, "Down quickly!" I saw that he and Leif had pieces of leather. They slipped them over the rope and flew down to the deck. I wondered how they would stop but, amazingly, they slowed and landed perfectly. They both ran to the two fore sheets and began to tighten them.

I landed and ran to the stern sheet on the steerboard side. I pulled on it but I had little effect. Leif ran from the forestay and said, "There is a trick to this." He pointed to a wooden cleat in the gunwale. "Wind it around this and pull." I helped him and found it much easier. We tied it off.

"Thank you!"

He smiled, "You will do but your cousin may struggle."

I saw that Siggi had made the mistake of passing too close to Ulf. He was hit on the back of the head with a piece of knotted rope, "Clumsy lump of crab bait! You are letting down the crew!"

Olaf stood by the mast fish and waved us over. "Come you three, it is knot time. Karl and Leif stand by Ulf."

Leif looked sympathetically at Siggi while Karl laughed. I knew then that Karl and I would come to blows. He might be older than me and a whole head taller but I would fight him!

We worked at the knots until our hands bled. To be fair to Siggi he found that much easier than the rest of the tasks and Olaf was able to praise him. When we had finished Olaf and the other two were sent to tighten and adjust the stays. We were given the job of taking ale and food to the crew. I saw the look of concern on my uncle's face as we neared him. He had a small jug and he said, "Here, Siggi, smear this on your hands."

Siggi nodded and said, quietly, "I am sorry, father, I have let you down."

"You have not, my son. I found it as hard and if it was not for Uncle Lars here, I might have never returned."

My father chuckled, "I sailed with our helmsman as a youth. Ulf North Star was younger then but just as handy with his rope. He learned then that my fists are like Thor's hammer." He smiled at Siggi, "When we have our own drekar this will not be a problem. I will steer!"

As we continued to serve food and ale, I realised I was learning as much about my father as I was myself. He did not like the jarl and he did not like the steersman. They did not like him either. Their looks showed that and Ulf's treatment of us. It was no wonder my father did not get on with either of them. This would be a difficult voyage.

By the time night fell we were exhausted. The jarl did not wish to stop and so we sailed through the night. Each of us took it in turns to stand by Ulf or the jarl at the steering board. Siggi woke me for my turn. There was an hourglass at the stern and a candle in a pot. We each did two turns of the glass.

When I reached the steering board, it was the jarl who was steering. "Go fetch me a horn of ale."

"Aye, jarl!"

I hurried to the barrel of ale which was close to the mast fish and ladled beer into it. I hoped I had it right. Some men like a foamy head and others did not. I handed it to the jarl and he drank. I had not displeased him and I felt some relief. It was a clear night and when he had downed the ale, he handed me the horn and looked up at the stars. He must have realised our course was not true and I saw him adjust it. After a while he turned and said, "So, Erik Larsson, what would you be, a mariner or a warrior?"

"Could I not be both?"

He laughed, "You are just like your father for to be both you have to have your own ship and crew. That is what your father wishes." He shook his head. "You have the blood of a Saxon and Norse. It seems that Norse wins." A strange smile came over him, "You just have to survive this voyage is all. I think, however, that you have more chance of that than your cousin. We will see."

And that was all that he said. I turned the glass when it needed and I watched the black night slip by. There was no feature save the sea. How did the jarl and Ulf navigate? Were they galdramenn? I determined to watch them. My father could tell me things but the jarl and his helmsmen had done this more than my father. I waited until the glass had run out and I had turned it before I went to wake Arne. The three newcomers had been given the most undesirable of watches. I thought I detected a slight smile on the jarl's face as I went to wake my brother. I curled up on the blanket he had left and pulled my own over me. I was so exhausted that I was asleep before Arne had reached the steering board.

Chapter 2

For the next days we followed the same routine. The three of us, as new boys, were run ragged. We passed up and down the drekar as well as up and down the stays. Hands became tougher and muscles grew. What had seemed impossible the first day became acceptable by the third. We also became invisible. It was though we could not be seen save as a hand which filled an ale horn or fetched some salted meat. I kept my eyes and ears open and I learned things. I saw that the jarl had a small band of warriors he kept close to him. These were not his oathsworn, they were men from the islands. Bjorn Bjornson was the closest. They did not like my father and I heard many disparaging comments from them. My father also sat with close friends. They sat forward of the mast and it was obvious that my father was leader. I saw his temper flare as he openly criticised the jarl and his choice of target. My father felt that the Mercians were more likely to yield treasure and grain. He was loud in his criticism and his voice carried down the drekar. The jarl heard. I also learned why none silenced him. He was acknowledged, even by his many enemies, as the best warrior on the drekar. The jarl himself tacitly admitted this when he came to my father and asked him and his oar brothers to be the first to land. Even when my father mocked the jarl's oathsworn the jarl took the criticism. It was then that I understood about my father's dream of a drekar. If he had a drekar then he would not need the jarl.

I asked Olaf, one morning as the wind took us and we had time to chat, how much it cost to build a drekar. "It is not something to be taken lightly. There are some things which any could get." He smiled, "Any who do not live on treeless Orkneyjar. You need good straight timbers for the keel and strakes. Then you need different wood for the decks. You need pine for the mast and spars. The last thing you need is time. It takes months, perhaps years to build a good drekar."

At last I understood. We now had a snekke which was almost ready to launch but it had taken a long time to build. As we sailed south, I grew up. Living on the farm with just my brother and cousin for company I had not had to interact with any. Now I had to endure the bully that was Karl. Not only was he bigger than we were he enjoyed special treatment. His father's friendship with the jarl meant he never had the hard duties. He enjoyed throwing his considerable weight around, sometimes quite literally. He would try to barge into us as we hurried down the decks. I learned to have quick feet and to dance around him. I did not know that it would stand me in good stead when I became a warrior. The Norns were spinning and I was being prepared to be a Viking.

We passed beyond the land of Strathclyde and headed towards the Land of the Wolf. We saw the land of the Hibernians to the west and I noticed that the crew became more agitated. Leif was always the easiest to talk with. Like Olaf he would soon be taking an oar. Karl had another few voyages left. I was not looking forward to the time when Karl was in charge. Perhaps my father would have finished our ship by then.

"Leif, why are the men sharpening weapons? We are not near the land of the Walhaz are we?"

"We are not but you are right. We have many more days before we raid. The men fear the pirates of Mann." He pointed south, "There it is. It is ruled from Dyflin and Veisafjǫrðr. Sometimes there is conflict in those kingdoms and when that happens then the folk who live on that island raid. Thorvald Asvaldsson and his crew were attacked when they passed the island six months since. Some think we should come and make war on them. It may come to that." He patted the seax he wore in his belt. "If we are attacked, I will defend myself but there will be no shame if you and the others hide on the spar."

I was outraged but I could not show it. If we were attacked then I would show them that even though I was young I could still fight. I might only have a sling and a bone knife but I was a Viking!

The wind was still with us and we had had little to do save reef the sail at sunset and loose it at dawn. It was now blowing from the north and east. We could still use the wind. Leif had told me that the wind was turning. The Norns must have been spinning for even as we headed towards the west to take the channel between Mann and Veisafjǫrðr the wind began to weaken. It was still sufficient so that we would not need to use oars but I saw men, my father included, taking out their swords and helmets from their chest. I saw some men touch their hammer of Thor. In those days I saw the sea but I did not understand it. The crew did. They knew what the change in the wind meant.

We could see Mann quite clearly now. It rose from the sea like a cow which was eating grass. The small island to the south was called the calf. I had heard the story. It had seemed charming and innocent but now that I was here it felt, somehow, sinister.

"Erik, you have young eyes, climb up the mast and tell me what you spy."

It was the jarl himself who had asked for me and I ran to the forestay and quickly climbed it. I could now climb with confidence. Even Siggi had managed it but he was still slow. I crawled along the spar and sat with my legs on either side of the mast. I looked to the island and realised that I could see much more from this elevated position. What I had taken to be a green lump rising from the sea could now be seen as having people and buildings. There was a harbour or port of some description for I saw stone and masts.

"I see masts!"

"Are they moving?"

I felt my heart sink. I was about to give my judgement on something. If I got it wrong then it could spell disaster for my oar brothers. That would be viewed as a comment on my character. My father was Lars the Luckless. I did not want to be Erik the Unlucky. With a nickname like that no one would sail with me.

"They are not moving yet!"

"Good. Shout if anything changes."

Ulf was trying to keep us out to sea but the wind, slight though it was had the effect of pushing us towards the land. The masts remained still. The spars had reefed sails. If they came out, they would be oared. I could not determine the size of the ships. I had seen few. How big was big? We drew closer and I stared intently at the island. I could now see houses dotted on the hillside below the mountain. There was also a hall. It looked to be above the quay. The ships were now clearer. They did not look to be as big as ours. Just then I heard from below, "Oars!"

I saw why. The wind was taking us even closer to the coast and Ulf wanted some sea room. I saw a movement in the harbour. A mast moved but I saw no ship's boys to unfurl it. "Ship leaving port!" Below me, the oars had begun to bite. I risked standing on the spar. I suddenly saw into the harbour. The ship which was leaving was a small drekar. I put her to be a threttanessa, thirteen oars on each side. "It is a threttanessa!" I saw other masts move and spied two smaller ships, they were large snekke, and they were leaving too. "Two snekke coming too!"

Jarl Eystein Rognvaldson shouted, "Olaf, get the boys on the mast! Take your bows!"

I had no bow but I did have my sling. Sitting, I took it from my pouch. I had twenty stones there too. Arne and I had tried to bring down a gull two days since. We had hit two but the fish had been the ones to benefit. I chose a good stone and fitted it.

Leif climbed first. He had a bow over his back and some arrows jammed into his belt. "Olaf will stay by his grandfather. You did well Erik." He stood and shouted, "A third snekke putting out!" He grinned at me, "Four ships for us to face on your first voyage. The gods have you marked!" Karl clambered up and he had a sling as did Arne and Siggi when they joined us. Leif said, "Siggi, come here to the mast. It is safer!"

Karl snarled, "He is of no use to this crew! Better to have brought his sister! At least we could have some use out of her!" My cousin Helga was considered beautiful. She was my cousin and I did not see her like that. To me, she was just someone friendly who made me laugh.

Before Leif could say anything, I said, "Do not insult my cousins Karl the Climber or you and I will have words!"

He pointed his finger at me, "Anytime!"

Leif shouted, "Silence! Siggi, come here. Erik, go to the end!"

I concentrated on moving along the spar. We were moving quite quickly now and the motion on the yard was extreme. I was grateful that Leif had allowed Siggi the chance to sit astride the mast. I saw that Ulf had managed to pull away from the coast but we were now sailing into the wind. There was little point in furling the sail for once we cleared the Calf then he could put the steering board over and lose these four terriers which would soon be snapping at our heels. They had men at the oars but the four were smaller and lighter than we were. We were carrying a month's supplies on board. I wondered if they would catch us.

I heard a shout from below but could not make it out. However, when half of the crew stood, I worked out what it was. The jarl was preparing for the men to fight. He chose my father and his oar brothers for the task. My father donned his helmet and took his shield from the steerboard side. Leif pulled back on his bow and an arrow arced. It was a ranging arrow. It landed just a few paces before the drekar. The three snekke were now spreading out to encircle us. The drekar would stop us while the snekke looked for a weakness at the steering board. Olaf would be in danger. He had neither helmet nor mail. I had been given no orders to use my sling but, as I had but twenty stones, I would need to be judicious.

Leif's second arrow hit a rower on the drekar. They were not wearing mail and his plunging arrow went into his shoulder. As the man slumped his oar caught the two behind. With three oars out of commission, the drekar began to slew around. I took a chance and hurled my first stone. I was helped by the height of the spar. My stone hit one of the rowers at the front of the drekar. He had a helmet but a stone could still hurt. I saw his head jerk forward. "Well done, Erik. The rest of you, aim at the drekar!" Leif only had ten arrows. When he had used them, he would have to use his sling.

We could not see what was happening astern. The drekar's slewed turn meant that she was just thirty paces from the larboard side of our ship. I saw men whirling grappling hooks. I threw my second stone. It hit one of those with hooks in the chest and he fell backwards, throwing the rowers into disarray. It was Siggi who sent the stone which thwarted the drekar. He hit the helmsman. The man had no helmet and the stone hit him hard on the cheek. The man let go of the steering board and the gap between us grew. As it did, I saw that we were almost abreast of the Calf. I threw stone after stone into the drekar. An arrow was sent from the drekar at us. It struck the spar. Leif leaned over and worked it free. He nocked it and sent it back at the drekar.

Ulf put the steering board over and we sailed dangerously close to the drekar. "In oars!" We now had the wind. The oars were shipped just a heartbeat before we passed the prow of the drekar. I had thought that we had succeeded for as I sent another stone towards the steering board of the drekar I saw that many of the crew had been hit by stones, arrows and oars! We had to turn to continue our assault and as we did so I saw that two of the snekke were within a length of us. They were gaining. By the time I had turned, the jarl had split the crew in two. I saw that my father and his brother were on the landward side. They stood together. The jarl and his hearth weru were on the steerboard side. The crews of the snekke were brave. They were trying to slow us down until the others could come and join them. I hurled a stone and was rewarded when it hit the warrior who was standing at the prow and holding on to the forestay. I hit his chest and he wore no mail. As he fell I thought, for a moment, that he would fall into the sea but he managed to hold on. He had to drop to one knee. I had hurt him. Our stones and Leif's arrows clattered into the snekke but they had learned and a wall of shields stopped any more injuries. From the two boats, four grappling hooks were hurled. They bit and even though men tried to cut them the damage had been done. The first warriors leapt aboard. Olaf, who was stood by his grandfather, took a hatchet and began to cut through the ropes binding the snekke to the drekar. A warrior stood on the prow of his ship and raised his spear. Without mail and a helmet, Olaf would die. This time my stone hit him perfectly. He had his arm pulled back and my stone hit him on the side of the head. He could not keep his balance and he fell into the sea. As he did so Olaf severed the second grappling hook and the snekke lost way.

The jarl led his men to go to the aid of my father. On the yard, we sent our last arrows and stones at those trying to leap the gap. When my father and the jarl slew the two men who had boarded, my uncle severed the ropes and the snekke had lost any chance of capturing us. I heard a cheer from below.

Leif said, "We did well, let us go down. Siggi, you have the place of honour. Your stone was the one that truly saved us."

By the time I reached the deck the snekke and the drekar were heading back to port. Olaf greeted us. He was our leader. "Siggi, all of your clumsiness is forgiven and Erik, I owe you a life."

I did not know what to say. My father strode up and picked Arne and me up, "My two little fighting cocks! You showed them all! My blood is the blood of a warrior!" He glowered and glared at the jarl. The jarl and Bjorn turned and headed towards the steering board. He had been insulted by my father. It seemed to diminish both our efforts and the victory.

Ulf shouted, "Ship's boys, serve ale and food."

I saw Leif talking to Olaf. Olaf nodded and said, "Karl, go and be lookout!" Giving me murderous looks Karl grabbed some stale bread and an ale skin. As he passed Siggi he deliberately lurched against him and knocked him into the mast fish. Siggi's head hit it hard. He laughed at Siggi and clambered up the backstay.

Olaf came over to me. "Karl can be dangerous. It does not do to antagonise him."

"I know you worry about me but if he hurts my family then, no matter how big he is, I will fight him."

"And you will lose."

I shrugged, "Perhaps but he will know that he has fought." I looked up at the mast and Karl's back. "Do you hear me Karl the Climber! Leave my family alone!"

Olaf laughed and shook his head, "You are your father's son. He does not back down either."

With the wind with us once more we sailed, a little more slowly, south. Once we had passed the island the Saxons called Anglesey the jarl decided to put in at a beach. He and Ulf had endured watch and watch about since we had left home. They knew of deserted beaches which could not be accessed from the land. He found one of those. We reefed the sail and we went in under oars. To me, this was all new. My father and uncle knew the beach. I thought it was a foreign land. As I stood by the prow, with the rope ready to secure us to the land, I tried to make sense of the water beneath our hull, the rocks which made white flurries. I looked at the size and shape of the sand and shingle. One day my father would captain his own ship and I would help him to steer. I needed as much knowledge as I could get. I spied what I thought was a flat rock as Olaf shouted, "Rocks!" The oarsmen backed water and I leapt in. I had been right, it had been a rock which was flat and allowed me to land relatively safely. However, the water came up, almost to my neck. Uncoiling the rope, I forced my way through the foaming water until I felt sand beneath my feet. I had spied a rock which looked big enough to hold us and I ran to it and put four or five turns around it. I raised my hand. Leif and Arne had followed me and they had secured the drekar. We were on dry land for the first time in a long time.

Karl had had the easier task of sitting on top of the mast and had not had to risk the rocks and the sea but he felt he had been punished and he blamed the three new boys. As he climbed down, he stared at us and he drew his finger across his throat. I thought it a dramatic gesture for he would not actually kill any of us. He just wanted to hurt us and show us that he was superior to us. Olaf led and Leif was his second. Until we had come aboard then Karl had been the dogsbody. He was making us miserable to give himself power.

The ship's boys were given the task of collecting shellfish for our meal. A fire had been lit and a pot filled with sea water. It would season the stew and save our precious salt. I went with my cousin and brother to the rock pools. Arne was older than I was and as we collected the shrimps and small crabs he said, "You are not Siggi's keeper, Erik, nor mine. We will fight our own battles."

I shook my head, "You are the elder but you are wrong. Together we are stronger. If Karl thinks he can pick us off one by one he will do but if he has to worry about his back, he may be warier."

"Or he may slip his knife in your back while you sleep."

I had not thought of that. Karl struck me as the sort who would do that. We had been told to bring plenty of shellfish back and the wooden pail was but half full. I was so determined to impress the jarl and the others that I did not notice that Arne and Siggi were no longer near me; nor were Olaf and Leif. I had wandered around beyond sight of the camp for I spied mussels handing down some weed. Mussels were highly prized and good eating. It was getting dark and I was alone. I was fortunate that I had my bone knife in my hand. I cut the mussels free and put them on the rock. I began prising limpets from the rock. I did not want to break my knife and I was concentrating hard. I worked my blade all the way around the shellfish to break the seal and used my left hand to ease the animal from the rock. I had six already. I also had a sea urchin. I knew that they were dangerous but there were parts on them that were delicious. I had managed to take the urchin without being stung.

Karl had a pungent aroma and I smelled him before I saw him. Even so he was quick and he grabbed my head with his two arms and began to squeeze my neck. "Your white dead body will be found floating in the morning. They will assume that you were as clumsy as your cousin. None will mourn you and you will join the gulls screeching in the sky!" He began to force my head towards the water. The waves splashed me in the face as I fought him. He was stronger than I was and, inevitably, he would win. I had my knife in my right hand but it was not sharp enough to cut through his breeks. I had to cut flesh. Instead of pushing back I leapt forward. He was taken by surprise and we both fell into the sea. The pool was deep. I had been expecting to be dunked and I was ready. He was not although he kept hold of my neck and continued his pressure. As the sea pushed and pulled us against the rocks and weed, I let my arms relax to make him think I had drowned. I held my breath and lay still. He relaxed his grip a little. I felt his right leg come close to my hand. I rammed my bone knife into the soft flesh behind his ankle bone. There are tendons there. He kicked hard with his good foot and my bone knife sank to the sea bed. Even below the water I heard his roar. His mouth filled with sea water and he let go of me. I kicked my legs and burst to the surface. I kicked towards the beach and began pulling Karl towards safety. I was hauling him on to the beach when I saw Leif and Olaf running towards us. They had heard Karl's cry.

Karl was still screaming as I dragged myself up. "Are you hurt?"

I shook my head, "I am not sure if Karl's foot struck a sea urchin or a rock. He looks in pain."

As Olaf dragged him from the water, he coughed and spluttered. He retched sea water. I managed to slip the dagger from Karl's belt. He was in too much pain to notice. My bone knife had ripped a jagged hole in his ankle. It was bleeding heavily. "Leif, help me carry him back to the drekar. He is hurt!" He turned to me, "Erik, bring the shellfish."

Arne and Siggi arrived. Arne said, "Where is your knife and why are you soaked?" I told them as we collected up the shellfish. "Then this will be a blood feud."

"Perhaps, perhaps not. I hurt him and I have this." I held his knife. "He will think he lost it beneath the water."

"But, cousin, if he tells the jarl…"

Arne shook his head, "Erik is right. Karl dare not do that. He will lose face and have to admit that he tried to kill Erik. But we all need to watch out for each other. We swear an oath. We will be brothers in blood." He took Karl's knife and made a cut in his palm. He handed it to me. I did the same. Finally, Siggi did it too. Arne and I held palms together, then Arne and Siggi and finally Siggi and me. "We swear to protect each other!" We both nodded.

I took back the knife. There was blood on the blade. I wiped it clean by sinking it into the sand. "This is an omen. Our lives are tied together from this day forth."

As we neared the fire Leif approached. "The rock has torn the tendon at the back of his leg. He will no longer be Karl the Climber, he will be Karl the Lame." He patted me on the back. "Had you not pulled him from the sea he might have been Karl the Dead! I do not think he will thank you. That is not his way." He took the pail of shellfish. "Come we will put this in the stew."

When we reached the fire, Karl was being tended to by his father. Bjorn Bjornson had just one son and his wife had died in childbirth. The result was that they did not farm themselves. They had two slaves who ran their farm for them and they took ship whenever they could. They lived on Orkneyjar close to the jarl. It was said that Bjorn wished to be the jarl of an island. Bjorn Bjornson raided more than most men and that explained why his son had such a fine dagger. Now secreted in the pail of shellfish I had to find somewhere to hide it.

The jarl was watching Bjorn as he sealed the wound in Karl's foot with a hot brand. He said to my father, "There is more to your son than a man would think. It appears he has saved Karl's life."

My father looked up from the bone he was carving, "Then he is a fool. Karl would have left him in a heartbeat." It was almost as though I wasn't there the way my father spoke. "If he thought to heal the rift then he was wrong." He shrugged, "It is his first voyage. He will learn that you do not help your enemies." His words told me much.

We carried on to the pot which bubbled on the fire. Salted meat and fish would be at the heart of it. Some seaweed was already in and soon would disappear leaving the stew gelatinous. The three of us began to drop the shellfish in the pot. The cook, Garðkell, was one of the oldest warriors on board. Leif had said he could still stand in a shield wall but he had no family. He liked to cook. He was talking with Ulf North Star and they did not see me slip the knife from the pail and into my breeks. I pulled my kirtle down to cover the shape. In the dark none would see the bulge but I had to get back aboard. I said, loudly, "This is a good beach for stones. I will collect some now and put them on the drekar. We may need them."

Garðkell was heading back to the fire, "You will be a good warrior, Erik, for you plan! Go, collect your stones. I will save some choice pieces for you. You have earned them and need fattening up."

Arne smiled, "Aye brother and when you go back to the drekar, fetch our bowls."

I was less than diligent when I picked the stones. I just needed ones of the right size and a quantity of them. Eyeball sized ones were best and the rounder the better. I carried them in the pail. We had a gangplank which led from the beach to the prow and I heaved the pail of stones. There was no one aboard. The three of us had the larboard side of the prow. Our blankets lay there. I slipped the knife from my breeks and pushed it as close to the strakes as I could get. I would not be able to leave it there for long as it was damp but it was hidden. I rammed the blankets against it and left the pail of stones there. Picking up the bowls and horns I hurried back to the beach.

The shellfish had not taken long to cook and by the time I returned the men were lining up. There was a hierarchy to the feeding. The jarl and Ulf were first followed by the hearth weru. I saw that Bjorn was behind the jarl and his men. Then my father and his brother. That told me much. As the three newest members we were at the back of the line. We would receive whatever was left! Karl was not in the line. He lay by the fire. He gave me a curious look as I passed. He was wondering why I had not spoken of the attempt on my life. Olaf shook his head, "Not even a thanks for a life. When you take over the ship's boys, Leif Ragnarson, you will have to watch that one. He has a bad seed in him."

"His father is a good warrior. Perhaps he will be one, too."

Shaking his head Olaf said, "I fear that Ran, god of the sea, has determined otherwise. He can stand and fight in a shield wall but how can he run?"

I touched my hammer of Thor. What had I done? I looked back at Karl. This had not been my doing. This had been the sisters. If he had not tried to hurt me, kill me even, then I would not have fought so hard and he would not be lame. I knew that our threads were bound together. The blood brothers and Karl were intertwined in some way. The spinning of their web would stretch into the future and across the sea. *Wyrd.*

Chapter 3

Karl's foot did not improve over the next few days and he was given the task of sitting by Ulf and either fishing or fetching and carrying for the helmsman. The five of us had an increased work load but we did not mind. We all managed to get on better without his abrasiveness. Even Siggi was less clumsy. More importantly, my knife remained hidden. Each night I took it from its hiding place and after drying it and cleaning it slept with it beneath my body. I needed a scabbard but that would have to wait.

It took another six days before we reached the river we would use to raid. This was the Sabrina. On one coast lay the Kingdom of Wessex and on the other the Kingdom of Gwent. We would raid Gwent. We ran out a sea anchor when we arrived at noon and we waited below the horizon. Olaf explained that the river had a powerful current. We had to time our arrival for the incoming tide and the hours of darkness. The Walhaz had watch towers. Our men would still have to climb a palisade but that would be easier under cover of darkness. The Walhaz had good archers. We respected them. I knew that when I returned home, I would be ready for my first bow. When Arne and I both had one we would practise. The hunting of birds would give us the skill to kill men.

As we waited in the estuary with our dragon prow facing upstream the men prepared. I saw that only four men had mail. The jarl, Bjorn Bjornson, my uncle and my father. Only the jarl had a full byrnie. The other three wore a short one which covered their chest and back. Their arms were unprotected as were their hips and legs. I saw some men applying cochineal and charcoal to their eyes and faces. My father and uncle did not. Only the jarl had a mask on his helmet. The rest had conical ones or round ones. My father and uncle had added their nasals themselves. My uncle had explained why before we left our home, "A one eyed warrior is at a disadvantage and a nasal can block the blow which would take out the eye and it saves the nose when you head butt an enemy. When we have the coin your father and I will have a mask like the jarl for they are even better." There was but one weaponsmith on our island and that meant that he could charge whatever he wished. He was the richest man apart from the jarl. It was why my uncle and father had adapted their helmets themselves. Every Viking warrior could work metal. The nasals were crude but effective.

The ship's boys had little to do until we moved off. The sail was furled and all that we would need to do would be to jump ashore and hold the drekar against the bank.

"Oars!" The sound of the jarl's voice prompted all of us into action. We ran to the centre of the ship and waited. Olaf would be at the prow looking for the land. It was too dark to use anyone on the mast. There were just four of us for Karl was still incapacitated. The rowers rowed silently. We had not needed a chant and now was not the right time. We were invisible but a chant would identify us as Vikings. The jarl stood with Olaf. He had his helmet in his hand and he sniffed the air. I now knew why. He was smelling for smoke and the smell of animals. Both would identify settlements. We knew which one we sought. We did not know its name but we did not need to. We would not be going there to speak with the people. We would just take their treasure and enslave their women. Traders had told us where it was. The King did not live here but there was a lord who ruled the area. He lived inland from the small settlement. The church there was one of many. It was a community of men. They were rich men for they had good candlesticks, holy books and fine linen. They also ate well. However, as my uncle warned, we did not know how many warriors would be there. If there were many then we might lose men. If we had to row home then that would be a problem. It was all in the hands of the Norns. They spun and trapped men in their spells.

I sniffed and I could smell wood smoke but I could see no lights nor could I see the shore. There was no foam breaking upon it. We were in an estuary. Olaf had told me that the estuary was as wide as the channel between Orkneyjar and the mainland. I saw Olaf wave and Ulf said, "Larboard oars in. Ship's boys, to the side."

We had to move quickly. I ran to the mast fish and tied one end of the rope around the lower support. Olaf, at the bow, would have to use a thwart as would Leif at the steering board. I wrapped the coils diagonally around my body and pulled myself up onto the gunwale and held on to the stay. I could now see the thin line of white which marked the shore. This was a river. The bank would be more likely to be mud than shingle or sand. Now that the larboard oars had been run in Ulf North Star was using the steering board to counteract the effect of the steerboard oars. We crabbed our way to the shore. The smell of smoke was stronger now and I detected the smell of both human and animal dung. There was a settlement close by.

Olaf whistled to get our attention and we all turned to look at him. He would leap and we would follow. All that we had to do was to find something to hold the drekar while the warriors leapt ashore. Then we would rejoin the drekar and turn it. Leif and Olaf, as the two biggest, would have to scull against the river. I saw a tree ahead of me. I had something to secure the drekar just so long as I could outrun Siggi and Arne. I saw Olaf leap and I was just behind him. I landed in the water and it was still deep and so I swam. It was easier. As I came up when the river was up to my knees and I saw that Arne and Siggi had struggled in the mud. I was glad that I was bare footed. Had I worn boots they would have been sucked off. I reached the tree and wrapped the rope around it. I went back to the river. The water washed the mud from me and I handed the end of the rope to my uncle. He and his shield brothers pulled. As soon as Olaf handed his rope to the jarl the drekar began to close with the bank. The warriors would not have to land in the mud. They could leap to dry ground.

The drekar was disembarked so quickly that it astounded me. Soon it was just Ulf and we, the ship's boys, who were left. We coiled the ropes and clambered aboard. Olaf and Leif were at the sweeps. Ulf North Star shouted, "Karl, you are an apology of a ship's boy but you are a sizeable lump. Go help Olaf. Arne, you help him too. Erik and Siggi help Leif."

Olaf and his helpers pushed the larboard side from the shore. Leif put the oar in the river and said, "Now push. We use a double steerboard." With Ulf pushing on the steering board and Olaf sculling, we turned.

Ulf seemed satisfied, "Now back water! The tide will turn before dawn. We have to save the warriors a walk."

31

It was hard work and we seemed to make little progress but when I saw my tree again, I knew we had returned to the mooring site.

"Arne, Siggi and Erik secure us tightly to the bank. Use a good knot but one you can slip if there is trouble." This time it was easier as the tide was still coming in and we were closer to the bank. I tied the rope and made sure that there was an end for me to pull. We used just three lines. "Now run out the gangplanks. There will be captives."

By the time we had done all that I was exhausted. Olaf and Leif grinned and Olaf said, "We deserve a reward, grandfather."

"Aye you do. Horns of ale for all of us! Even the lump of lard that is Karl."

"I am wounded, Ulf North Star!"

"No, you are not! You cut yourself on a rock and you are milking the wound for all that it is worth. You make the limp more exaggerated when the jarl is watching! I know you! Give him half a horn. I do not like his attitude."

As we drank the ale and chatted, I felt good. Karl would not sail with us again, not as a ship's boy at least. My life and those of my blood brothers would be safer. I had always thought I would like the life on a drekar and now I knew it for certain.

Suddenly we heard a cry and then the sound of a church bell. There was a roar upriver and then a clash of steel. Ulf nodded and hung his empty horn from around his neck. "Arm yourselves, spread yourselves out and watch for enemies. We have to defend the drekar until the jarl and our men return."

We all had more stones but I had no knife. I wondered about retrieving my hidden weapon and then changed my mind. Karl would recognise it. I needed to change the handle before I dared wear it. I picked a good stone and sat on the mast fish. I was elevated and could see further than those lower down. There were seven pairs of eyes watching the shore although I was unsure whence would come our enemies. The sounds of fighting reached a crescendo and then there was a cheer. We could not tell who cheered. It was unlikely but our men could have lost. If they had then I would expect them back soon. No one came and I saw, in the east, dawn begin to break.

I had just turned my head when I saw a movement to the north, in the land of Gwent. I did not see it again and I thought I had imagined it. I would appear foolish if I was wrong. Better foolish than lose the ship. I hissed, "I saw a movement on the bank!"

"Stand to!" I saw Olaf nock an arrow as did his grandfather. We four whirled our slings slowly above our heads. Ulf North Star shouted, in Norse, "Speak or die!"

No one spoke and Ulf let fly with an arrow. Perhaps he had seen a movement or perhaps he was trying to make the watcher move. The watchers moved and began to run towards the drekar. I had a good view of the gangplank and I saw the five warriors run for it. While Ulf nocked another arrow, Olaf sent an arrow at the leading man who had a small shield. The warrior took the arrow on the shield. I was above him and I sent my stone into the side of the head and he fell from the gangplank into the mud. The Walhaz warriors would have been better using both gangplanks but they were eager to capture the drekar and kill ship's boys. Ulf's arrow caught the next warrior unawares. It hit him in the shoulder. He had leather mail but Ulf was less than twenty paces from him. It spun him around and he landed in the mud. Olaf sent an arrow into the warrior I had hit. He was rising from the mud and had no protection. At ten paces Olaf could not miss and I saw the arrow enter his forehead and emerge from the back of his skull. Leif and the others sent their stones to hit the fourth warrior. I had a stone in the sling and I sent it at the last one. It hit his right hand and I heard a cry. When Olaf and Ulf sent arrows into the shield of the nearest warrior one of them shouted and the four survivors ran for the bank. They did not escape unscathed. One was knocked to the ground and did not move. One of the others picked him up as an arrow from Olaf hit his calf. Arne's stone smacked into the back of another. Then they disappeared in the undergrowth.

The dead warrior lay face down in the mud. He had a shield, a sword and, I guessed a knife. I was new but I had helped to kill him. Perhaps Olaf would let me have something. Ulf shouted, "Can you see any more?"

Olaf shouted, "I do not think so."

"Erik and Leif go and check. The warrior should be dead but make certain!"

I slipped to the deck and almost ran down the gangplank. The light was getting better. You could make out shapes. I ran to the body. The arrow had hit so hard that there were pieces of bone in the mud. I saw that there was also blood close to his ear. That was where I had hit him. Leif appeared, "That was a good strike. He would have died from that wound." He took his sword belt and sword. He handed me his dagger. He slipped the sword and belt around his neck. He tugged the leather boots from the body and then searched his clothes. He found a purse and a metal cross. He took them and put them on the gangplank. "Come, let us search the path."

I slipped the sling into my leather pouch and held the dagger before me. I was pleased that the light was better. We reached the path and saw nothing. Leif turned and shouted, "They have gone."

Just then a hand appeared from the undergrowth and grabbed Leif's ankle. Without thinking I raised the Walhaz dagger and plunged it into the warrior's neck. The blade cut an artery and blood spurted. The tip had gone in quicker than I had expected and I felt it grate off bone. The warrior's death had been so quick that he had not uttered a sound.

Leif said, "Thank you, Erik. That was my error." He handed me the sword and belt and then stripped the body. He took the Walhaz sword, belt, dagger, coins and boots. We had not raided the settlement but we had treasure! "Come we have pushed our luck and I hear the Norns spinning."

When we returned to the drekar Ulf said, "What happened?"

Leif nodded to me, "A wounded Walhaz grabbed my ankle. Erik slew him. He is blooded!"

I saw the admiration in the eyes of all but Karl. Olaf said, "We will share the booty when we have time."

Ulf nodded, "Your last voyage as a ship's boy has shown that you have wisdom, grandson, I will miss you next time."

"Do not worry, grandfather. We have good ones to replace us."

"Even me?"

"Even you, Siggi the Clumsy." Although Siggi was pleased to be accepted I saw him worrying that his nickname would stick.

We heard noise coming from upstream. "Stand watch! This may be our war band but it could be the Walhaz. Be prepared to slip the ropes!" Olaf took his bow and we ran to the ropes. The light was better now and I recognised Karl's father leading animals down the path. There were pigs and sheep. Olaf shouted, "It is friends!"

We had wounded too and they came on some horses which had been captured. I saw Ulf frowning. Pigs and sheep were one thing but cows and horses were difficult to transport. As Bjorn Bjornson and his four men led the animals to graze on the grass, we went to help the four wounded warriors. One, Eystein, had lost fingers on his left hand. I wondered how for he had had a shield. He had no shield now and perhaps that was the story. Petr Petrsson had a gashed leg. It looked bad but it was on the fleshy part of his leg and my father said those wounds were the best to have. The other two, Folki and Benni, had both been laid unconscious. It was hard to see what their wound was. They were too heavy for the three of us and so we saw to Eystein and Petr.

Petr said, "Your father, Arne and Erik, is almost a berserker. He is relentless once he starts laying about him with his sword. Poor Eystein tried the same and when he tried your father's trick of sweeping aside the sword, the man he fought took his fingers from the inside of his shield. He will have to be a farmer now. At least I can still row and fight!"

His words told me that my father was alive and that was good news. It took until noon for the drekar to be loaded. The tide was racing out and Ulf was becoming quite agitated. We did not take the three horses. There was no room. With five women and four children, not to mention the sheep, pigs, and fowl, we were well loaded. The sacks of grain, hides, the carcasses of slaughtered animals, looted treasure, weapons and helmets were all stored beneath the deck. Our little haven by the prow now became crowded for we had the captives there too. Olaf and the rest of us were their guards. Ulf North Star annoyed Karl by telling him that he was no longer his assistant, he was in charge of the captives for the rest of us would be needed to trim the sail.

I had little chance to speak to my father but he smiled at me as he came on board. Ulf shouted, "Lars, your son did well. He killed a man and saved Leif from injury. You should be proud of him."

I saw my father nodded and his smile became broader, "I am always proud of my sons but today my chest swells just a little more!"

We managed to make the tide. The five of us swarmed up to the spar. It was daylight and we did not need a lookout. The river was wide and the current and the oarsmen took us. Our warriors did not row hard. It was to keep way. We sat on the yard for although the wind was against us once we turned to steerboard to sail along the coasts of Gwent and Dyfed we would have a breeze pushing from the south and west. The warriors would still need to row but it would be with just half of the rowers. Ulf North Star was confident that, at this time of year, the winds and the current would be from the south and west. I had asked him many questions about being a navigator. At first, he seemed to resent my questions but now he was almost resigned to them. He told me that there was a warm current to the west which pushed all the way around to our home. I wanted to sail that current. Was it made by the gods? Perhaps that was how Ran navigated. There was much I did not know but I had learned so much on this one voyage and there would be more.

I was between Leif and Olaf. They seemed happy to talk with me. "How long will it take us to get home, Olaf?"

"Faster than the journey here. We will have the wind and the current. We will sail closer to Hibernia in case the dogs of Mann are hunting. My grandfather thinks that the jarl will make war on them."

Leif asked, "With one drekar?"

"There are other drekar on the islands."

"But not enough to destroy the pirates." Olaf was silent. "Perhaps, if it is not for some time I may be old enough and strong enough to take an oar."

Leif's father had been killed fighting alongside the Danes. Leif had never known him. His mother had brought Leif and his sisters up alone. They were poor. He lived on Orkneyjar and I knew that the other families looked after them but Leif wanted to take care of his own family. He could not do that as a ship's boy. It was another reason why the two dead Walhaz were so important. We had not spoken of it but I knew he wanted the sword. It was mine by right for I had slain the Walhaz warrior but Leif needed it more than I did. Besides I would not be able to use it. I had decided already that I would let him have it. There were two daggers from the dead men and I wanted just one of them.

I looked to steerboard and saw that the land was flying by. Our rowers were barely stroking. I now understood how our drekar were able to cover such vast distances so quickly. We truly were the master mariners.

Sitting so high up we were aware of where we would make our turn and also the effect of the freshening wind. I was now used to the motion and even Siggi, now that his hands were healed, seemed easier. Part of it was that there was no smirking Karl just waiting for us to make a mistake.

"Let fly!" Ulf's voice was a relief. We took all of the reefs from the sail and then slid down to tighten the stays to the satisfaction of the helmsman. There were squeals from the captives as the drekar heeled over at an alarming angle. They thought we were going to capsize. We were not. For some reason that made me laugh. Ulf shouted, "Have some ale, you have deserved it!"

The oarsmen had already broached the ale we had taken from the men of Gwent. I took my horn from my neck and scooped a hornful. This was not the watered beer we had at home. This was man's ale. I knew it and drank carefully. I would normally add water but I had killed a man. I was almost a warrior. I did not count those I had hit with stones. They might have lived. My father came over to Arne and me. "Are you watching over your little brother Arne?"

He laughed, "He needs no one to watch him. Leif would have been hurt but for his reactions." He put his arm around me. "He will be my oar brother."

My father shook his head and lowered his voice. "Better that you become Siggi's oar brother. Erik is strong enough in the heart to row with any but Siggi needs you, Arne. It was not right that the younger of you defended Siggi."

This was the first time that my father had ever criticised either of us. He must have heard what I had done. The drekar was a small place to hide secrets. Arne nodded. "You are right father but Erik thinks quicker than I do. If I had been given time then I might well have done what Erik did. Erik can be a little reckless." He gave me a look. My father did not know but I did. He was talking of my wounding of Karl.

"I am reckless. I confess it. I will try to curb it."

My father took me by the shoulder and shook his head, "It is part of you. You cannot change what you are. I have the same nature and I find it brings me into conflict with others." He threw a glance at the jarl who was watching us. "I will have much coin from this raid. We will take our snekke with my brother and the five of us will sail to the mainland. We will take timber. You can now sail and I know that you can fight. I will build a drekar. There are men will follow me. I would rather have twenty good men to follow me than a whole crew like this one." Although he was speaking quietly, I saw his brother look over and frown. Uncle Snorri got on with everyone. He was popular. He did not rise to anger as quickly as my father and he tried to see good in all men.

"And I, for one, look forward to that day. Father, I see Olaf and Leif. They are dividing the treasure."

He laughed, "And here am I planning your future. Go!"

Arne followed behind. I knew that he was envious. Perhaps he and Siggi might be given something. Leif and Olaf were sat by our shelter. Karl was scowling at all and shouting at the captives. It was to no avail for they did not understand any of his words. We ignored him and the three of us sat before Olaf and Leif. Olaf had laid out everything that we had collected. The two pairs of boots were too big for me. The two swords were too big but there were two daggers and I would have one. If I could have some coins too then that would be good.

Olaf said to me, "You helped to kill one warrior and you slew a second on your own. One of these swords is yours by right. Which will you have?"

I shook my head, "As much as I would wish a sword, I will not be able to use one for some time. Leif needs a sword. I would that Leif has one."

Leif's face lit up. "I will ever be in your debt."

Olaf looked at the two and took the better one, as was his right. "I choose this one." Leif nodded and greedily grasped the sword, scabbard and belt. Olaf held the two daggers and smiled, "You wish one of these?"

"Aye." I took the longer narrower one. I had Karl's which was a short dagger. This would be like a short sword. In addition, the longer one had a scabbard.

The weapons out of the way the rest were divided between the three of us as well as Siggi and Arne. We all had coins. Olaf and Leif took the cloaks and boots. Siggi and Arne were given the metal crosses. I was given one leather jerkin and Leif took the other. We were all happy. Karl was not.

I said, quietly, "Should we not give coins to Karl too? He was with us when they attacked."

Leif shook his head, "You did not see, Erik, but he never even took out a sling. He sat behind Ulf North Star. Ulf knows this and that is why Olaf's grandfather put him in charge of the captives. He saw what Karl did. He will not sail again with Ulf as a ship's boy."

Karl was staring at me and hatred burned in his eyes. I had made an enemy. I took off my belt and slipped the scabbard through it. When it was fastened, I took out the blade. It was narrower than most blades. I knew that would be a weakness. It could break more easily. I touched the edge it was sharp. I had wanted to sharpen it. Instead, I held it in my hand and felt the balance. My pleasure was ended when Ulf shouted, "Ship's boys!" We went back to work.

On the voyage back home, I felt my body changing. At home, Arne and I ran everywhere. We used our slingshots and we climbed but here on the ship we spent even longer each day running down a crowded deck or clambering up the stays, sheets and mast. I knew I was becoming stronger. Even Siggi looked different. His hands had now healed and he was able to reach the yard almost as quickly as Arne and me. By the time we saw Orkneyjar in the distance, I knew that the boy who had left Hrólfsey was now lost at sea. When Karl and I had fallen into the sea it had changed us both. It had made him weaker and made me stronger. The ocean was my friend and I did not fear her. I had been reborn. As yet I had no name although some on the ship called me fearless while others used the name, Walhaz Killer, but I knew that one day I would have one. Hrólfsey was not going to be enough for me. I had seen the sea and it had an attraction for me I could not explain. What lay beyond the horizon?

Chapter 4

We called at Dyflin on the way back and the surplus captives were sold along with the holy books and goods from the church. Only the jarl and his hearth weru went ashore. I was not sure why but my father saw a conspiracy in this. He was loud in his criticism. The chest of coins they brought back told all that we had done well. The jarl had also made representation about the attack from Mann. He told us that he was given a satisfactory answer. My father did not believe him.

We left to sail the last part of our journey. We were dropped off first. There were just four men and three boys who would disembark. I had seen my father, uncle and the jarl in deep conversation during the latter part of the voyage. It had looked animated. The booty had been shared out and perhaps my father thought it was an unfair division. I knew from other warriors that my father and his oar brothers had borne the brunt of the fighting. My father and uncle had a small chest of coin and two sheep. The two had also captured weapons and daggers for themselves. They had purses they had taken too. We unloaded our goods on the jetty. The two sheep hurtled off. My uncle laughed. "They cannot go far and we know who they belong to. Besides, Loki, the ram will find them soon enough!"

Olaf and Leif came to clasp our arms as we lifted the chest from the drekar. "We would sail with you three again. More, I would stand in a shield wall with you, even you Siggi Deck Crusher! You could have given up but you did not. You worked hard and showed courage."

Snorri Long Fingers nodded, "Siggi Deck Crusher, I like the name, my son."

"And it is better than Siggi the Clumsy." Siggi nodded acceptance. Like my father a man did not choose his name, others did.

In truth it was a good name for it was like a riddle. Men would ask how he got his name and when Siggi told them they would smile. A boy who fell from a stay and survived was a lucky man.

As we headed up the hill towards our farms my father spoke to all of us. "The jarl wishes to make war on Mann and to punish them for their attack. He does not have enough ships and so he will be sailing the islands to gather support. I do not think that he will have enough men until the next raiding season. We will sail to the mainland to get the timber we need for the keel. We have the winter to begin to build our drekar."

Arne said, "It took a long time to build the snekke. Is there any point?"

Snorri Long Fingers laughed, "We had but two men and a slave. Now we have three voyagers who have shown they are not afraid of hard work. It will take a year, no more, but first we have to collect the timber." There was a sack on the chest they carried. "We took wood axes from the Walhaz as well as two swords. We can hew our own timber."

Karl's dagger was wrapped in the blanket I had tied around me. I wondered how to tell my father. I could not keep the blade hidden forever. I decided that I would tell him at Samhain. That was when we made our bone fire and prepared for winter. I would make a sacrifice to Odin so that the Allfather would help me with my father.

We separated at my uncle's farm. Helga ran to meet her father and his wife waved at us. Siggi and his father took their share from the chests and the sack. Arne and I helped my father to carry the lighter chest. We had collected the sheep and driven them to join our herd. The two additions would improve the herd and meant we could slaughter our oldest ewe. Loki would cover the two new ones so that we would have spring lambs. Edmund was tending the vegetables as we strode up to our longhouse. Edmund never smiled. I think he might have run away if it was not for my mother. Edmund and she had some sort of connection. I never discovered what it was but Arne and I thought they were related in some way.

My mother appeared in the door. She looked happy to see my father. Even though she had been taken as a slave my father had married her and I think that she liked him. Certainly, she smiled more than Edmund. She threw her arms around him and kissed him. "You have brought my boys home! They are safe!"

My father put his arms around us and said, "More than that they have fought our foes and Erik has killed a man!"

My father was proud but my mother was a Christian and her hand went to her cross. She then held me. "You could have been killed yourself!"

I shook my head, "No, mother, for the Allfather guided my hand."

She was disappointed. She had tried to make us Christian but failed. "Come, I will make the meal while you empty your chest."

Arne and I were eager to see what weapons he had brought back. Apart from the two wood axes there were just two swords and a couple of poorly made daggers. Arne and I were disappointed. My father smiled, "I know, you hoped for more. What can I say, the Walhaz have poor weapons. The other three swords your uncle and I captured had bent in battle. They are fit only for melting. As we have no weapon smith we will have to wait."

"What of helmets? Surely they had helmets too."

"No Arne, not ones which were worth taking. Why do you think we lost no men and the ship's boys killed two warriors?" He ruffled my hair. "The Walhaz are poor enemies. I told the jarl to raid the Saxons. They have better weapons. He did not listen to me. He seeks easy foes."

"And what of the men of Mann?"

"If he ever manages to get enough ships then that would be a raid which would be worthwhile. Arne, this sword is yours. Erik has his dagger and that will have to suffice." I saw Arne give me a knowing look.

"That is good and I am happy."

Time passed and we grew. We were no longer children. Not yet men, we were learning to behave as men did. My father had decided that we needed to sail the snekke. Arne, Siggi and I had learned much on the drekar. Now our lessons would continue on *'Jötnar'*. We were busy preparing the snekke for sea. We had trees to harvest before winter. The Norns were spinning for Gytha discovered that she was with child. The baby would be born at the end of Þorri. My mother would give birth just a short time before.

The brothers were pleased but father made a blót to ensure that it would be a healthy baby.

We were hunting seals. The Allfather had not given us many trees nor cattle but he had filled the islands with grey seals and they were ours to harvest. They were our bounty. We delayed our departure as the grey seals had come ashore to give birth to their young. We relied upon the seal for food, oil and skin. They were hard to hunt at sea but when they came on land then they were easier to kill. We rose in the middle of the night. They were easier to hunt in the early morning. The seals had all given birth to their young and some had been weaned already. We had a short time to hunt them. We needed to do so when the pups were able to fend for themselves. We needed at least ten seals to sustain us. Our fathers carried a spear each. The three of us each carried a spare spear. I had my dagger and Arne took his short sword. I saw that Siggi wore a dagger which his father had taken. We also had our slings. They would distract the seals while our fathers slew them.

We heard them long before we saw them. They were basking on the rocks as the sun came up in the east. Already some were heading for the sea. They were a vigilant animal and they had sentries watching. They would be the first ones we would hunt. After they had been killed the slower ones would be hunted. It made the seal herd stronger and we would have better meat. The three of us would approach first and throw stones at the nearest sentry. When he came towards us then our fathers would slay him. By moving along the shore line, we made the most of every opportunity to take seals.

We came at them so that we could smell them and they could not smell us. We came from the dark of the west. We were just ten paces from the first of the sentries. He sat atop a rock. We laid down our spears and took out our slings. Behind us, our fathers approached with spears ready. The seal detected them when they were just four paces away. Even as the sentry seal started to bark two spears were thrown and the seal was knocked to the sand. Our fathers each grabbed a second spear and hurried to the next sentry. He had seen them and began to race towards them. They were faster than one might have expected and had sharp teeth. Our fathers wore leather but it would not stop a seal bite. The three of us hurled our stones and they smacked into the animal. It had a thick layer of blubber which meant our stones did not inflict wounds but they made the seal turn and that allowed two more spears to end the sentry's life.

"Spears!"

While Siggi took the last spears to our fathers I went to the first seal to pull the spears from its body. It was dead. The spears had not penetrated deeply but one must have struck the heart for there was a great deal of blood there. I did not want to damage the heads of the throwing spears. If I did then I would have to repair them. As I pulled it from the seal's body, I felt it strike a bone. I turned the head slowly and pulled each time I turned. Eventually, it slid out with a satisfying slurp. The second one was easier.

"Spears!"

I rant to my father and uncle and handed them the two spears. They had killed another seal. By the time the tenth had been killed the beach was empty. The seals had fled to the sea. They would return when it was safe. This was when a horse would have been useful. While Arne, my father and uncle took back two seals at a time Siggi and I guarded the seals' carcasses which we had gathered together. Already seabirds were swooping. We took out our stones and killed a herring gull, a skua and two sea gulls before they decided to find other hunting grounds. It took until late afternoon for us to take all of the seals back and begin the work of skinning and butchering the animals then rendering the fat. Siggi and I plucked and prepared the four sea birds for a stew. We would all eat in our longhouse. The rendering and butchery would take a couple of days. The stink from the fat rendering made the two pregnant women ill. We were used to the smell, as were they, but as Snorri said, "Women change when they carry a child! It is their lot to bear such adversity stoically!"

The two men skinned the seals. Such work was skilful. We needed the skin in one piece. Our job was to cut up the meat and the fat. When the skins were taken, they were placed on drying frames before we began the process of tanning. We had a clay and rock lined pool. We all made water in it and then soaked the dried skins before drying them for a second time. All in all, it took fourteen nights before we had all of our tasks completed. The fat took time to render but when it was done, we not only had fuel but delicious and crunchy fat which we ate liberally spread with sea salt. The bones would not be wasted. When the nights became so long that there was almost no daylight, we would carve the bones into useful implements: combs, pins, knife blades and handles, sewing needles, fishing hooks. There was no end to the uses to which we would put the bone. I was determined to make even better fishing hooks than I had before. On the raid I had not caught as many fish as Siggi. I blamed my poor hooks. Ulf North Star had suggested using five or six hooks on a line with something shiny. I had found a coloured misshapen stone on the beach when Karl had tried to kill me. I knew that I could polish and make a hole in it to attract the shiny fish which made such good eating. Siggi had risen in the estimation of all by his skill at fishing.

And then, when days lengthened, it was time to go for timber. Until we used the new seal skins to make our boots and capes, we would be barefoot and have to use our old capes. We were hardy. Leaving Karl's dagger under my sleeping cot I took my new one and we boarded the snekke. We had sailed her around the island when we had been seeking seals but we would now be sailing her out of sight of land. She looked remarkably small. My father had named her *'Jötnar'*. It was a joke for she was hardly a giant but my uncle pointed out that the jötnar swam through a flood of Ymir's blood and that this was a good omen for we would sail through a sea of our enemies' blood. I liked the name. I also liked the fact that we did not have to climb the mast. We were able to raise and lower the sail by lowering the spar. She was lively and we could sail almost into the wind. We would, however, be learning to row on the snekke. While one of us steered the other two would row with our fathers. That way we learned to row and we learned to steer. Those two days as we sailed to the mainland were amongst the best I could remember. The weather was good and we were all in a good humour.

We had just two shields on the side. One day there would be another three there. One of my tasks this winter was to make my shield. It would not be as big as my father's but big enough. The two warriors had also brought their swords and spears. Spears were useful. If game came close by then we could hunt it.

We spied the trees as soon as we saw the coast. They seemed to rise like a wall from the sea. We had to sail a little east before we found a bay which was free from inhabitants. We used the sail to sail her in and ground up gently onto the soft sand and shingle. While our fathers took their bows and climbed to the cliff top, we hauled the snekke clear of the water. We would be using her as our home for a few days. We used a piece of old sail and made a shelter for us. By then our fathers had returned.

"We spied neither houses nor smoke. There are good trees and we can use the cliff to lower them to the beach. This is a good place to hunt timber. Fetch the rope and axes from the snekke. There is enough daylight for us to hew a couple before dark."

We had three tree axes and three hand axes. I saw that my father had already spied two trees. Snorri patted one almost affectionately, "This one is close to the edge and, if we hit it right, it will roll down to the beach."

My father shook his head, "That matters not. This one will be the keel. It is perfect. You three stand to the side and we will show you how it is done." They first hacked a cut as wide as a hand on the seaward side of the tree and then they alternated hits on the other side. They made it look so easy. "Stand clear!" There was a crack and then the tree began to topple. As Snorri had predicted it fell down the slope towards the beach. As it hit there was a series of cracks as the smaller branches were broken off. It slithered and slid until its top was three paces on the beach. "You three go and hack off as many of the smaller branches as you can and then attach a rope to it. The other is there." He pointed a little way further along. They would be able to fell that one and we would not be in danger.

I was confident that we would be able to strip the smaller branches and I envisioned us pulling the trunk to the snekke. How wrong I was. What had seemed easy when the brothers had done it now seemed almost impossible. The ones the width of a sword hilt were easy but it took many blows to sever the ones as thick as my arm. We heard 'Stand clear!' and looked up as the second tree was felled. I was just pleased that the others were finding it as hard.

Snorri reached us first for my father had begun to take off the lower and larger branches of the other tree. He took his axe and said, "There is a technique to this. Learn it now for when you are older this will help you wield a Danish war axe." He put one hand at the end of the axe haft and the other near the head. "See, as I swing, I move my right hand to join my left. I let the weight of the axe head do the work. If Siggi and Arne work in a pair they will be able to take some thicker branches. Erik, go and join your father. Take the smaller branches for him."

I was not happy as I wandered to my father. I had failed and been given a lesser task. I determined to do as well as I could and impress my father. It came on to dark and I still had not finished. My father stretched. "Come we have done enough. Give me the axe and then go up the slope and find as much dry wood as you can. We will have food. We have done better than I hoped. Three or four days should give us enough timber for the skeleton of the drekar!"

I did as I was bid and I took the wood back to the beach where I made a fire. We would light it later. I headed back to my father. "I am not tired. I can hew some more."

"Good, the more we do tonight the sooner we can head home."

"We do not get all of the timber now?"

"We would struggle to take it back. We will need at least three journeys." He talked as he hewed. I used the technique my uncle had taught me and it was easier. Gradually the pile of branches grew and the trunk became more like a usable piece of timber. "We need to use the wood while it still has the moisture of growth within it. When we tow them back it will help us. We will strip the bark to reveal the bast fibres and they will make rope. The first two trees will give us the keel, the bow and the stern as well as the cross pieces. It is why we chose the two largest trees. When we return it will be for the wood for the strakes and they need to be young and supple that we may shape them to make a drekar." He paused and wiped the sweat from his brow. "I have waited my whole life to make a drekar. Every one in which I have sailed I have studied. I have spoken with shipwrights. This is good that our family builds the drekar for our toil, sweat and, I have no doubt, our blood, will be within her. With such a ship we can sail anywhere we wish."

The sun set and although we had not finished, we headed for the beach where Snorri had used the kindling we had brought to get the fire going. I saw Arne and Siggi collecting limpets and other shellfish. With the salted meat we had brought we would eat well. My father took out the whetstone and carefully sharpened all of the axes. He took my dagger and Arne's sword. "Come and watch. I will give you a lesson in how to sharpen a blade."

I smiled, "My blade is sharp!"

He laughed, "When you can shave my beard with it then it is sharp." I watched him work the stone. He spat on it every now and again. He tested the sharpness. He handed Arne his sword, "Here, test it." As Arne did so he cut himself and my father laughed. "That is sharp!" As he dabbed a piece of cloth against the wound, he saw the scar down Arne's palm. Although Siggi and I tried to hide ours they were seen. My father nodded, "It seems our sons have sworn a blood oath."

Snorri asked, "Did you?"

We all nodded. We were fearful of the consequences of our admission. My father said, "Did you spill the blood beneath a cut turf and then replace the turf?"

Arne shook his head, "It was on a beach. The tide came in and washed away the blood."

"Ah, then Ran will control your destiny. You are now tied to each other and the sea. You can return from such an oath."

"We do not want to!"

He nodded, "Erik, the Norns are listening. Be careful what you wish for." He began to sharpen my blade. "Check the stew. I have an appetite."

We were too few to keep watch and besides it was remote. We slept well and woke with all of us safe and sound. The fire had died and so we put some stones in the embers and a piece of salted meat on the top. It warmed it through and the smell made it even more appetising. We had just dragged the two timbers and trimmed branches to the snekke when we saw the fishing ship. It appeared in the bay and there were two men in it. It did not stop. My father said. "We cut two more timbers and then raft up what we have."

Arne said, "It was only a fishing boat with two men within it."

"And they will return home and tell others. It may be that the men who live here may not mind sharing their timber but as they are the people who fled when we came to Orkneyjar I would not count on it."

We had started work earlier in the day and we had felled the two trees and stripped the wood by noon. I know my father had planned on felling more but we had been seen. As he and his brother used the rope to make a raft, we stripped all the foliage from the branches. We would take them home and utilise every single piece of timber we could. We piled the green foliage next to the embers of the fire to begin to dry them. We stopped for food in the middle of the afternoon. My father had us relight the fire and put on a pot of water. "I plan on sailing at night. Tomorrow there may be visitors and I would be gone. We will have a hot meal and then sail. Come Snorri, let us launch the raft. When it is done load it with the other branches and secure them with ropes."

Even on the drekar I had never worked as hard. We did not wish to be caught on this shore by angry warriors. We had just tethered the raft and begun to eat the stew when the warriors appeared on the cliff top. There were just six of them. It did not matter if it was six or sixty for we only had two warriors. My father turned, "Take the pot back to the boat. You boys launch the snekke. Tie the raft securely to the stern rail and untether her. When I give the command then lower the sail."

"But…"

"Do as I command, Arne!" There was steel in his voice. We worked hard. Our time on the drekar paid off for we worked together well and soon Siggi was holding the tiller as Arne and I tied the raft. We heard a shout and the five men ran at my father and uncle. Arne shouted, "You finish here. I will help them!" He drew his sword and ran.

I quickly tied the knot and then took my sling from the snekke. I ran towards the skirmish. My father and uncle were back to back. They were taller than the five warriors who came at them. I heard the ring of steel on wood. My father had a leather jerkin and it could take a blow from a sword. Eventually, however, it would succumb and a blade would find flesh. I saw Arne dash, like a hound to hack at the back of the leg of one of the attackers. There was a roar of pain and the man he had wounded and another turned to face Arne. My brother was in danger although my uncle now had just one man to fight. I put a stone in my sling and hurled it at the unwounded one fighting Arne. It was a hurried throw and I only managed to hit his arm but it must have hurt. Arne swashed his sword before him as Snorri hacked into the leg of his opponent. As the man fell to the sand Snorri went to the aid of my father. I stopped and fitting another stone took aim. The man whose arm I had hit turned and my stone smacked into his forehead. He fell down. The wounded man took to his good leg and he ran. As my father slew his opponent the three who were still able fled.

I ran to Arne. "Are you hurt?"

He shook his head but I could see that his hand was shaking. He held his sword aloft and I saw blood upon it. "I have blooded the blade! I have wounded a man! I am catching you, brother!"

My father's voice was angry, "And you could both have been killed. You disobeyed me. Get back to the snekke and prepare to cast off."

"But father, they are fled!"

In answer, my father pointed to the cliff. There were men there. This time there were many more than five. "Arne, obey me!" He ran to the fire and dumped the green foliage upon it. Smoke began to billow along the beach.

We ran to the snekke. Already the tide was taking it away. Only the weight of the raft kept it close. Siggi had done well. As we clambered aboard Arne and I took the ropes which would release the sail. Our fathers were running towards us. They had taken the discarded weapons. The men chasing them were just two hundred paces from us.

"Lower the sail!"

We did not wish to risk my father's anger again and so we did as he said. *'Jötnar'* was ready and she leapt forward like a greyhound. The raft was a dead weight and I felt the rope tighten. My father and Snorri threw their shields, boots and the captured weapons on the raft and then began to swim to us. The pursuers had reached the shoreline. As my father and uncle clambered aboard my father shouted, "Arne, Erik, slings!" I took my sling and whirling it around my head, threw a stone at the leading warrior. It was a hasty strike but Ran was guiding me for it hit the water before him and skimmed up to strike him in the face. He fell backwards clutching his face. Arne hit one on the sword hand and the sword fell beneath the water. Then the wind caught the sail fully for Snorri took the helm. The raft floated and moved easier. We had escaped but we would not be able to return to the bay again. We would have to find somewhere else for the rest.

Once we knew we were safe my father began to laugh, "Brother what have we bred here! Perhaps we should swear an oath too eh?"

Chapter 5

We made it home in three days. The raft was a dead weight. We finished the food we had brought after two and had to fish. I quite liked raw fish and I was hungry enough to eat it all. I kept looking at the weapons we had captured. There were three short swords and two long daggers. I hoped that Siggi and I would be given a short sword each. As we watched Hrólfsey grow closer my father said, "We have the keel, the prow and the stern. We have the crosspieces. Those two timbers should yield forty planks. That might be enough."

"We need pine for the mast and yard anyway. The best is in Norway." Snorri was eminently practical and positive.

"Aye, I know. We cross that bridge when we come to it."

When we reached the shore, our problems had just begun. We had to drag the raft ashore. My father came up with the idea of tethering it at high tide and when the tide went out it would be grounded. We could then take off the ropes and haul the timbers above the high-water mark. We had the help of Edmund and Gava, Snorri's slave. It was dark by the time that the four timbers, the cut branches and the trimmed wood were safe and secure. I was almost asleep on my feet as we reached our longhouse. My mother was normally subservient to my father but she stood up to him, "These are little more than children and they are almost asleep as they walk. For shame on you."

In answer he grabbed us both around the shoulders, we were still a head shorter than he was, and kissed my mother. "You are right. I forget for they do not behave as children. They draw weapons and face their father's foes. They are Vikings but I will put them to bed!"

I do not remember falling asleep. The next morning, when I awoke, I reached under my cot for Karl's dagger. It was not there. I jumped up. Arne was still asleep. I shook him awake, "Karl's dagger! Where is it?"

"I know not, he said sleepily! I have a sword! I need no dagger!"

I searched our sleeping chamber but could not find it. Had Edmund stolen it? I clambered down the ladder to the main hall. My mother and father sat at the table. They were eating freshly baked bread and runny goats' cheese. The dagger was forgotten until I saw it on the table between them.

My father chewed and swallowed. He washed the bread and cheese down with ale and then he leaned back, "Tell me all and do not think to lie." He stared at me as though he could see into my heart. I told them all, leaving nothing out including the oath we had sworn.

My mother rose and held my head to her bosom. "He tried to kill you!"

"He tried but he failed for I am the better warrior."

My father said, "Sit, wife. We have a warrior for a son. Both our sons are warriors but Erik here has seen death and defeated it. I have never known this in one so young. You know that if you had told the jarl then Karl would have been banished?"

I nodded, "I thought I had done more wrong in taking his knife!"

My father laughed, "By the Allfather you have honour! Do not hide the dagger. If Karl the Lame claims it then he will be the laughing stock of Orkneyjar for he will be admitting that he tried to murder someone younger and failed." The smile left him and he became the warrior I had seen fighting. "Never hide anything from me again! Do you understand?"

"Yes, father, I do."

"Good. Now we must make a scabbard for this. It is a good blade. His father took it from a Northumbrian Eorl. There is writing on it. Wife, you can read the Saxon squiggles, what does it say?"

She peered at it, "Rædwulf had me made."

My father frowned, "Rædwulf? I have not heard of him."

She shrugged, "Nor have I."

Edmund rarely spoke but he did now, "He claimed the throne of Northumbria. My father told me about him. He ruled for months but he had weapons made for him with his name upon them. He was desperate to remain king. This is an old blade. May I look at it, lord?"

My father put his hand on his own seax as he said, "Aye, but tread carefully, thrall."

Edmund nodded, "See that there is a hawk carved in the handle. That was his sign. This is a well-made weapon, Master Erik."

I looked at it in a new light. The gods had sent it to me and I would look after it.

That day began many days which started with the sun rise and ended when it set in the western seas. We stripped the bark from the timber and collected the bast fibre. My father began to carve the prow while we helped Uncle Snorri to make the join which would fit it to the keel. Each day we soaked the other timbers with sea water. The days were getting shorter and the time of the bone fire approached. It was as if we were in a race with nature itself.

I now had a scabbard for the dagger. I knew its story and that made it even more special. A king had owned it. I knew not the story of how it had come into the possession of Karl's father but I felt that it had sought me out and that made me special too. The scabbard was relatively plain. I did not wish my enemies to know that the blade was worth stealing. I doubted that Karl had known its true value. I made the scabbard at night when we had finished labouring with the drekar. By the time it was Ýlir there was shape to the drekar and we had begun to fit the planks. My father used wooden trenails rather than iron. We had no smith and it was easier. My father also thought it would be better. As the winter solstice drew closer then we knew that we would not be able to source the mast and spars. We needed pine not just for the mast and yard but also the pine tar to seal it. We had the teased wool but without the pine tar, the drekar would not last long in our harsh northern seas.

My father was philosophical about it. It meant he could spend longer carving the dragon prow. The drekar might not be a big one but the dragon prow would be intricately carved. He and Snorri worked at it during the increasingly short days of winter. My father had a name in mind for the drekar but he told no one. He considered it bad luck. He did not want the Norns to know. Snorri thought it foolish as the Norns had already spun the web of our paths and the drekar was there, taking shape before our eyes. I think he just wanted to wait until the ship was finished and he could announce it to the world.

When Yule came and the days were so short that the sun barely made an appearance my father gave me one of the swords we had taken from the Picts. The scabbard was crudely made and it was a short sword but it was a sword. "It is not as good as one made by your mother's people but, for a first weapon, it will do. As your brother showed even a poor weapon, so long as it is sharp, can do damage to one of our enemies."

I held the blade and felt the edge. He was right, it was not sharp and needed to be sharpened. "Thank you, father, I now have a fine dagger, a good knife and a sword. When next we sail, I will feel more like a warrior."

Arne had been given a Pictish dagger and he took out a whetstone to sharpen it. As he did so he asked, "When will we sail again?"

"We need pine and that means either trading with someone from the Baltic or sailing to Norway and taking some. This is the time of the winter storms. This is the time when ships which sail do not return. We have enough wood to finish the drekar and that will take until the new grass. The deck, the mast, the yard and the oars can wait."

Once the days lengthened, at the end of Mörsugur, my father returned to the drekar where the tasks required just one man and Arne and I began to train as warriors. Part of that was building up our arms. Arne was older than I was and had grown more than I over winter. I was growing too. We had our progress marked on the wall of our long house. I was as tall as Arne had been at the same age. I would be as big as he was. It was a spur to me. We used the adze and axe to finish off timber for my father to fit to the drekar. He gave us two hunks of offcuts to carve into wooden swords. None of us had enough confidence in the Pict and Walhaz swords. We had to use the wooden ones for practise. I had been desperate to make a shield but my father told me to wait until we could get willow. We had two small Pictish ones we could use in the meantime. Every moment of every short day was spent in working either with wood or with weapons. Arne and I were evenly matched for although he had the strength and height, I had cunning. I had the little flick to the knee. I had the foot hooked behind him. He won. I won. We both won for we were getting better and we knew the way that the other fought. When we stood in a shield wall that could only help.

My uncle came over to visit with us at the start of Þorri. They had yet to divide the coins that they had acquired in the raid on the Walhaz. I had few coins. They were meaningless to me. There was nowhere to spend them. The largest place on the island, Westness, had no market. The hersir who lived there, Sigurd, was now a greybeard. He did not go to war. His sons had left the island and never returned. Westness seemed to be a place filled with the old. He brought Helga, my cousin, over. Siggi stayed with his mother. My mother was almost due to give birth. Normally Gytha would have been there to help but she was also large with child. Helga would stay with us until the babe was born and then go back to her own mother. Helga got on well with my mother. I think my mother enjoyed the company of another female.

Arne and I sat with my uncle and father as they stacked the coins. The designs of them were different. Some were from the Walhaz and some from the Picts but most were Saxon or Norse. The two brothers stacked the coins so that they could count them. There were far more than I expected.

"Are we rich?"

My father laughed, "It looks to be a great deal of silver but it will soon go. The sail for the snekke was woven by your mother and aunt but we do not have enough wool for a drekar's sail. The seal oil we rendered will make it stronger and weather resistant but we need more rope too. If we are to sail a drekar any distance then we will need a spare sail. We need a spare yard and a spare mast. If we had more men we could sail to Norway and simply take the wood we need but I fear that we will have to trade. That means coin. He handed coins to me, Arne and Siggi. I clutched them tightly for they were the first coins I had earned.

Uncle Snorri tapped Arne's sword, "And the three of you will need a better sword. For that we need a weaponsmith. That means going to the jarl's stad. The weaponsmith works for him and it will not be cheap." He glanced at my father. My father shrugged.

When you are young, adults assume that you do not understand silences and looks. Arne and I did. We often spoke about them. We knew that my father and the jarl did not get on. We had learned that on the raid. The men of Hrólfsey who sailed on the drekar had all kept close to my father. When they had returned from the raid they had been as one. They rowed on chests which were close to each other yet my father was not even a hersir. Even the jarl's words to me had suggested animosity. The jarl needed my father as a warrior and a leader but my father needed the jarl for his ship. When our drekar was built then my father would not need the jarl. It was as though that thought process generated an idea for I suddenly blurted out, "When we have a drekar will we leave this island?"

My uncle's hand went to his hammer of Thor. "Are you galdramenn?"

My father said, irritably, "Snorri, the boy guesses! He is clever!" He nodded, "We may do. But you can say nothing to any of this. There are lands which have more to offer than Hrólfsey."

"Aye, the Land of the Wolf is one."

My father shook his head, "No for that land is ruled by the wolf witch. It is said that she has woven spells with the Norns and I would not risk falling foul of her. There are other lands. Just south of there is good land with forests close by. The Mercians used to hold it but now, thanks to the raids from Mann and the Warriors of the Wolf, it has Vikings there."

"Are they not a danger to us, father?"

"No Arne. I might fear a witch but there is not a warrior alive that can best me." He ruffled my hair, "At least not yet. Now when you two grow…" My uncle left when the coins had been counted and shared.

My brother, Fótr, was born after a day long labour. We were not allowed near to the birth. That was considered bad luck. Helga was the one who stayed with my mother. We heard the screams and cries as we waited outside. The cold wind from the east chilled us to the bones but I wondered if the chill in Helga's heart was that she would have to endure this to have a child. She came out and was as bloody as a warrior after a battle. She smiled, "Uncle, you have a son. He has the right number of hands, fingers, toes, feet, eyes and ears. He is healthy and he screams for milk!"

We were just relieved that it was a boy and healthy. I knew that my mother yearned for a girl but the Norns had spun. Edmund seemed to be as excited as we were about the birth. After Helga had left to return to her mother, I caught the old Saxon speaking with my mother. I saw him dip his finger in water and make a sign on Fótr's forehead. I did not understand it. My mother saw me and waved me over as Edmund guiltily slipped out of the room.

"Come Erik, see your brother." I went to look at the little red and to be honest, ugly little bundle. Mother saw my frown and laughed, "You looked like this once. Do not worry he will grow and become as you." The babe's mouth opened and closed and my mother began to feed him. "You were the special one, Erik. You were born on the longest day. Gytha was before the door which faced west and when you were born, she moved and a light from the west shone on you and lit your face. You were a golden child. That was God smiling on you. He has great things planned for you."

I frowned, "The Allfather, Odin?"

She squeezed my hand. "It is the same one. We choose different names for him, that is all."

"But what of the White Christ? The one with the cross?" I pointed to the metal cross she wore about her neck.

"Does not Odin have a son and do you not wear his sign about your neck too?"

"Then Thor is the White Christ?"

She clutched her cross and said, "I did not say that. You are young but you are clever. When you next sail and you keep watch think on these things. Make up your own mind and when this one grows then you must protect him. Swear on your hammer that you will." I did as she asked. I would have done so without her urging. We were a clan, albeit a tiny one, but we would grow.

Seven days later and Siggi had a brother. Tostig was born. He was a little underweight and the women worried about him. My mother took my new brother to offer her help and so we had a house of men. I had been busy in the winter carving the bone from the grey seals we had hunted. I was proudest of my fish hooks. I was determined to catch more than any other ship's boy. My comb had taken longer. The sea tangled my hair and I had discovered that a daily combing made it easier to stop the tangling. I had used my father's before. Now I had my own. I had made some needles. They varied from smaller ones to repair my kirtle up to bodkins to sew seal skin. I now had seal skin boots as did Arne. When we climbed the rigging, we would not wear them and when we waded in the water, we would be barefoot. The boots made us feel more like a warrior. The sealskin cape would be our most useful tool. It would keep us dry and we could use it to make our prow shelter even cosier.

My mother had been home for ten days and it was Einmánuður. We were considering sailing to find more timber when a messenger arrived from Jarl Eystein Rognvaldson. We were summoned to his stad on Orkneyjar for a Thing. I knew that my father did not like being summoned but we had to go. We loaded the snekke and set sail. I did not mind for it meant we might be able to buy things. His stad had a market and we had coin. We had taken it from the men of Walhaz. They were few in number but most boys our age had none. Arne and I were already spending the coin as we tacked and sailed around the island to Orkneyjar. My father brooded and that was not good. Uncle Snorri tried to banter him out of his mood but he was having none of it. Having the skeleton of a drekar he wanted it finished. He only brightened when Snorri said, "There will be pine tar we can buy. When we shear the sheep, we will have wool. We can seal the hull." That took the scowl away but I knew that beneath the surface he was angry. One day I would discover why he and the jarl did not get on.

There were knarr and snekke in Hamnavoe. The jarl's stad was on the south of the island but he had a good anchorage. It was safe and ships could land in any season. I saw men working on his drekar. There was also a much larger drekar with twenty oars on each side tied up. There were visitors. Snorri said, "That is a Norse ship. I recognise the pennant. The sign of the red dragon comes from Oseberg."

As we tied up next to another two snekke my father said, "Keep silent and listen. Erik if Karl the Lame is here, I want no provocation."

I squirmed under his fierce gaze, "Aye father. Do we carry our swords and daggers?"

He smiled, "Is Rædwulf's dagger in your boot?"

I smiled. I had anticipated that Karl might be here and I had hidden it in my boot. I nodded, "It is hidden."

"Then you may carry your swords but do not unsheathe them unless I tell you."

We climbed across the two snekke and up the wall to the stad. There was a gate and two warriors lounged there. I recognise them as hearth weru. They grinned when they saw Arne, Siggi and me, "You boys have grown! They feed you well on Hrólfsey."

Arne said, "It is a good island and we eat well." My father nodded his approval. Arne had said the right thing.

The jarl's hall was full already. There were almost a hundred and twenty warriors there. They milled around. Many had horns of ale. My father's friends all cheered when we entered and we walked over to them. Thralls brought ale and we held out our horns to have them filled.

"What is this about?"

Asbjorn Blue Eyes shrugged, "We think the jarl plans a raid or a war, Lars."

Butar Beer Belly emptied his horn and held it out for the thrall to fill, "Did you see the drekar, *'Cold Drake'*? She has come, they say, from the King of Norway."

My father wiped the foam from his beard, "Harald Fairhair has been so called king for less time than my son has been alive. He calls himself King of Norway but that does not make him so."

Finn the Scar shook his head, "You never change Lars. Keep your voice down. We do not need to antagonise another drekar captain! It is bad enough that Jarl Eystein thinks so little of us."

Instead of scowling my father smiled, "Then know that I have the hull of my drekar laid. This time next year we can raid without the say so of Jarl Eystein."

For some reason that made the three warriors smile. The conversation lightened as they asked my father and Snorri about the ship. My coins were burning a hole in my purse. Arne was the same and as more men joined our fathers and their oar brothers we were crowded out. "Father, can we go to the market? It will make more room here and we have no voice."

He looked down and spoke to Arne, "You are in command. Make sure your little brother does not do anything foolish."

"Me!"

Snorri laughed, "Aye you, nephew. You are the most unpredictable youth I have ever met."

We left the hall and headed to the market. In the time which had passed the three of us had grown. We did not have to move out of the way of men we met. Traders, anticipating sales at such a large gathering, had come in great numbers. When I saw the timber merchants, I knew that we had been meant to attend. If my father had brought coin then he could buy the pine and pine tar he desired. There were swordsmiths selling weapons. We could not afford them. We could only stand and look at them. They were longer than the swords we carried about our waists. The sword smiths were happy for us to handle them even though they knew that we would not buy them. They hoped we would tell our fathers. Despite the length of the blades they felt well balanced.

"Who are your fathers?"

"Lars Ragnarsson."

"Snorri Long Fingers."

"You mean Lars the Luckless?" The weapon smith turned to his companion, "Now there is a swordsman. He hewed more Saxon heads than any other when the Great Army swept through Northumbria."

"I thought he was jarl now?"

The swordsmith shook his head, "Ivar the Boneless did not like Lars. It was said he was envious of his success. He forbade the men to elect him. They chose Eystein Rognvaldson instead." He turned back to us. "He was a great warrior." He reached beneath the table and pulled out a finely decorated seax sheath. "This is for you if you recommend us to your father."

Arne took it, "I will do so."

We would have much to talk about. The next weaponsmith sold bows. He had a Saami bow. I had heard that they were the finest bows that could be had. When we asked the price, we discovered that they were almost the same price as a sword. I considered buying a yew stave but realised I could have one for nothing. Most Saxon churches had a stand of yew. When next we raided, I would simply take one. I did buy a bow string. It cost me but a half penny and I knew that it would be better than any I might make.

I wandered over to the timber merchant. When my cousin and brother had finished, they followed me. I saw pine there. It had not been turned into planks yet and that would suit us. I also saw willow boards. Arne had a sheath and I saw a way to profit from my visit. "My father seeks pine for a mast and for decking. What is the price?"

He told me but I had no concept if it was a good price or not. My father would haggle but I would be able to give the price to my father.

"And how much for willow boards?"

He frowned, "Your father wants a shield?"

"He has a shield but I want one."

"You are a little young to be a warrior."

Arne said, defensively, "My little brother has killed at least one Walhaz warrior with his bare hands."

The timber merchant looked impressed. "Then aye, I do. I can do you a good price."

I smiled, "You can do us all a better price if we tell our fathers that you are a fair man."

He laughed, "You are a Viking! You know how to trade. Tell me how much is in your purse and I will tell you if you can afford the boards needed to make a shield."

I halved the number, "Four silver pennies."

I saw him considering. He said, "And you two?"

"The same."

He held out his hand to me, "Then you have a deal but you drive a hard bargain!"

We spied a smith selling metal items he had made. He had some metal nails. They were long ones with a flat head. We each purchased some with our horde of coins.

We carried our purchases to the snekke and covered them with the seal skin cover we used to protect the cargo. Arne said, "You are clever little brother and now we have coin left."

I nodded, "And I am hungry. Let us see what delicacies our coin will buy us."

Our noses took us to the bakers and there we each bought two honeyed oat cakes. We had no bee hive. Our bees had died in a bad winter two years since and the honeyed cakes were like nectar. We sat on the sea wall and ate them slowly savouring each crumb. It was late afternoon when the warriors emerged from the hall. They came out in knots and most headed for the stalls set up by the ale wives. My father and his friends came out and, spying us came over to speak. Snorri sniffed, "I smell honeyed oat cakes! Our sons spent their money well!"

I nodded, "And we bought willow boards for our shields. There is a timber trader here, father and he has plenty of pine!"

My father's face had had a scowl upon it but now he grinned. "Then let us find him."

"And there is a swordsmith. He gave me a sheath for my dagger if I would tell you."

"Then you have told me and you have your honour. Come let us buy pine. The day may not be totally wasted!" They headed off with Finn the Scar. Butar Beer Belly headed for the ale wives but Asbjorn, who was the youngest of my father's friends stayed with us.

We saw Karl the Lame and his father. They emerged with the jarl and a warrior in the finest mail I had ever seen. Upon his helmet was a flying bird. I gasped out loud. Butar shook his head, "The helmet is for show. If you fight in a helmet like that you will lose the bird or your head. That is Halfdan Halfdansson the nephew of King Harald of Norway." We watched as they walked the finely dressed warrior and his men to his drekar. "The King of Norway offers his ships and the jarl has accepted. Your father is not happy. He believes that Harald Fairhair has ulterior motives. We agree with him. However, as we get to raid Mann and kill pirates then we will go along with the jarl." He pointed to the market, "And if your father can get the timber for the mast then we can do without the jarl."

Siggi was thoughtful, "This might cause trouble with the jarl."

Asbjorn shrugged, "There is but a hersir on Hrólfsey. He has no children. Those on the island could choose your father as hersir and besides, it does not matter. None of us have sworn an oath to the jarl. We choose to sail with him. There is no dishonour in sailing for ourselves."

The afternoon was getting on and I wondered what my father could be doing. Eventually, the three of them returned. Asbjorn looked up expectantly. My father's smile told me all that I needed to know. "We have the timber and for a good price. I have paid him a sum to ensure he delivers it to our beach and there I will pay him the remainder." He turned to Finn and he clasped his arm. "Thank you for your help there. You have honeyed words."

Finn the Scar shrugged, "Your brother does too. You tend to speak too plainly."

"It is my nature."

"Aye, we know. Well, Asbjorn, should we join our oar brother and sample the ale?"

"That is an appealing idea. Fare well and we shall see you on the drekar when we raid Mann."

That was the first time that we were spoken too as equals by a warrior and it changed me. I had no beard but I was no longer a boy.

We passed the jarl, his hearth weru and Bjorn and his son as we headed to the snekke. The jarl stopped and asked, brusquely, "So despite your words to our honoured guest you would fight on my drekar and obey my orders?"

I was aware that my father was trying to remain clam, "I will sail on your drekar and I will help you to defeat these pirates but that does not change my suspicions about the King of Norway."

Bjorn Bjornson snorted, "You know nothing. Why should the King of Norway be concerned about our little islands? He is a friend and helping us to rid the sea of pirates. Would that there were more like that."

My father shrugged, "And why should I fear a wolf when it smiles at me and invites me into its lair? Simple. I know that the wolf cannot change its nature and it will eat me. However, so long as he aids us and sends men then I will go along with you."

"And that is so good of you!" The jarl's words were heavily laced with sarcasm.

It was dark by the time we reached home. Although we were all weary Arne and I carried our willow boards as though they were a new born babe. We would not need a shield yet but we would one day and we would be ready.

Chapter 6

The trader arrived the next day just after noon. He was on his way to Dyflin with the rest of his cargo and my father's purchase meant that he had a smaller cargo to carry and that meant a fast voyage. We had been able to get a good price for the masts which we had purchased and the yards were not big enough for most drekar and would be too big for a snekke. For our ship they would be perfect. The money was paid and we were able to begin work on the deck and the mast. This was intricate work. The mast had to fit perfectly and yet be easily removed. It was skilled work and the three of us would just get in the way. While my father and uncle worked on the drekar the three of us made our shields. When we were bigger, we would need a much bigger shield but until we were fully grown there would be little point. As my father had said the exercise of making a shield would help us to understand how to use one. I used the stones on the beach to make a base for my shield. Laying the board on the stones I used a piece of cord to draw, with charcoal, a circle. I then sawed through the wood to make a roughly rounded shape for the willow boards. I made a hole for the boss and then repeated the process. The second, round board would be laid on the first with teased wool between them. It would help to absorb blows. We then drilled holes for the metal and wooden pegs we would use to hold the shield together. We could do no more until the pine tar was ready and we would only be able to have that once the hull had been sealed. When we had been attacked by the Picts our fathers had managed to take three small iron pot helmets. As helmets, they were next to useless, but as a boss for a shield, they were perfect. We each had to adjust the size of the hole to accommodate the pot.

"We are ready to apply the pine tar and wool!" My father's voice summoned us to the keel.

This was a messy job but we were eager to help for the little pine tar that was left would allow us to stick the laminated shield together. The pine tar had a strong smell. We three rammed and jammed teased wool between the strakes and then my father and uncle used the hot pine tar to glue it in position. Once it had set we would put the hull in the water to allow the wood to swell and for us to test for any leaks. It was almost dark by the time the three of us glued our roughly cut shields together.

The next morning all of us were up early. We had to drag the drekar over wooden rollers to the sea. Tethered to two posts she floated in the bay and we watched. After a short time, my father said, "There is little point in watching. We will return this afternoon and discover if we have made a ship." He smiled, "You have shields to finish, do you not?"

We had no anvil but we had a large tree trunk. We each had four precious nails. We would use them first. We drove them through the two alternating boards and then hammered the heads flat. In a perfect world, we would have used ten or so but we could only afford four. Then we hammered four wooden pegs through the holes we had drilled. The last part involved fitting the boss and fixing it into place. The final shaping would have to wait for the next day.

The next day was a nervous one for all of us. As three young Viking warriors, we each had a shield to hold and see if it had stuck together and we all had to see if the drekar leaked. The boat was the priority and we hauled her back to the beach. She was whole and there was just the rain in the bottom. My father tested it by drinking it. "The ship is sound! Now we begin the rest of the work." He smiled, "You boys go and test your shields."

We went and picked them up. It was obvious, when we did so, that Siggi's was not circular. It was not a disaster. He would reshape the outside but it would take work. They were all glued. I took the adze and began to make the rough round edges smooth. When I tired I handed it to Arne so that he could work on his. I had some strips of leather and I nailed them on to the back of the shield. They would be for my arm. By the time Arne had finished it was time for Siggi. He would have the most to do. I took the dagger I had taken from the Walhaz warrior and I used it to smooth off the edge. I really needed a metal strip around the edge of the shield but that would be a luxury. In lieu of that I needed leather but that was also in short supply. For the time being, I would have to heft the crude willow board shield. I did not care. I had a sword and I had a shield. I was a Viking.

There were not enough hours in the day as we worked on the drekar, the farm and prepared to raid Mann. This time although we were going as ship's boys we were going with arms and experience. There would be no fear. There would be no Karl. Surprisingly none of us feared the pirates of Mann. They were Vikings but they did not raid. They were not the wolf they were the crow which picked on flesh. There was a difference.

It was the start of Harpa when we heard that the fleet of fifteen drekar had begun to gather at the jarl's stad and we were told to come to the drekar. My father was dismissive of the numbers. "When Ragnar Lodbrok raided Paris he took three hundred and fifty ships. This King of Norway toys with our jarl. He gives him scraps and Eystein will lose all that he has!"

Arne screwed up his face. "Then why go, father?"

My father grinned, "We make coin and we take metal. We need coin so that we can buy the last pieces for our drekar." He ruffled our hair, "And you two may gain more skills. I need not ship's boys! I need warriors!"

Both Gytha and my mother had recovered from the births. The babes were growing and were healthy. Edmund and Helga would have to watch over them while we raided Mann as the proximity of the island meant we would be away for a shorter time. My uncle had no idea what sort of punishment our jarl intended for the pirates of Mann. "I cannot see that he would try to control the whole island. He barely controls Orkneyjar."

My father snorted as we marched towards the drekar, "The King of Norway might like the plum that is Mann. If he controlled that island then he could threaten the Land of the Wolf and the Viking land of Hibernia. You would be wrong to underestimate the ambition of Harald Fairhair!"

I learned later how right my father was but then I knew nothing. Then I was a ship's boy with two daggers, a sword and a shield. I thought I was Thor himself sent to slay the giants. How little I knew. My body had grown much. Now almost fourteen summers old I knew that I would soon need to groom my straggly beard. That would be the sign that I was a man.

Before we left we secured the half-finished drekar. The rain would not harm her but the winds might and we tied her down well. We ensured that my mother and Edmund had plenty of food. We did not want Edmund hunting food and leaving my mother and baby brother alone. Then we trekked across the island to the muster. This time we would be ferried to the main island and march across that to the jarl's stad. We left at dawn for it would be a long journey. The three of us had more war gear but not enough for a chest. Arne and I had the wood for our chest but we had had no time to build it. We each had a sack slung across our back and we walked in our seal skin boots.

"Will there be more ship's boys, Snorri?" As Arne and I now had hair on our faces my father and uncle thought that when we were on the drekar we should use their names. We were not going on the drekar as their children but as members of the crew.

"There may be but if not then the three of you will have to help Leif to do the work of six!"

I did not mind. The extra work would be better than having to endure Karl as one of the ship's boys. When we had seen him at the market I saw that he had grown. He now had a groomed beard and a sword. Would he be one of the rowers? That might be difficult. I put it from my mind. In the months since our encounter I had grown. I was sure that within a short time I would have a groomed beard. The work with the axe and the adze had broadened my chest and made the muscles on my arms thicker. The three of us chatted easily as we walked across Orkneyjar. We were excited. A raid against the Walhaz was one thing but a war against Vikings was something else. We had picked up men walking across Hrólfsey and more joined us as we tramped across Orkneyjar. There were twenty of us when the lights of the stad glowed by the sea.

Although it was dark as we marched down to the drekar I was overawed by the sheer number of drekar. I had only ever seen two before and here were gathered fifteen, many of them far bigger than *'Moon Dragon'*. The stad was bustling. Even as we headed towards our drekar I saw another two drekar appear. They were both smaller ones. We had to pass *'Cold Drake'*, she was the ship of the nephew of the King of Norway. As we did so I heard a familiar voice call out contemptuously, "Ship's boys still! I am a warrior now! I take an oar!"

We looked up and saw Karl leaning over the side of the Norse ship. Even though it was unnecessary he was wearing his helmet. My father turned and said, "Shout again, Karl the Lame and you shall be wearing that oar up your arse!" It made the men with us laugh and I watched as Karl's head disappeared. Bullying and humiliating us was one thing but he would not risk the wrath of my father.

Snorri laughed, "Well, at least we will not have to endure him and his father this time!"

My father nodded but said, with a note of caution in his voice, "Our jarl is a fool. Bjorn Bjornson has ambition to be a jarl. Why does he sail with the King's nephew? If I were Eystein I would watch my back." He looked at me. "The family have a habit of attacking from behind."

Only half the crew were aboard *'Moon Dragon'*. The rest lived in the warrior hall and would be the last to join. Ulf North Star was one of them and as Leif was now senior ship's boy, he took charge of us when we boarded. As our fathers headed for their oar Leif smiled, "There are just four of us on this voyage. It is good that it will be a short one for we will have much to do. Arne, you will be with me as steerboard watch and Erik you and Siggi will be the larboard watch."

Siggi frowned, "Why do we have watches this time Leif? Do we no longer work together?"

"The jarl has decided that it is unseemly for him to stand a watch." His words were guarded and he was hiding something. "Olaf Olafsson will share the watch with his grandfather and Arne and I will help him. Erik you and Siggi will be on the night watch with Ulf North Star."

I realised that meant we would have even less sleep on this voyage. Leif was right. It was fortunate that we had such a short journey south ahead of us.

He smiled, "At least we will have more room. I managed to get a piece of old sail. We have a better home at the prow. Go and sort your war gear and then return here. I would talk with you." There was a change in Leif. He now spoke as a man. His beard had been sparse on the last raid, now it was thicker. He had groomed it. His manner was that of a man.

As we passed my father Arne said, proudly, "I am to watch with Leif!"

My father nodded, "Well done, Erik."

Arne frowned, "Did you not hear my words? I am with Leif."

"Aye and that means that Leif trusts Erik to supervise Siggi." I saw realisation hit Arne. I had not thought of it either. Although Siggi was a little older than me we both knew that I was better as a sailor. He had improved but Ulf, Olaf and Leif had always asked me to perform the more difficult tasks.

As we packed our war gear I said, "It does not mean Leif thinks less of you, Arne."

He nodded, "I know but our father is right as is Leif. You are the better sailor. I will be the better warrior!"

Siggi said, "We do not compete with each other. We are the brothers of the blade." He held up his palm. "See the scar is still there. It may fade but it will always be a reminder of the oath. We watch out for each other. We are family!"

He was right and I clasped first his and then Arne's arm. We had each other and together we were like iron; we would not break.

Leif told us what he knew of the jarl and prince's plan. "We land on the north west coast of the island. There are many small settlements but the jarl wishes to capture the one which attacked us. Bergil the Fearless rules there. While the men march south the drekar will use their sails to approach from the sea."

I nodded, "A good plan for the pirates' eyes will be drawn to the fleet and not to the warriors who march south."

Siggi, thoughtful as ever, said, "What if they attack us? We will have but five of us to defend the drekar."

Leif shrugged, "Then we might die but they cannot attack us and defend their home." He shook his head, "Siggi Deck Crusher, you see everything as half empty!"

Siggi smiled, "That way I am never disappointed."

"And Ulf has made some improvements since last we sailed. He has not been idle. We now have a halyard so that we can raise and lower the spar." He laughed, "Perhaps he did not want his ship's boys to crash on to his deck. The only time we have to climb the spar now is when we are lookout."

I nodded, "That is easier."

Siggi smiled, "Until the halyard breaks!"

We all laughed for Siggi was mocking himself and that was no bad thing. We returned to the prow to organise our beds and our gear. We used ropes between the timbers to make nets to hold things in place. We put our seal skin boots there and jammed our swords and scabbards behind them. We covered them with our seal skin capes. If we had a bad storm, we would wear them but they were too cumbersome to wear when working.

Ulf North Star and most of the crew arrived not long after sunset. Ulf shouted, "We leave on the next tide. The jarl will be here shortly."

Olaf Olafsson came to speak with us. He had a simple pot helmet and a leather jerkin. His sword and seax were at his side. He looked like a warrior but I could see that he was nervous. "I take the place of Bjorn Bjornson but my grandfather says that I can row close to the men of Hrólfsey." I was pleased. My father would look after the young warrior who had been so kind to us.

The drekar was a hive of activity as men placed their chests and secured them in their rowing positions. Those like my father and uncle who had arrived early were able to sit and chat. I saw that Finn, Asbjorn, Butar and Galmr were gathered closely about my father. When our drekar was finished then it would be they who would sail it. There would be others but the six of them would form the heart of the crew. I hoped that, by then, Arne, Siggi and I could row too. Asbjorn and Galmr had young sons. We would only need a couple of ship's boys on such a small drekar.

The jarl and his hearth weru brought their war gear and chests aboard and we were ready to sail. The jarl stood and shouted loudly. I think he was speaking for crews of the other drekar to hear his words, too. Only three other drekar were from the islands of Orkneyjar and the rest were from the King of Norway. "Today we sail for Mann. The King of Dyflin cannot control them and so we must. We will all return from this voyage rich warriors and we will be able to sail the waters safely! May the Allfather be with us!"

Men banged the deck and they all chanted, "May the Allfather be with us!"

Ulf shouted, as the jarl and the hearth weru went to their places, "Ship's boys, prepare to cast off."

There were just two ropes tying us to the quay. Arne and I ran down the gangplank. Leif and Siggi hauled the gangplank aboard and we loosened the ropes and held them against the wooden bollards.

"Oars!"

The crew grabbed their oars and sat with them in the air. The steerboard side would not be able to run them out until we were away from the quay. All along the quay there was the same sound. Some drekar were moored two or three deep. There was a small drekar outboard of us. They gradually moved away from the shore. "Untie the mooring ropes." I quickly unwound the rope and coiled it as I ran to the side. I hurled the coiled rope to Siggi who managed to catch it and I leapt to the gunwale. "Oars out." The steerboard oars pushed against the quay and we began to move. I clambered over the side and then helped Siggi to coil the rope and hang it from the cleat. The yard was resting across the sides of the drekar. We had never hoisted it with a halyard and so we went to the ropes ready for Ulf's command. We gradually moved away from the quay.

"Raise the sail!" The halyard had been greased with seal oil and moved remarkably easily. The four of us pulled the two sheets in unison. Ulf shouted, "Tie it off and secure the stays!" As we did that he shouted, "Oars!" To give the beat the jarl banged the haft of the spear on the deck. I glanced ahead and saw a mass of drekar masts. It seemed inevitable that we would clash with one or other of them. Then I saw that the two drekar which were ahead of us were Orkneyjar boats and they knew these waters. The high tide meant that we were safe from the rocks and shallows.

"Erik, lookout!" Leif commanded us now and he would assign our tasks. As he gave his instructions to Siggi and Arne I made sure my horn was secure around my back and then climbed up the fore stay. I slipped my legs around the mast and stared ahead into the darkness. Except it was not truly dark for each drekar had a glowing pot hung from the stern post. It was not much of a light but it showed each drekar where the next ship lay. I saw that there were just two lights ahead of us. Leif was at the prow and I heard him shout, "*'Wolf's Teeth'* ahead, *'Moon Dragon'* steer to steerboard." Despite my father's opinion the fleet was commanded by Jarl Eystein and the drekar ahead pulled to the steerboard side of us and we surged a little further ahead. Once we cleared Graemsay we would have open water to the west. I looked forward to seeing the fleet at sea.

We were able to ship the oars within a short time. We had the wind and the jarl did not want to lose any of his ships. Behind was darkness save for the occasional sight of a white sail. My horn of ale had a cap. I had made it over the winter using a piece of sheep bone. I flipped it open and drank sparingly. I knew why I had been sent to keep lookout even though it was dark. It was to have a pair of eyes as dawn broke. It was unlikely that the Picts would have ships ready to attack us but unlikelier things had happened. My eyes were salt rimmed and tired as dawn broke. Ahead of us was open water. I looked to my left and right. The fleet was spreading out so that we were the tip of an arrow. It gave all an equal share of the wind and while we had sea room it was the most efficient way to sail.

It was the third hour of daylight when I was relieved by Arne. I did not use the leather strap to slide down the rope. There was no hurry. When I reached the deck Leif said, "Have some food and rest. I will wake you when it is time for your watch."

I had been told that it could take up to two days to reach Mann. We did not need to strike at night. Our plan meant that if we were seen it would not harm us. I had finished my horn of ale and so I refilled it at the barrel. I took a piece of bread and some salted fish. The bread was hard. I would pour some ale on it to soften it. When I had eaten I curled up and slept. The motion of the ship helped and when I slept, I dreamed. I had had the same dream almost every night whilst aboard the drekar. I had not had the same dream on the snekke but then I had not slept for long on the snekke.

The land was covered in ice and snow. There were few trees. Steam spouted and sprayed from the bowels of the earth. There was a smell like rotten eggs in the air. Great white bears twice the size of the bears I had seen rose and roared.

The dream was vivid. Each dream added more detail. What I had not seen in the dream was people. From what others had told me Norway was a land of ice and rocks but not of steam rising from the bowels of the earth. I wondered if this was the land of the gods. Was I dreaming my death? Valhalla was reserved for warriors who died with a sword in their hand. I was a ship's boy. If I died what would be my fate?

It was towards late afternoon on the second day of our voyage when we saw the mountains of the Land of the Wolf to the east of us. Mann was ahead. Siggi was the lookout and he shouted, "Land ahead!"

"Where away?"

"The dragon points the way!"

That meant it was directly ahead and Ulf nodded. He turned and said to the jarl, "The gods favour us. We did not need to row!"

"It is good." Cupping his hands, he shouted, "Prepare for war!"

Men opened their chests and took out their byrnies and weapons. Ulf looked at us, "And you ship's boys had better prepare. When we sail into their lair we may have to fight." He laughed, "Even you Siggi Deck Crusher! Perhaps we should have you as lookout and then we could always fell them from above!"

Siggi and I went to the prow. Leif was already there. "Ulf said to arm."

Nodding he took out his sword and strapped it on. He strung his bow and jammed five arrows in his belt. I put my sword belt around me. The sword felt weighty. I liked that. With no seal skin boots I could only have one dagger and so I chose the Walhaz one. That was good enough for pirates. I tied back my long hair. I did not want it flapping in my eyes. Finally, I took my sling and tied the stone bag to my belt. I carried Arne's war gear to the mast fish. All down the boat men were arming. Some had rituals. They varied from chants and prayers to putting on their war gear in a particular order. The last thing which every warrior did was to collect his shield from the side. I stood with Siggi at the base of the mast. Ahead I would see the island.

Ulf shouted, "Arne Larsson, your duty is done. Prepare for war."

I helped Arne to arm. Leif used his arm to direct Ulf. Leif and Ulf were the two most important men in the fleet. They had to find the beach upon which we would land. We had armed because we would not need to secure the drekar. The warriors would land in the water and make their way ashore. The four of us would have to use the sweeps to move us away from the landing site. We would then have to shift the sail to enable us to sail down the coast. Ulf was looking for the beach which lay just a couple of miles north of their stronghold. When we had been attacked, we had seen the island with the palisade and tower. We were to make a bridge of drekar to enable our warriors to cross to the stronghold.

Ulf shouted, "Prepare to land!"

The jarl led the warriors to the prow and the landward side of the drekar. I thought that this was the riskiest part of our plan. Ulf was trusting that there were no rocks beneath the water. Perhaps he had more knowledge than I thought for as the waves threatened to broach us the jarl leapt into the sea. My father and his men were close behind. The ones with longer legs landed in knee deep water. Some of the shorter warriors spluttered to the surface as they landed in deeper sea. They were hauled to their feet. Ulf shouted, "Loose the steerboard back stay. Tighten the larboard forestay."

Siggi and I went to the nearer backstay. As Leif and Arne tightened the forestay the sail twisted and shifted. The breeze caught us and pushed us away from the land and towards the sea. Already the two smaller drekar had disembarked their warriors and were also pulling away. The other drekar would tack and land in turn.

"Tighten the steerboard back stay. Loosen the larboard forestay." As we adjusted the sail and it became square to the drekar our speed became more even. I saw the smoke in the distance marking the settlement. It was then I saw how clever was the King of Norway. The risks would be taken by the first ships and the first men. They would be the men of Orkneyjar. His nephew had the largest ship. They would have more ship's boys than we. In that moment of clarity, I knew that my father was correct. The King of Norway was plotting. We were collateral damage.

Ulf shouted, "Once we get close to the land I will shout and I want the sail down so fast that the pirates will think we have Loki aboard."

Leif had strung his bow and had it about his back. He would have no time to string it when the action began later.

The adjustments that Ulf had made slowed us down to allow some of the other ships to close with us. I saw that he had donned a helmet and had his war axe close by. The masts of the ships in the harbour could be seen. Leif had told me that there was a river and many boats could anchor there. It was why the first Vikings to conquer the island had chosen this as their stronghold, that and the fact that it faced Dyflin and they had the support of the Dyflin King. As Ulf put the steerboard over to begin to enter the channel between the island and the mole, we slowed. I was being given a lesson in sailing. Without us having to do much he was commanding *'Moon Dragon'* to obey his wishes. I heard shouts from ahead and saw men rushing to the mole.

"Leif, use your bow whenever you can. You boys have your slings ready." I wanted to use my sword but that would have to wait until I was face to face with a pirate. I chose a good stone and began to whirl the sling above my head. Ulf shouted, "The steerboard side. There are men in the stronghold. We ran to the other side and I saw the wooden palisade. There appeared to be a church there too. Men lined the palisade. I counted ten of them. Leif's arrow flew and was blocked by a shield. The three of us whirled our slings and threw our stones. You can see an arrow coming for you but a stone is harder to spot. One of our stones hit one of those on the palisade and when he dropped the others pulled up their shields. "Now! Lower the sail and be as quick as you can."

We dropped our slings and bows and ran to the sheets holding the mast and sail. We normally lowered it slowly but we needed to do it quickly. We did it so quickly that the rope burned our hands but it came down and we slowed dramatically. We had enough way to reach the beach below the palisade. We would be on our own until the other drekar made a longphort for the warriors. Five of us had to hold off those from the stronghold until help came. I had barely picked up my sling when arrows and spears were hurled at us. I saw the door opening. They were going to sally forth and attack us. Such danger makes a warrior do things he thinks are impossible. My stone cracked off a helmet on the wall. I saw the gate open and I already had a stone whirling towards it before I could see a target. The pirate who emerged was struck in the chest by my stone. He fell writhing to the ground. No one else risked it. Leif's next arrow hit an arm. Siggi and Arne were sending their stones at the helmets and shields on the walls. We slid on to the sand and shingle. I felt a bump as a drekar ground next to us. Then there was a cry as Ulf was hit in the leg by a spear thrown from the palisade.

I was the nearest to him and I ran to his aid. He had fallen with his back to the gunwale. The spear had been slowed by the leather breeks. I saw Ulf tie a piece of cord above the wound. He said, through gritted teeth, "Erik, pull the spear out. Keep it straight. It is touching the bone!"

"Aye Ulf." I braced my right foot against his knee and using both hands pulled. At first, I thought it was not going to move and then, with a slurp and a puddle of blood it popped out. I grabbed a piece of linen and roughly tied it around the wound. He nodded. "Go back to the fight." He handed me the spear. "Send this back to them eh?"

In the few minutes I had been seeing to Ulf, events had changed dramatically. Leif had run out of arrows and the stones from two slings had merely encouraged the pirates. They ran from the stronghold. I saw that they carried torches. They meant to burn us. The boys and helmsmen from the two drekar which had tied to us had not reached us yet.

"Erik, with me. You two, aim for the ones with the fire!"

I held the blood smeared spear in two hands and joined Leif at the prow. He stood on the gunwale. "You have the spear. Stab the ones who fight me! They will be above you. They wear no armour down there!"

We both thought we were going to die. It was boys against men but we were Vikings and these were pirates. We had to believe that we would win. Arne slung his stone and hit one of those with a brand and as a second bent to retrieve it Siggi hit him on the side of the head. Even twenty paces away we heard the crack as his skull was broken. It gave us encouragement. "Well done Siggi! One for the Blade Brothers!"

A pirate who was wearing a half mail byrnie jumped up on the gunwale and swung his sword at Leif. The blow was so hard that, when it hit his shield it knocked Leif against our dragon. As the warrior raised his sword to finish him, I rammed the spear two handed between his legs. He squealed like a pig being butchered. I twisted and pulled hard and quick. I now knew how much force it took to remove a spear. He fell and landed with a splash in the sea. Only our bow had grounded.

The next to come had shields with them. One of the brands had fallen into the sea where it had spluttered and died. One remained and they had men protected by shields coming to us. I had felt a series of bumps. I assumed that others had joined our longphort. Two of the ship's boys had also clambered aboard. One had a sling and the other, who was older, joined Leif above me.

The rattle of stones on shields continued. One of the stones hit a helmet. As the man dropped another stone hit his right shoulder and spun him around but inevitably the pirates drew closer. With shields before them they swashed their swords at Leif and the other boy. Leif jumped to avoid the sword but the other ship's boy was hit in the leg and fell. I barely managed to step from his falling path. Leif's sword rang against his enemy's weapon and as the pirate who had felled the boy and another man of Mann reached the gunwale I lunged with the spear. I struck one in the right shoulder as he tried to climb aboard. He fell but tore the spear from my hand. Even as I drew my sword the other slipped over the side.

I heard, from behind me, "We come to your aid, brother. Others are coming!"

I was encouraged by the words and as the warrior jumped down, I slashed with my sword. I tore across his shin and he screamed with rage. My arm jarred as I ripped through the skin on the shin and grated against the bone. He swung his sword as he landed and I barely had time to block it. As I fell Leif jumped to the deck and brought his sword against the man's back. He wore a leather byrnie and turned. I rose and lunged at his leg. This time the tip found the soft flesh of his thigh and as he turned to swing his sword at me Leif hacked into his neck. Blood spurted and spattered across the deck and our faces.

Ulf North Star crowed, "Show them ship's boys! We are *'Moon Dragon'*. Stop them burning our ship!"

Arne and Siggi had joined us and I heard more stones rattling against the enemy. We were no longer alone. Leif shouted, "We can take these bilge rats!" He raised his sword and blood ran down it.

I drew my dagger for the joy of battle was upon me, "Aye!" We ran to the side just as the next four warriors arrived. They had the brand. It was easier for us to climb on the gunwale and Leif and I stood on the gunwale and then jumped down. The four held locked shields before them and slashed blindly. The Norns had been spinning for they missed and we landed on the shields. We were heavy and the four of them were knocked to the ground. Before they could rise Siggi and Arne had joined us as well as two more ship's boys who stood on the gunwale. The four of us had little skill but the four men were held on the ground by our weight and their shields. I plunged my dagger into the throat of one and repeatedly smashed my sword against the others. Arne and Siggi's swords scraped across throats and the four lay dead or dying as blood oozed from mortal wounds.

That was when we should have stopped. We had done all that we had been ordered. We had done better than expected but when the two ship's boys we did not know jumped from the drekar and ran to the open gate we had no choice. We rose to our feet and we followed them.

The four of us stayed together. We were not as reckless as the other two. As we entered the gate, I heard a cry. Turning into the open space before the church and tower I saw the two boys as they were butchered by three more pirates. The pirates came towards us. We could have run but we did not. The three had shields and we did not. They had helmets and we were bare headed. They wore boots and we were barefoot. All three had leather vests but we were bare armed. None would have blamed us if we had run but we did not. We prepared to die.

Leif saw that I had a sword and dagger. He pulled out his own. "Do as Erik does! Use your dagger as a shield."

The three men began to run towards us. The surface upon which we stood was rough. I knew, although I knew not how, that we had to use our speed across the uneven ground to outwit the men. We outnumbered them. "Fight as a watch! Two to one!"

As the three came towards us I ran to the right and hoped that Siggi would follow me. He did. As the two warriors closest to us tried to turn, their boots skittered on the stones. It made them falter and allowed Siggi and me to turn and face the nearer of them. I swung at his shield as Siggi hacked at his sword. His companion was turning. I stabbed down with my dagger at his knee. The blade went through the breeks and into the flesh behind the knee. I felt it grate on bone. He opened his mouth to scream as the second warrior brought his sword to hack across Siggi's neck. Then Siggi showed that he was not clumsy. His sword and dagger made a V and blocked the sword. The man smashed the boss of his shield into Siggi's face. Blood spurted and he fell. His fall, however, allowed me to swing my sword at his left arm. It was without protection. I half severed it with the force of the blow. He dropped his shield. I turned for the man whose knee I had stabbed was trying to rise. I used my legs as a weapon. I kicked his good leg from beneath him and as he fell it made the wound in his knee worse. He screamed and fell backwards. I ran to him and putting my sword into his neck put all of my weight upon it.

Leif shouted, "Erik! Beware!"

I turned with just my dagger in my hand as the man whose shield arm I had half severed came at me with his sword. Although I blocked it with my dagger I was off balance and I fell over the man I had just slain. He stood over me and I knew that I must die when Arne's sword appeared through his chest as my brother saved my life.

I scrambled to my feet and ran to Siggi. His nose had been broken. He opened his eyes, "Am I alive?"

I laughed, "Aye, cuz."

Leif shouted, "Before we get too cocky let us search for more pirates."

The only ones we found were dead or dying. Our stones and arrows had wreaked wounds. We climbed the palisade and saw that we had won. Across the harbour, we could see our men as they put the heads of pirates on spears. We had not been in the main battle but we had done our part and we had fought. I could see the bodies of five ship's boys who had obeyed orders but would now never be a warrior. It was a lesson learned.

Before others could reap the benefit of our combat, we stripped the dead of weapons, coins and treasure. We took their boots and we took their cloaks and brooches. By the time we reached our ship it was getting on to dark and already rats were coming forth to feast on the flesh of the dead.

Chapter 7

Ulf North Star was being tended to by the helmsman of the small drekar which had tied next to us. We were elated and loud. I saw Ulf give a slight shake of the head. We became serious. Ulf said, "Thank you, Einar. I am sorry for your loss."

"It was I who promised my brother that his sons would be safe and now they lie dead."

"They died well. He can father more children."

Einar nodded and turned to us, "You four showed great courage. My nephews died in good company. I thank you for avenging them. If there is ever anything I can do for you then just ask."

Leif said, "It was our honour. Had they not joined us then we would be dead too. It is we who are in your debt."

Ulf winced, "I am going to be in pain tonight. Erik, Arne go back inside the tower. They must have some means of cooking. Prepare food. The jarl and the Prince will be too busy celebrating to think of us."

Einar said, "And I will get the other crews on this side of the longphort to throw the dead pirates into the sea!"

When we reached the church, we saw that it was no longer used as a church. There were beds for sleeping, war gear, a table and pots for cooking. There was a fire and a pot of water upon it. They had not yet begun to cook. "Let us see what they have, little brother."

We found some bread and a leg of salted pig. There were some sad looking cabbage leaves and some dried beans. We emptied them all into the pot. That done we searched the building which was obviously used as some sort of guard room. We searched it and it was I who found the treasure. At least I thought it was treasure. There was a wooden compass and an hourglass. Ulf had both and he guarded them with his life. Arne found coins and a good dagger. He said, "Do you want the dagger? We can split the coins."

"No, you keep the dagger and I keep these."

He looked at them dismissively, "We do not need them!"

"If we are to sail beyond the sight of land we will. I am content. Are you?"

"Of course. This dagger is much better than the one we had."

I nodded, "And the swords we took, which Leif now guards, are better than this Walhaz one." I took it from the scabbard. It was bent! "It is fit for melting down and using to strengthen our shields and making arrow heads." I looked at the coins. "We will give a share to Siggi too."

Two of the pots the guards used were metal. We would take them with us. Our mothers would find them useful. There was a barrel of ale. We stoppered it and rolled it down to the drekar. Ulf's eyes lit up, "This will ease my pain. When the food is ready fetch it here."

It was dark by the time that the food was ready. We ladled half of it into a small pot to make it easier to carry and took that to the drekar. More than half of the ship's boys and helmsmen had gathered on our drekar. Ulf frowned when he saw the pot. "This will not feed us all!"

Arne said, "And it will not need to. There is another pot. We will fetch that." Arne spoke up to Ulf more now. He would not suffer a smack to the head any longer. When you have sunk a blade into a man's flesh it makes a change in you. As you hear the last breath slip from a warrior's mouth you truly understand mortality. Life becomes ever more precious.

Ulf had had a great deal of ale and after he had eaten, he fell asleep. The four of us sat together by the prow after the others had returned to their own drekar to sleep. If Ulf had been awake then he would have had us clean the drekar. He was not and so we enjoyed a rare piece of peace. We drank the ale, examined our treasure and spoke of the battle.

Leif examined the sword he had taken from a dead pirate. "Two swords! When we went to raid the Walhaz I did not even have one." He picked up the pot helmet. "And a helmet. I just need a helmet liner and I can wear it."

Siggi said, "What about the one the warrior wore?"

Leif shook his head, "It was bloodied. Better to have my mother make me a new one. That way she can weave protection into it."

We all touched our hammers. Women had great power and when they wove, they were like the Norns or volvas. By weaving strands of their hair into the weft they added strength and power.

Siggi had also drunk too much for his tongue was loose, "When we sail our drekar I will not be a ship's boy. I will pull at the oar."

Leif turned sharply, "Drekar? You have a drekar?"

I clipped Siggi about the back of the head as Arne said, "We have spilled blood together, Leif Ragnarson. Our cousin cannot hold his ale. We would ask you to swear to keep this a secret."

Touching his hammer, he said, "Of course. You are my shield brothers. I would sail on your drekar with you."

Relieved Arne said, "My father will be captain but I am sure he would have someone with such a stout heart." He added quietly, "You would leave the jarl's service? Did you not swear an oath?"

He shook his head, "My mother farms the land with my sisters. He takes me out of pity. The jarl has his favourites. The ones on the front eight oars are the ones who are given the choicest treasure. Why do you think Olaf sits with your father at the rear?"

"But I thought that Ulf and the jarl were close."

"They were, Erik, until the jarl's son, Haaken, was ship's boy and Ulf smacked him. Since then Haaken has not sailed with us and Ulf has received less treasure. I fear this wound means this will be his last voyage with the jarl. He was old anyway but the wound will make him slower."

I nodded, "Aye the spear touched the bone and my father said such wounds never fully heal. The cold gets to them. The damp makes them ache. I fear you are right."

"Fear? Ulf is a bad-tempered helmsman."

Leif said, "I know Arne but we know him. What of one we do not know? Besides, he owes us a life now. Had Erik not pulled the spear from his leg and bound it then he might have bled to death. I would rather sail with your father than another man. I do not believe he is luckless. He slays more than any other on the drekar and yet he has the fewest wounds. I would call him Lars the Skilled."

It was later, as I rolled into my blanket and recently acquired cloak, that I wondered who had given him the name. In truth, until I had seen five summers, I had not heard it. No-one who had visited the farm, save the jarl, ever used it. When I had the chance, I would ask him.

We were woken in the middle of the night by a rain shower. Leif roused us and we used the time to clean the ship and to put a seal skin cape over Ulf who continued to sleep. We stored the pots we had taken below the deck. We managed to return to the prow to catch an hour or so of sleep before dawn and a chill wind from the north east woke us.

Einar the Helmsman came to our drekar as the sun began to rise over Mann. He went to Ulf to tend to him. He spoke over his shoulder, "We had a message last night after we left your ship. The jarl and the Prince wish us to take the drekar into the river and tie up. Can you four manage the drekar? Ulf North Star will be of little use for a while. The old take longer to recover from such wounds."

"We can, but what of you? You have no ship's boys."

He stood, turned and smiled, "I should have been honest with you. I would steer your drekar and we can tow mine."

Leif looked relieved, "Then let us do so sooner rather than later. That way we can have the better berth."

Einar nodded, "Erik, go and loose my drekar from the next one. Arne, tie a rope to the prow of my drekar and Siggi secure it to the sternpost of yours. Come, Leif, we must be ready to push us from the island."

The small drekar next to Einar's looked empty but it was not. The helmsman and the one remaining ship's boy slept. I untied the rope from the cleat and, after coiling it, dropped it into their drekar. I went to the prow and helped Arne tie the tow rope to the prow. Einar shouted, "You two stay on my drekar. Use the steering board. It will make it easier if we are not fighting her."

We ran, eagerly, to the steering board. I had always wanted to steer a drekar and now I had the chance. We stood on either side of it and waited for *'Moon Dragon'* to begin to move. The sun was a little higher but with rain clouds scudding in from the north east it was hard to tell. Slowly, *'Moon Dragon'*, slid towards the river as Einar and our two shield brothers used oars to push her from the island. As soon as she was no longer next to us then the small drekar, we learned she was called, *'Wave Dancer'*, began to bob on the water. We pushed the steering board over to keep us from grounding. Erik and Siggi each had an oar and Einar steered *'Moon Dragon'* as he headed into the wind to cross the mouth of the river. Bodies bumped next to us. Some we had thrown into the sea and others were from the battle on the land. We only had a hundred odd paces to travel but it would feel like ten times that to Leif and Siggi. There was a jerk as the slack was taken up and then we began to move slowly across the water. The drekar was easier to steer than I had expected although the land protected us from waves. I saw that Einar was taking us to lie alongside a large drekar. It looked to be the same size as *'Moon Dragon'*. As they bumped next to it, we put our steering board over to put *'Wave Dancer'* next to the knarr.

"Arne, loose the tow. Erik, tie her to the knarr. You both did well." That was praise indeed. Ulf North Star would have said nothing.

Anxious to return to our ship we did as we had been instructed and then crossed the knarr to the stone quay. There the bodies still lay. I guessed that they were pirates. When we reached the large drekar we found more bodies. As we crossed to *'Moon Dragon'* I spied two dead pirates. They still had their helmets although their swords, daggers and purses had been taken. "Arne, treasure!"

"We did not earn them!"

"What, brother, steering a drekar here does not deserve payment?"

He grinned, "You have a clever mind, brother." We took the two conical helmets with nasals. Like Leif we would have mother weave us a skull protector.

Einar nodded as we boarded, "Good. You earned those. And now I go back to my ship. Was there aught on the knarr worth taking?"

"We did not search it."

"Then I will do so. You are welcome to join me."

Leif said, "Whatever you find will be weregeld for your lost boys. We are satisfied with what we have."

We spent almost seven days on the island. We had much to gather and to store beneath the decks of the drekar. We saw little of the jarl. He was aboard one of the captured drekar with the nephew of the King of Norway. The loading of the drekar was left to my father. I watched as he did so and I learned much. The crew returned laden with treasure and some animals. Olaf Olafsson went directly to his father. Ulf was asleep. When he learned what we had done he swore to repay us. It was the next morning when we left the river. The jarl and the nephew of the King of Norway took as many slaves as they could. I knew that my father would not have any. A Norse slave would often be a danger. Saxons were safer. Four ships were taken and they were laden with treasure. The rest were burned along with every building. Many people had escaped and would be hiding on the island but they would not be able to raid for many years. The jarl and his hearth weru did not sail back with us. They sailed on one of the captured drekar. The Prince and the jarl were heading for Dyflin. My father was not happy about that but as he had a drekar to sail he accepted it. We had half a crew and each oar was manned by one man. Despite that, we were all happy for my father was given command. The jarl had little choice. Ulf was in no condition to stand. We left Mann individually and our men had to row. Leif took my father's oar and I was allowed to stand next to my father. I was the one who wished to be a navigator and Arne knew that. I was given the spear to keep the beat.

"When we have our own drekar we will have a chant. The jarl does not think of such things. A good chant can keep a man rowing for longer."

I nodded, "Will we have to row all the way home? This wind feels like it is here for a while."

"You have the sense of a navigator already. No, my son, we row into the wind and then turn to sail along the coast of the Land of the Wolf. It will take us north and west. Once we pass the island the Irish call Beinn na bhFadhla we may have to row again but that is many days hence."

The rowers settled into an easy rhythm. I watched my father's every move. "Leif would sail with us on our drekar."

He turned and gave me a sharp look, "You told him?"

I would not use Siggi as the cause, "It came out that is all but he swore to keep it a secret."

That seemed to satisfy him, "He is a good lad. His father was too. He is handling my oar well. It is good."

"He said he did not think that you were luckless." My father's eyes burned but he said nothing. I summoned up the same courage as when I had faced the pirates. "How did you get the name?"

At first, I thought that he would either strike me or not speak but he eventually nodded, "It is right that you know. It was the jarl who gave me the name. We had raided and were sailing up the coast of Northumbria. My brother had been wounded and I rowed alone. Ulf and the jarl should have found a beach on which to land so that we could rest but they did not. The jarl did not row. I was tired and my oar struck another and sheared. A wave swamped us and took four sheep over the side. I was blamed and the jarl called me luckless."

"But it was not your fault!"

"It was my oar. That makes it my fault." He stared ahead, "Now go and take ale to the rowers. Perhaps you can relieve Leif."

"Aye Lars, I will!" I now understood the name and also the animosity my father felt to the jarl and Ulf.

I reached Leif and said, "My father said to relieve you." I saw the doubt on his face. I said, "Just until you have had a drink and made water."

He nodded and I slipped next to him. I had watched rowers do this and I knew the procedure. I got into the rhythm and nodded. Leif lifted his hands and then slipped out. I had rowed the snekke but this was different. I had taken barely ten strokes when I felt my shoulders burning. Leif came back and smiled, "It is not as easy as they make it look, is it?"

I shook my head and I was fearful of speaking. I did so anyway, "Another fifty strokes eh?"

By the time I had reached fifty every muscle in my back and arms was aching. My legs felt as though I had run across our island. I was relieved beyond words when Leif sat next to me and nodded. "Thank you, Erik."

They did not have long to row. My father shouted, "Ship's boys raise the mast. Prepare to come about!" This had to be timed well. As the three of us hauled the yard up my father began to turn the steering board. He shouted, "Oars in!" He chose the perfect time. The yard locked into place and, as we turned, the wind caught us and we moved north and west. It was not fast but it was quicker than it had been with the oars. More importantly, the men could rest.

We reached Orkneyjar three days later. We had no captives aboard the drekar and only twenty sheep. There was one sheep for each of the rowers. Ulf North Star had begun to improve over the last day. He was able to thank my father for handling the ship. My father was unrelenting. "I did what any man would do for his oar brothers. You should thank Leif for he took my oar despite being just a ship's boy."

"I do, Lars. You have good sons. They do you credit."

"And I need no foresworn helmsman to tell me that." Father did not forgive.

We off loaded all of our treasure. There was too much to carry across the island. Leaving it with Olaf and Leif we trekked across the island. We needed the snekke. We sailed her back to the port. It was late at night when we finally unloaded all that we had taken from the raid. We did not know it then but that would be the last time we would raid with the jarl and the men of Orkneyjar. The Norns were spinning and the King of Norway was plotting. We just got on with our simple lives.

Skerpla was always a busy time for us and with two new sheep which needed to be covered by the ram, crops which needed tending, a ship which had to be finished. The days were not long enough. Siggi, Arne and myself had become men on the last voyage. Arne had a groomed beard now and mine and Siggi's were not far behind. Our chests were broad and our arms becoming knotted with muscle.

The drekar was finished by the end of Skerpla. My father had kept the figurehead covered until we were ready. The two families and their thralls gathered at the beach. My father made a blót. It was a fowl we had taken from Mann and seemed appropriate. Mother and Gytha had woven a pennant for the masthead. It was not merely to give us the wind direction, it would protect us for they had used hair from all of our heads in the spell. They had dyed it with the blood of many beetles. The red pennant would stand out. The sail also had red lines in it. It would mark the drekar as ours. My father had kept the name secret from all, including his brother.

As he sacrificed the fowl he intoned, "Allfather watch over this drekar. Ran keep us safe when we sail. I name this ship *'Njörðr'* and ask that god to help us find a safe way through the seas."

We celebrated with a special barrel of beer. Half was spilled over the dragon prow so that Njörðr could drink the libation. The next day began the work of sailing her. First, we filled her with ballast. That took half a day. When my father and his brother were satisfied with the trim, we raised the sail. We sailed her around our bay to see how close she could sail to the wind. Larger than the snekke but smaller than a threttanessa, she was lithe and lively. A sudden gust of wind took the gunwale close to the sea but she fought the wind and did not broach. By the time night fell we knew our drekar a little better but it would take years to understand how she would truly sail. We anchored her in the bay and, that night, the men gathered in our hall to speak of our plans. I say our plans but they were my father's. Even his brother went along with them.

"I would raid the land of the Saxons before the end of summer. The lands north of the land of the Walhaz are ripe. The wars between Wessex and her neighbours have weakened them. They have churches which are filled with silver and fine metals. They have holy books. The slaves there are hardier and less likely to run. When we go to the midsummer Thing we will speak with our friends."

"How many do we need to crew, father?" We had finally settled on ten places for oars on each side. If we had them all manned, we would be crowded but my father and his brother had planned for the future.

My father smiled at Arne's question. "The three of you can take an oar with Snorri. You are small yet but I believe you have the heart." I beamed. I would be a warrior! "We have four rowers. Butar, Finn, Asbjorn and Galmr make eight."

"Do not forget Leif." My father nodded. "And I think Olaf Olafsson would sail with us too."

"Then ten would be a good number. Finn and Galmr each have a son. They could be the boys. We now have to make twenty oars. We do not need them all yet but if we do not make them then we will need them; the Norns will see to that."

Once again, despite the long days of summer, there were not enough hours left in them. We worked from sunrise to sunset. The three of us needed a leather byrnie. We had the tanned hides but they needed to be cut and stitched. We had the poor swords taken on earlier raids. We made a fire and melted them down. It was hard work. We made a mould from clay for the strips and studs which would adorn the jerkin and our shields. We had each painted a design on our shields. Mine was a yellow dragon head with red eyes. When the studs were made, I would use them to fashion the dragon's eyes. We poured the metal into the moulds. It had to be thin enough to be malleable and yet hard enough to blunt a sword. We sewed them on ourselves. Our mothers had made our helmet protectors. We could now wear our helmets. The leather straps had to be adjusted but I felt like a warrior when we wore them.

We sailed for the Thing on the day before midsummer's eve. This was the largest Thing of the year and there would be a huge market. We had great quantities of coin. We intended to buy as much as we could to give us the greatest chance of success with our raid. The one thing we were uncertain of acquiring were maps and charts.

When I had shown my father my compass and hourglass, he had been more excited than I had ever seen. "This saves us much coin. I will use them but they remain yours, Erik. They are your treasure."

"Then show me how to use them for I would be a navigator too."

He shook his head, "That is a lesson for the days at sea."

When we sailed, we did not take our helmets and shields. A Thing was a time for peace. Disputes between warriors and farmers were settled. It was a time of negotiation and reconciliation. It was also when the summer raids were decided. We reached the stad at sunset. As we entered the bay, I saw that there were two huge drekar in port. It was fortunate that we were not a drekar for we were the only ship small enough to find a berth. We recognised the pennant, it was the King of Norway's ship. The symbol of the king was a hawk with talons clutching a serpent.

My father's mood became black immediately. "What is he doing here? He will detract from the Thing."

My uncle was ever the peacemaker, "Perhaps he comes to reward the jarl for our defeat of the men of Mann."

"I see a more sinister side to this. Come we will see our friends before the Thing." As we passed the feasting hall of the jarl, we could hear the sound of men celebrating. That would be the King, his nephew and the jarl. "We will sleep this night on the snekke. I will not beg for a bed from the jarl."

We found an ale wife who served the beer my father and his brother enjoyed. Butar and Finn were there already. They were gloomy. We bought a jug of ale and my father asked them why the black mood.

"We thought to enjoy a feast in the jarl's hall but we were told that he had honoured guests from Norway."

"Honoured guests! The King of Norway is little better than a pirate who has stolen the lands of others. It is said that men flee his land and seek new homes."

Finn nodded, "I heard that they have found a land far to the north. It is a land of ice and fire. It is in the middle of the seas to the west. A man called Naddor found it."

I suddenly shivered. A land of ice and fire sounded like my dream. I paid even more attention.

"And why is he here?"

"None know. His nephew and the jarl spent seven nights in Dyflin and the word was that there was some sort of agreement over the future of Mann."

My father seemed mollified by that. "Then if the King of Norway is here to guarantee that the pirates will no longer raid then I am happy." The others nodded.

A voice from the dark shouted, "Lars! Well met!" It was Galmr and Asbjorn. They had a young warrior with them.

"Come join us this is an appropriate time. Snorri, more ale."

Asbjorn said, "This is Harald of Dyrøy. He came to our farm seeking someone to follow."

My father's eyes narrowed, "Is there no jarl on Dyrøy to follow?"

"There was but Jarl Bjorn has given his allegiance to the King of Norway."

Finn the Scar shook his head, "Then you have come to the wrong place. The King of Norway may not rule here but he, too, is an ally of our jarl."

Asbjorn said, quietly, "I have spoken to him of your plan, Lars."

"You should have asked me first."

"Lars, we are too few in number to raid. We cannot turn down any who wish to raid with us."

"Perhaps. You are welcome, Harald, but keep what is said here in your heart."

"I will and I am an honourable man. It is why I left my island and my jarl. I would not raise a sword against him but I do not like this Harald Fairhair. It strikes me that he is a man without honour."

The beer arrived, "Well, friends, the drekar is built. She floats and she sails like she was born to be upon the water. I intend to raid the land of Mercia."

"Mercia?"

"Aye, Butar. There are many rivers there. The land south of the Land of the Wolf and north of Ceaster is without strongholds. The farm land is rich and there are few warriors. A small band such as ours could use a river for a raiding camp and then raid up and down the land."

All of the assembled warriors seemed in agreement and nodded. Butar said, "Saxons make good slaves. They are easier to train and I like their churches."

"Then after the Thing, I will tell the jarl that I raid."

Finn said, "You will ask his permission?"

My father laughed scornfully, "I am informing him as a courtesy. We have no king here. None of us have sworn an oath to him. We tell him that is all. Perhaps there may be others who might wish to join us."

Harald said, "There will be. Many young warriors left Dyrøy at the same time as I did. I found a berth on a knarr. Others went to the Land of the Wolf while one crew sailed south to the land of Göngu-Hrólfr Rognvaldson. It is said he will soon rule the land of the Franks and there he has no king."

"Then I hope there are others of the same mind. We had oars to spare and twenty men will be better than the handful I have."

I suddenly became concerned. If all the oars were taken by grown warriors, I would not have an oar. I would be a ship's boy still. I hoped that we would not have more men wishing to ship with us. I knew that I was being disloyal but I could not help it.

Finn the Scar said, "Have you heard about Ulf North Star?" We all shook our heads. "The healer the jarl sent over was not as diligent as he should have been. Ulf's leg went bad and they had to take it off." He saw the look of dismay on my face and he patted my arm. "This was not your doing, Erik. Ulf said that had you not pulled out the spear then he would have died. This is a bad healer and the Norns."

Despite the words, I felt responsible. I drank less as I brooded.

The ale and beer flowed. Plans were made. The more the men drank the grander became those plans. I drank little for I still brooded about losing my chance of an oar. Siggi and Arne were drunk as we headed back to the snekke. Snorri carried Siggi and my father and I held Arne between us. My father was never drunk. I had seen him consume a firkin of ale and he had not appeared drunk.

"You were quiet this night." I was silent. "Come, my son. We must have honesty between us. Speak the truth and I will not think badly of you."

I was not drunk but I had drunk enough to have Frisian courage. "If we take on more men then I might not have an oar. I would be a warrior."

He nodded. We neared the sea. We stopped while Snorri lowered his son into the snekke. "You do not want to be an oarsman."

"I do!"

"I thought you wished to be a navigator."

I was confused, "That too!"

"Which is it, navigator or oarsman?"

"You do both!"

"Not out of choice. Ulf North Star was the navigator. He is not as good as me but he was a friend of the jarl. If we fill the benches then you will learn at my side."

I suddenly felt foolish. "I am sorry I..."

"Always speak what is in your heart. It is my way. I know that others might be upset by your words but not I. Anyway, let us worry about a crew after the Thing."

We rose early and prepared ourselves for the Thing. Despite the low opinion my father had of both the jarl and the King of Norway he wanted us to look our best. We wore our finest kyrtles. We had combed and oiled beards and hair. Our boots were without dirt and we strode to the ale wife to meet our fellows. My father wished to be surrounded by allies. We had a horn of ale and then went to the market to buy that which we needed. The market was always better first thing and when we had bought all that we required the men returned for another horn of ale while Siggi, Arne and I took our purchases back to the snekke to store them below deck.

Despite the feasting and the carousing, the hall was already filling with warriors when we arrived not long before noon. Most of the tables and benches had been removed save for one large table and a bench. We were at the rear and we heard a cheer. The jarl, the King and the King's nephew stood on the table and then Bjorn Bjornson clambered up too. What was Karl the Lame's father doing there?

The King of Norway stroked his hair as he looked down on us. He was ever a vain man. He and his nephew wore golden mail. It was not gold, of course. It was ordinary mail made to look like gold. His helmet was also golden. I guessed it was copper. My father was right about this King.

The jarl held up his hands. He spoke first of all the success they had had and then flattered, uncomfortably so, the King of Norway and all of his achievements. Men became restless and so the jarl moved on to the meat of his words, "Hersir, bondi, warriors and friends, welcome to this Thing. I have spoken at many of these but today, thanks to King Harald, what I say will ripple through the ages. Today we become part of the Kingdom of Norway!"

If he thought his words would result in a torrent of cheers and applause, he was wrong. I saw the King of Norway frown and the jarl looked nervously at Bjorn Bjornson.

He ploughed on through waters which were becoming increasingly stormy, "More, we have been honoured by the generosity of King Harald. He has accepted that the King of Dyflin accepts his suzerainty. King Harald has made Bjorn Bjornson, Jarl of Mann. No longer will men fear to sail those waters."

The silence was deafening. This was not the response either man expected.

A voice from close to the front shouted, "Why do we need the King of Norway?"

Behind the table were the hearth weru of the King. I saw them bristling. The King did not seem happy either. The jarl looked panicked, "We need fear no enemies!"

My father shouted, "We fear no enemies now! We need no king! I will follow no king!"

The silence which had greeted the jarl's announcement was now replaced with a roar as warriors cheered my father. This was not going the way the jarl had expected. The King, embarrassed, made to leave but the jarl restrained him. He held up his arms, "Lars the Luckless knows nothing. As part of the Kingdom of Norway and the Isles no one will dare face us. The Picts will be ground underfoot. Already the King of Dyflin prepares an army to take Hibernia. When that is done and we are ready then Mercia and Wessex will fall beneath our heel!"

For the first time there was a murmur of approval from some. Butar Beer Belly shouted, "And who will pay for this army? This protection?"

The jarl made a major mistake, he answered him, "The taxes we will all pay to the King will suffice!"

My father shouted, "I have heard enough. I go to my home. If any tries to collect my taxes they had better wear good mail!" His answer was greeted by a cheer.

I watched the King of Norway bend down to speak with the jarl. The jarl nodded and turned. Pointing to my father he shouted, "Lars the Luckless is banished from Hrólfsey and Orkneyjar! He is declared outlaw! That is my decision and any man who sides with him is also declared outlaw!"

All eyes turned to my father, "So be it! You were ever a faithless jarl and now all men can see the colour of your heart!"

He turned and we all followed him from the hall. Others, not just my father's friends, joined us. Once outside my father said, "Any who wish to follow me to a new land come to Hrólfsey. I will not stay here to be crushed beneath Fairhair's foot. There are new lands without kings. I will find one!"

My father had cast the bones and my future changed irrevocably on that Midsummer Day.

Chapter 8

We had parted at the quay. The hall had spilled out and men had milled around debating the words of the jarl. Now I understood the need for two huge drekar. The King's hearth weru had been inside but outside there were more than a hundred Norwegian warriors. No matter what had been said at the Thing Norway had taken over Orkneyjar. The King had doubled the size of the land he controlled. My father spoke to his friends and to the many others who came with us. They organised the opposition to the King of Norway. Arne, Siggi and I prepared the snekke. We could not stay on Orkneyjar. We might resist the jarl but the King of Norway had too many men for us to fight. We would die. If we sailed away then where would we go? The annexation of Mann and the neutralising of Dyflin limited the places we could go. Before we had attended the meeting, we were planning a future of raiding. Now we had to seek a new home.

As my father and his brother descended into the snekke Asbjorn said, "You are not alone! There are others who will not stand by and allow you to be driven from this land. We will join you at your farm"

My father said nothing but he raised his hand. He took no pleasure in being proved right. Instead of taking the steering board he waved me over, "Let us see if you can be a navigator. Take the steering board. Arne, Siggi, raise the sail. We will watch your brother sail."

All thoughts of the future fled from my head. I had a snekke to steer. I had sailed her before, in our bay, and I had taken her for short periods to give my father some relief but this was not the same for we were in a crowded anchorage. There were many men watching us. When we reached the channel, I was relieved. While my father and Snorri talked, I concentrated upon keeping the sail filled and our course true. I did not have the open sea to contend with. I had to sail around Orkneyjar and then north to sail around

Hrólfsey. I would have to tack so that no one needed to row. Time was unimportant. No matter how badly I sailed we would be home by morning. I had to ensure that we reached there safely.

Snorri tried to be the voice of reason, "We cannot fight the jarl, brother. He has the King of Norway at his back. We would kill many of them but we would be killed and our families enslaved."

"I know Snorri but we have other matters to think on. First, it will take time to collect what we need for a new life. Will we be given that time? We have to be ready to fight. Then, where do we go? Mann or Dyflin were possibilities but the King of Norway's web has ended that hope."

I looked up at the pennant and adjusted our course. The sail snapped as the wind pushed us. My father smiled and nodded.

"Then that leaves Land of the Wolf or the land of Göngu-Hrólfr Rognvaldson."

My father shook his head. "The Land of the Wolf, since the Dragonheart disappeared, is less friendly than it was. The best land is already taken. They are real warriors. Do you wish to tangle with the Ulfheonar?" My uncle shook his head. "And it is still a little too close to the lands of Norway. As for the land of Göngu-Hrólfr Rognvaldson, that is a possibility but it is two moons south of here. We need somewhere else." He looked to the north and east. "The land we heard of, the land ice and fire, sounds attractive. There are few men there and land to be had. I would go there but it is the unknown. If we had no wives then the five of us could go there but we have womenfolk and bairns to consider."

Snorri laughed, "Then, big brother, tell me where we go, for I know that you have decided already."

"The land south of the Land of the Wolf and north of Ceaster is without strongholds. Instead of just using a river as a base we build a new home there. True, the King of Norway will control the land to the west of us but not the north, east and south. Our drekar has a shallow draught and we can find a river which has no Vikings living there. We make a home which can be defended. We raid. When we are stronger then we decide where we go next."

"Next?"

"Yes, brother. The King of Norway seems to me to be an ambitious man. Did you not hear the jarl's words? Already he casts his eye upon the Saxon kingdoms. Guthrum almost defeated this

King of Wessex, Alfred. The King of Norway would do the same. We need a home which is far from his tentacles." He turned to me, "You have done well but it is coming on dark and I will take a turn." He took the steering board. "When we sail, we will have a drekar and a snekke. Both will be full and the snekke will need a helmsman. I have felt the snekke beneath my feet. *'Jötnar'* likes your hand upon her steering board. When we leave Hrólfsey then this will be your ship to sail."

I saw the envy on the faces of Siggi and Arne. I nodded dumbly and went to the mast. I would be a navigator. Was I ready? Arne and Siggi came to sit with me. Arne put his arm around my shoulder, "I envy you brother but I would not exchange places with you. Siggi and I will be your crew when we leave our home."

"Thank you, brother. I am not sure that I am ready."

Thoughtful Siggi had mulled our future over in his mind, "Erik, it seems to me that we are in a Norn's web. None of this would have been the course our fathers chose. This was chosen for us. We thought to spend our days on Hrólfsey." He swept an arm to the west, "Our future lies out there somewhere. We are not farmers. We are Vikings. Each of us has skills. Our fathers are two halves of a whole. There is a future out there but we do not yet know what it is."

We parted at the beach. Arne and I amused our baby brother while my father explained to my mother and Edmund what we intended. Neither had any attachment to Hrólfsey but the thought of a voyage of many days filled them with dread. "Can we take all of the animals?"

My father shook his head. "We take the milk cow, the ram, the three most fertile ewes and as many lambs as we can manage. We take the fowl for we can eat the eggs on the voyage. The rest we slaughter and salt." She nodded. "We take that which we need for a new life. We take tools and what we need to cook. We will hew timber in the new land to make beds and furniture."

"And when do we leave?" My mother was ever practical.

"That I do not know. I think that we will have to leave by the start of Heyannir. The jarl will be anxious to show the King of Norway that he can rule these islands for him. We have friends who will come with us. Our drekar will be crowded."

97

We began to prepare the next morning. There were enough barrels for we often took them from our enemies when we raided. They needed to be cleansed. We had to prepare salt and so while Edmund cleaned out the barrels, Arne and I made salt pans on the beach to make the salt that we would need to salt the meat and the fish. When we had finished, we went to the drekar and the snekke to lift the decks and to prepare the hold for cargo. My father and Snorri came down to help us to remove some of the ballast. I knew that my father was worried that while we had spare spars and a mast, we did not have a spare sail.

When we ate that night, the meal was tinged with sadness. We would be leaving the only home Arne and I had known. Each meal would be a time to remember the turf hall which was so familiar. Even our beds would be left behind and as I lay on mine, I wondered about the future. Would I live, one day, in the land of ice and fire?

The next day the first of my father's friends arrived with their chests and war gear. Butar Beer Belly and Sigismund were unmarried. They brought with them Harald of Dyrøy. Butar said, "We had no need to debate our future. I will not follow a king. We will follow you, Lars. Where do we go?"

"The land south of the Land of the Wolf and north of Ceaster. We are preparing to gather what we will need."

Herald said, "Then I would hurry for I heard that the jarl and the new lord of Mann wish to punish you for your opposition."

My father had already considered that. "We cannot leave until we have a crew. You three are a start. We will begin to fill the hold. We have one barrel of ale brewed already and some fish are dried. We stack those in the hold first."

The next day more men arrived. This time there were women and children too. Galmr, Asbjorn and Finn had wives and children. Two had sons of seven and eight summers. Galmr's was just four. They would have to be ship's boys. Galmr had a daughter too and Finn the Scar had twins. The women and the girls went to my uncle's hall. They would be safer there. Even as they were heading across the pasture to Snorri's hall three figures approached. I shaded my eyes against the sun.

"It is Leif, Olaf Olafsson and another I do not know."

My father stopped and we awaited them. Olaf spoke for them. "Lars, we would sail with you. My grandfather died and I had nothing left on the island. Leif would follow you as would Sven Svensson." Sven's father had been killed on the Mann raid. I could see that he would not be happy to remain on the island.

"You are welcome. There is little room in my hall and I would have you sleep by the drekar."

"That is good. Others are coming, Lars. They share your view that this is bad for us. We need no king."

With so many men and women now available we were able to slaughter the animals and fatten up the ones we would be taking. Nothing would be wasted from the animals. Finn led the men to hunt more seals. The seals were the gold of the islands and there would be none in our new home. We needed their oil, bones and meat. Another handful of men arrived two days later. We now had enough men to crew the drekar. Gandálfr, Benni, and Ragnar all came from the jarl's stad. As we ate a fish stew on the beach by the drekar they told us of the changes wrought by the King of Norway.

"He taxes those who live by the port. The ones who object are ejected from their homes. We each had a small farm which gave us vegetables. We had little coin and we could not pay. It is not right. We would have fought but…"

I looked at Gandálfr. He had a poorer sword than mine and his pot helmet was battered. My father nodded, "You need numbers to fight. That is how this King has gained such a large kingdom. He picks off individuals. We leave in ten days. By then we will have fattened up the animals and that which we take will be ready. We have many mouths to feed."

Now that we had more men my father had begun to allocate men to oars. Asbjorn was given the snekke. I would steer but Asbjorn would command. I was happier about that. We had the younger warriors as our crew: Arne, Siggi, Olaf, Leif, Ragnar, Harald and Gandálfr. We would also have the fowl and the sheep. The next days saw us all draw closer together as we continued our preparations. More men arrived. They came in ones and twos. I wondered if we had enough space for all of them.

My father and Snorri were at the hall studying a chart which Olaf had brought. He had inherited all of his grandfather's goods. He had a compass too but no hourglass. The rest of us were loading barrels into the hull of the drekar and snekke. It was a painstaking business. Badly stacked cargo could cause a ship to broach and sink. Einar Finnsson came racing down to us, "Father, Jarl Eystein has sent men. They are heading from the south. Our lord needs you armed."

We needed no urging. All our war gear was by the drekar and I grabbed my helmet, shield and sword. I had no time to don my jerkin. Finn said, "The jarl does not know we are here. Let us give him a surprise. Asbjorn and Butar, take half of the men and sweep around to the west. The rest come with me and we will go to the east."

I followed Asbjorn and we ran along the beach and then up the western path. I knew this land better than any save Arne. He had gone with Finn. I said, "There is a piece of dead ground ahead. We can use it to rise like wraiths behind the jarl's men."

Asbjorn nodded, "This is your land and we will follow."

This was the first time I had run with a shield on my back and without a leather jerkin it chafed. I was just glad that I had my protector under my helmet and that the strap fitted well. I heard the raised voices before we were seen. I held up my hand and walked slowly up the slope from the dell.

My father's voice sounded controlled but I knew it was an illusion, "Tell the jarl we are leaving Hrólfsey, Agner Shield Bearer. There is no need to fight."

I heard Agner Shield Bearer. He was one of those who dutifully followed the jarl. He and my father did not get on. As I recalled he had a mail byrnie. He laughed, "It is not enough that you leave. You must be punished. The jarl wants the heads of you and your brother to show others that he is the one who rules here."

We neared the top. "And is that why he is not here with you? Does he fear to face me beard to beard?"

As we rose up on the small ridge, I saw that Agner Shield Bearer had twenty men with him. These were the warriors who lived close to the jarl. They did not farm. They raided and spent the rest of the time drinking away their profit. Agner Shield Bearer raised his sword. The all had their backs to us but I saw that my father and uncle had seen us. "Lars the Luckless, the jarl is too important to soil his hands on a farmer. Prepare to die!"

Asbjorn shouted, "You first!" He ran down the slope and we followed.

Agner was a stupid man. He must have known that the number of women who had emerged from the hall meant there were more than two men who would fight him. He knew that Arne, Siggi and myself lived here. He turned and stared in horror as we tumbled down the slope. Then Finn shouted, "Kill them!" and led the rest toward the jarl's killers. Four of Agner's men took to their heels. My father ran at Agner. He was going to kill him himself.

Asbjorn and I had outstripped the others. I saw Petr Snorrison brace himself. He was facing me and had a shield and spear. He had seen thirty summers and knew how to fight but he had a beer belly. I ignored everyone else as I ran at him. I only had a small shield and Petr had a long spear. I saw him pull it back to strike at me. One advantage of my smaller shield was that I could move it easily. As the spear head came towards me, I flicked with my shield and then swung my sword. The shield deflected the head easily. My sword strike was badly timed but I hit the shield of Petr and knocked him to the ground. I fell too, winded. I rolled and rose.

Petr's spear had fallen to the ground. He took out his sword. He swung his sword in a long sweep. He would hit my little shield and this time I would have no protection. I brought my sword over. As his blade hit my shield my sword rang off his. I had a better sword than Petr. As he stepped back, I saw that it was no longer true. I took heart from that and swung at his head. He had a pot helmet and no protector underneath. His left arm was too slow to raise his heavy shield and he had to use his sword. The bent blade did not stop my strike and I caught his helmet. I punched with my small round shield and he reeled. He was on a down slope and I saw him lose his balance. I lunged with my sword as he fell and it went into his open mouth. It scraped off his teeth and then tore through the back of his head. He fell to the ground, dead.

I turned and saw my father block Agner's sword strike and then backhand his sword across the neck of the jarl's man. The body fell to the ground. I saw that we had killed eight men and the rest had run. Sigismund had a wound to his leg and Gytha and Helga were tending to him.

My father's head whipped around. He saw me and smiled. On the ridge line, Arne and Siggi raised their bloody swords. My father said, "They will be back. We leave tomorrow. Take what you need from the bodies."

Snorri asked, "Do we bury them?"

"They do not deserve it. Leave them where they lie!"

I went to Petr. As I expected he had no coins and his hammer was wooden. I took his sword and dagger. They were poor but we could melt them down. His shield and his spear were worth taking. The bodies were soon searched and all of value taken. Siggi and Arne were keeping watch from the top of the ridge. Arne shouted, "Men approach!" We all grabbed our weapons. Had the jarl sent more men? Then Arne shouted, "It is Faramir and his family."

Faramir farmed the land to the south west of us. My father and Snorri came towards me. My father said, "You did well. Petr had fought in many battles."

"He was old and he was slow."

Snorri laughed, "He was of an age with me. Am I old?"

"I am sorry."

"I am just teasing." I saw that Faramir had a cart. He was bringing all of his family. They led a pair of goats. "I think, brother, that we have more folk for our journey."

My father frowned. He feared we would be overcrowded. We might have to remove more ballast and as we had already begun to load beneath the deck that would be a problem. He shrugged, "We cannot turn any away. This is the work of the Norns."

Faramir had a wife, two grown sons, one of whom was married, and two unmarried daughters. When he reached my father, he gave a bow. "Lars we had nowhere else to go. We would come with you."

"You know not where I go."

"Wherever it is will be a better life than here. I have stood in a shield wall with you. That is more than can be said for the jarl. His men came yesterday and demanded taxes for living on my farm. We did not raid with the jarl. My sons and I have no coin. They took our thralls, cow and pigs as payment. They would have taken the goats but they ran off."

My father smiled, "Then come with us and welcome." He pointed to the dead, "If you need weapons or aught from the dead then take them."

His son, Fámr, shook his head, "My brother, Folkmar, and I have helmet, sword and shield. We can fight for what is ours. Perhaps you will be a better jarl."

My father shook his head, "I am no jarl."

Faramir said, "By leading this new clan you are a jarl whether you will or not."

I could hear the Norns as they were spinning. Faramir was correct. We did have a clan. I was not sure how I viewed the prospect. We had lived alone and we were comfortable with ourselves. Now we would need to build a palisade, a hall and live close together.

We shared the watch that night but I was relieved for I was needed in the hall. My father was there with the other senior men of our new, as yet, unnamed clan. The hall had been stripped of everything that would be carried. The women and the children were already wrapped in blankets, skins and furs as they enjoyed their last night on land for some time.

"Erik, I need to ask you, are you still happy about sailing the snekke?" I saw that Olaf was in the hall but not around the table. He had more experience than I did. My father smiled, "No one wishes to take the helm from you but there will now be more people and you have a greater responsibility. If you are not sure then speak."

"I have sailed the snekke, '*Jötnar*' speaks to me. I am content and I will have Asbjorn to command if we have to do battle."

"And that may be truer than you think, my son. You will have ten warriors on your snekke. All of the oars can be manned. You will have the goats too. My intention is to sail west and get as far from Orkneyjar as we can. I do not think that either the King of Norway or his new Lord of the Isles will let us leave peacefully. By heading into the western sea, we may lose any pursuers. Then we sail south between Dún Lethglaise and Ljoðhús. If we have to, we can then enter the narrow channels between the islands there."

Faramir had not been party to the earlier discussions, "And where do we land?"

"There are two good rivers, the Loyne and the Ribble. We choose the one with the fewest people." Faramir nodded. My father turned to me. "You know that we may well become separated on this journey?"

"Aye."

"You have the compass but I will take your hourglass."

"That is at it should be. We will manage." I sounded more confident than I actually was. Had Olaf been able to secure the hourglass of his grandfather then all might have been well but the jarl had it in his possession. The Norns!

We spent some time studying. I had a piece of cloth I had taken from Petr's body. I had intended to use it to clean my mail but as it was light coloured, I took a piece of charcoal and made a rough copy of my father's chart. It was crude and had no distances upon it but it showed the north and that was all that I needed. I marked with a cross Dún Lethglaise and Ljoðhús as well as wriggly lines for the two rivers. Thankfully they looked closer together. I did not sleep in the hall that night. Instead, I went over every piece of tackle on the snekke. The deck was in place and small barrels of ale and food were secured at the side. The two goats would be tethered by the prow.

Arne and Siggi came to join me. "Brother, will you not sleep in the hall tonight?"

I shook my head, "I need to become as one with '*Jötnar*'. She must be in my dreams and in my head. She must know my fears as well as my hopes. I did not ask for this, brother, but I know that it is my destiny. When I sail west tomorrow it will be the start of a journey which will take a lifetime."

Chapter 9

It took longer to load the drekar than my snekke. I let Asbjorn assign the oars. I hoped we would not need them. Siggi and Arne had the ones at the prow and they would also have to watch the goats. Olaf and Leif were the next pair. Harald and Gandálfr the next and finally Asbjorn and Sven Svensson. They were balanced and the snekke still felt light. I now had a chest which I shared with Arne and Siggi. My compass was with me at the steering board. We had four bows amongst the crew. I had used Petr's shield along the side. It gave more protection than my small one. My shield was lodged next to the stern post. I could use it to lean against.

My father and his brother were the last to board the drekar. They fired the two halls and then boarded *'Njörðr'*. We had already cast off and were waiting to hoist the sail. My father came to the steering board and looked over. "You will follow. May the Allfather be with you and if we become separated…"

"Then we will wait for you at the Loyne."

He laughed, "You are confident!"

"I am your son!"

The drekar was slower to move than we were. I gave it four lengths before I said, "Raise the sail!"

The lively snekke leapt forward. Asbjorn laughed, "I can see that you named this one in humour. She is no slow giant! We could overtake the drekar any time we choose."

"I think that is why my father has us as a follower. I do not mind." He went to sit by the mast with the others. It gave the snekke a better balance. I said, "Olaf Olafsson, would you join me?"

He came and smiled, "You have come far in the last couple of years. Not quite a full beard and yet you steer!"

"I know that it is in your blood and I thank you for not asking for the helm."

He shrugged, "I would be a warrior. I do not mind steering but I would not be my grandfather."

"Yet I hope that you will share the watch with Asbjorn and me."

"Of course."

"And," I reached down and picked up the sealskin pouch, "mark the compass for me." He nodded and took out the charcoal and compass. "I gave the hourglass to my father. When you see them turn it you could take a sight for me."

"Of course."

And so we settled into a pattern. I steered and the others trimmed the sails and chatted. Olaf watched the drekar and when my father took a sun sight then so did he. We were lucky that there was a bright sun. We headed north and west for most of the morning. With the wind from the north west we had to tack for most of the morning but once we cleared the north west corner of Hrólfsey we were able to take advantage of the wind as we sailed south and west. I smiled. My father had planned on a westerly course but the Norns had been spinning. We sailed close to Orkneyjar. The burning of the two farms had not been done out of sheer malice. We wanted eyes drawn there. My father believed that the jarl would send more men to punish us and burn our ships. This way we would have a good start over any pursuit.

As the wind filled our sails and the drekar sailed as she was intended, I was able to look at her critically. She was lower in the water than we had planned. Her decks were crowded. There were women, children, animals and cooking gear. We anticipated landing where we could cook and have hot food. If we had been heading for a raid with an almost empty drekar we could have done the journey in two hard days. As it was, we would have to double that. We were plodding rather than racing. The sun was at its height when we saw *'Moon Dragon'*. She was well astern of us. It was Olaf's sharp eyes which spotted her on the horizon. He knew her well. His grandfather had sailed it for many years and he recognised the red sail. I sailed directly for *'Njörðr's'* stern. *'Jötnar'* was like a horse which was eager to open her legs. We reached the drekar in a few heartbeats.

Olaf cupped his hands and shouted, "Jarl, *'Moon Dragon'* is following!"

"We will use our oars and head between Ljoðhús and Skíð. We have a shallower draught than *'Moon Dragon'* and we can lose her in the small islands."

Olaf waved his acknowledgement and I tacked us to allow him sea room. The oars came out and as my father turned the steering board the wind and the oars bit together and *'Njörðr'* began to draw away from us. We were now heading south and east. Asbjorn shouted, "Olaf, join Erik and watch for him."

Olaf stared astern. "Your father has built two good ships. Already I can only see the mast head and top half of the sail. We will outrun her."

I clutched my hammer. "Do not tempt the Norns, Olaf. We know not what is ahead."

I saw that my father had sent Finn's son up the mast to act as lookout. Olaf shouted, "I can no longer see them." I looked at the drekar and saw that the oars were being drawn inboard. Rowing on such a crowded drekar was to be avoided. Finn's son must have seen that we had lost them? My father then headed south and west. It was getting on to dark when we spied the coast of north Uist. I saw my uncle waving and so I took us closer. "We are going to find a beach to land."

Siggi waved and then came aft to tell me. I stretched my arm, "And right glad I am! My back aches."

Olaf said, "I would have relieved you had you asked."

I laughed, "Do not worry, next time I will not be such a hero! I need to make water!"

We found an uninhabited island with a good beach. It lay to the south of Ensay. I saw the sails lowered and then the oars backed her towards the beach. My father turned her so that they could run out a gangplank. Once I saw they were safe I raced into the sand, "Prepare to lower the sail!" Leif, Olaf, Siggi and Arne were all ready. I knew my little snekke now and when it seemed we would fly onto the sand I shouted, "Down sail!" And as it came down put the steering board over. It was almost our undoing for the weight of the men and chests nearly capsized us. It did not and we rested in ankle deep water.

Asbjorn glowered at me, "Do not show off Erik Larsson! You are a better sailor than that!"

"I am sorry." The apology was to the crew and the ship. I had learned a lesson. Arne, Siggi and I secured the snekke and while I went to make water, they began to light the fire on the beach. We would need many fires to feed all the people. When I had finished, I walked back to the snekke.

I thought that my father would be angry for he had seen my landing but, instead, when he strode over, he just smiled. "It is good that you are getting to know the limitations of both yourself and your ship."

"She is fast!"

"I know. She is like a terrier. Other ships will be bigger but you will be able to dance around them."

Snorri joined us. They both looked north and east. I asked, "Do you think that we have lost them?"

"I thought to make them believe we had gone to the land of ice and fire. Now they know where we sailed and they will follow. We will have to be vigilant."

"You are riding lower in the water than I expected."

"I know, my son. I can see that you are a navigator. We have too many people on board. We will have to rest ashore each night. We had to bring all who wished to do so. I could not leave them to be persecuted by the King of Norway and his lackeys."

We sat by the fire and watched as the food was prepared. Arne came to join us. "I have looked at the chart. Mann is not far from this new land you wish us to use. What is to stop Bjorn and his men coming to attack us?"

"Nothing, Arne. In fact, I expect that once he knows where we dwell, he will come to try to destroy us." Arne frowned. My father smiled, "There is nowhere else for us to go, my son. Yes, we may well be attacked but it will be not for a while. It is one thing to make Bjorn Lord of Mann but another thing entirely to expect the ones who live there to accept his rule. We destroyed the pirates and their ships but there are other Vikings who live there. We have made our choice and now we must live with it. We are Vikings. If we were not, we would live like the Saxons and tend fields. They sailed the seas once but now have given up."

We ate well and we drank good ale. I slept on the snekke. Arne and Siggi tried to persuade me to sleep ashore. "No brother. I know it may sound foolish but when I sleep in the snekke I dream and my dreams are of the future. I do not understand them yet for they are like pieces of a torn piece of manuscript. I need to put them all together. *'Jötnar'* is speaking to me and I must hear her." They nodded and they left. Siggi and Arne were less worried about the snekke and more worried about those pursuing us. I saw them hold their swords and scabbards as they curled up before the fire. My sword lay in my chest. I would not need it.

I had woken, after my first night aboard, with a vivid picture of trees laden with fruit. It was not the land of ice and fire but where was it? When we had slept on the snekke in the jarl's stad I had dreamed of trees with trunks so big that it took ten men holding hands to surround one. I was looking forward to the picture I would be sent this night.

When I woke I stared west. I had seen the sun set over land in my dream. The land was a forest. Did they have such forests in Hibernia? If it was not Hibernia then where was it? Was this the snekke or was it the Norns? I knew not but I woke each day and I was excited to be alive.

Once again it took longer to load the drekar than it should. We had tethered our two goats to graze on the salt grass. Siggi milked the female before we loaded the two of them. We gave the milk to the children on the drekar. There had been surprisingly little dung from them and Arne and Siggi had disposed of it at sea. The cow on the drekar was a different story. I had seen the two ship's boys cleaning the deck while we ate.

Once again, we resumed our course south and west but as the day wore on my father made it more southerly and then, finally, south and east. We were heading for the coast of the Land of the Wolf. Once it had been a land which had welcomed Vikings. That had been when the Dragonheart ruled. No one had seen him for many years. My father said that he had to be dead. If he was alive then he would be more than a hundred years old. Yet no one had seen him die. His sword, the one touched by the gods, had disappeared and his granddaughter, Ylva, the most powerful of witches, now ruled the land.

We would use a beach which had no access to the land and we would trust the witch left us alone. In the end, we did not reach the Land of the Wolf. It came on to dark as we neared the islands called Suðreyjar. The beach we found was long and empty. More importantly, as we had sailed south, we had seen little smoke from the island and none on the west coast. The snekke made a more sedate landing. I received smiles from the crew rather than scowls.

That night I slept aboard and I dreamed again. This time I dreamed of dragonships. There were three of them. They came towards my snekke and I was mesmerised. Their prows crushed our little boat. It was so vivid that I woke with a start. The night was pitch black. I rose and after taking off my breeks walked into the shallows to empty my bowels. I had just cleansed myself when I heard a creak. To a Saxon or a Pict, the sound would be dismissed easily but I knew that it was the sound of a drekar. It was out at sea but I knew the sound. When I had stood a watch, I had heard it. I stared out to sea but it was so black that I could see nothing. Was it a dream? I felt foolish. I returned ashore and donned my breeks. I could not get the thought from my head and so I went to the drekar. My father was not sleeping on board. He was rolled in his fur on the beach.

I shook him awake. "What is it? Trouble? Does the weather or wind change?"

"No, but I woke and I am sure I heard a drekar pass by."

He frowned. "You were not drinking heavily? Sometimes drink makes a man think he sees things."

"No, but I had dreamed of drekar."

He touched his hammer, "Then perhaps you were warned and it was not a dream. There may be enemies ahead then. Tomorrow, be ready to race to our aid if danger strikes."

"I will."

As we set sail the next day, I realised that I was now totally in tune with the snekke. My back had not ached as much the previous day as on the first. I was able to make minor adjustments calmly. I confess I was not sure that we would ever need to use the oars unless we were trying to get up a narrow river. We could use any wind even one from our bows. I told the crew about my dream and what my father had said. All of us knew the power of dreams. It was how the gods, the spirits and the Norns spoke to us. They planted seeds in our sleep and let them grow. The wind had changed to one from the west and north. It was stronger and felt slightly warmer. It would help us as we headed towards a beach in the Land of the Wolf. We could have sailed further south but we knew of treacherous sands which lay north of the Loyne and we wished to avoid them. This way we would arrive at the Loyne in daylight. That was always better.

It was getting dark when we spotted the two drekar. They were following us. We were close to the Land of the Wolf which lay just over the horizon. Olaf had just used the compass and it was he saw them. "There are two drekar. We had better tell the jarl."

He hurried to the prow as I stopped tacking and used the wind to sail directly towards the stern of *'Njörðr'*. Olaf cupped his hands and called to my father. The wind took the words from me but Olaf heard them. I saw the oars being run out.

"Your father is going to sail due south. We are to keep four lengths astern. As soon it is dark, he will head due east and sail for the Land of the Wolf. He said we should keep sailing south. When the light has disappeared, we can lose them."

Asbjorn nodded, "It is a good plan and the jarl does us great honour but it means that you have much upon your shoulders."

"I know."

Arne said, "This is your dream, is it not?"

"Perhaps the Norns are testing us. We will do as he says. Asbjorn, I can sail but all else will be up to you."

"I know. Get your bows and slings. Siggi, you had better stay with the goats. When Erik begins to throw this snekke around then they may become distressed and we will have enough to deal with fighting two drekar."

He glanced astern. "They are following and they have their oars run out. They are catching us."

"And we cannot show them our turn of speed yet. I would have that come as a surprise. Arne, watch them for me."

'Njörðr' was slicing through the water and I allowed her to move away from us. She would still be visible to the two drekar but as soon as dusk came then they would be lost in the murk of a darkening sky. A turn east would make them vanish as though by magic. The trick would be to distract them. Olaf had not recognised the drekar. That meant they were the King of

Norway's. They knew neither my father nor me. I would use that uncertainty to our advantage.

"Brother, they are splitting up to come on either side of us."

"How far back are they?"

"Ten lengths or more."

"Tell me when they are five lengths from us. Siggi, can you still see *'Njörðr'*?"

"Barely."

It was time. "Asbjorn I am going to turn into the wind and head west and south. I want them to think I know not what we do. When they begin to turn too, I will race across their bows and head north and west as though we are heading back to the north."

"It is a risk, Erik."

"Trust the snekke, Asbjorn."

He laughed, "It may be a short life but it will be exciting. Ready bows and slings."

When I judged that it was dark enough and my father's ship was hidden, I put the steering board over and we almost stopped. "Leif let out the forestay."

We caught a little more wind and began to head south and west.

"Three lengths and closing. They are turning!"

It was working. They could no longer see the drekar and assumed that we were mirroring their course. I put the steering board over hard to head north and east. Leif's action gave us a huge burst of speed. As we whipped around, I saw the prow of the nearest drekar. It was a skull with a hawk on its head. The men on the drekar were not expecting such a manoeuvre. The four bows and our slings sent a torrent of missiles at the drekar. I saw the bow of the drekar. It was less than a length away and beyond it I saw the second drekar. A mad idea came into my head. I would sail between the two ships. The prow of the first drekar was less than twenty paces from our stern as I turned. The huge drekar tried to turn to cut us off. Asbjorn and the others enjoyed free rein to rain arrows and stones upon the crew of the first drekar. The second Norwegian was turning. The sun was a glow in the west and, to the east, all was darkness. We were skimming over the waves now. The first drekar had men who had been hit. As we sailed past, I saw oars in disarray. The second drekar was turning and so oblivious to all but us that they did not seem to see that they were heading for their consort.

Arne was still whirling his sling but I was not certain he was close enough to hit. Suddenly he shouted, "The prow is going to foul the back stay!" I could not resist turning to see the two drekar become entangled. Oars were shattered and then the two ships disappeared into the darkness. I tweaked the steering board a little to larboard and the wind pushed us into the dark. We could hear the shouts from the two drekar as they tried to disentangle themselves. We had been lucky. Had they had archers or slingers ready then we could all have been slain as we sailed perilously close to the two of them. We were not safe yet. They were close enough to follow.

Asbjorn came to the stern. "You are right Erik, this is a special boat. We had better follow the jarl."

I shook my head. "We are still bait. Let us head due east and find somewhere to land. My father will not light a fire. They will eat cold this night and we will not find them. Let them look for us."

"How can they follow in the dark?"

I pointed to the water behind the snekke. Small as we were, we had disturbed the water. There was some sort of light which followed a ship when it sailed in the dark. A lookout would see the direction we had taken. "Eventually we will be far enough ahead for them not to see our wake but until we see the coast we would be better staying on this course."

He shook his head, "How do you know about this?"

"When we sailed to Mann, I was lookout. I saw the trails behind the other ships."

"Then we will head east."

"Leif, tighten the forestay again."

I heard him laugh in the dark, "Aye, Captain!"

I began to worry about sailing in the dark. It had been a clear sky when the sun had set but clouds had arrived and I could not see the stars. I think Asbjorn was worried too. "Erik, let us stay here for a while." I looked at him. "We both know that a drekar under sail makes noises even above the noise of the sea. If they come close then we will hear them."

"Arne, Leif, lower the sail." We had a bag of oiled wool with a hole in the end. It was tied to a piece of rope. I threw it astern. It would not stop us moving but it would slow down the movement and keep us pointing with the wind. As soon as the bag filled the bow swung around and our movement became easier.

Olaf handed me the ale skin. We said nothing for we needed the silence of the night to hear the approach of the drekar. I drank deeply and handed him back the skin. Like the others I made water. I saw Asbjorn tapping most of the men on the shoulder and miming for them to sleep. He came aft and sat by me. Our backs rested against the strakes. Once I had attuned to the sound of the night and satisfied myself that the drekar were not close I relaxed a little. How had I known what to do? I had never been in the position before. I thought back to that day in the bay when I had found that piece of wreckage. Where was it now? Perhaps in touching the wood and sitting upon it I had been touched by the builder of the unknown ship. I would be a navigator but I knew that would not be enough. I had to be a warrior too. We were a small clan. Each of us would have to fight. When we reached our new home then I would learn.

After a while, Asbjorn touched my shoulder and said, quietly, "I think we have lost them. Let us sail south and try to find the drekar. They will be worried."

I nodded and began to haul in the woollen anchor. Two years earlier I would have had to call Arne to help me but now I was able to drag the dead weight from the sea. I emptied the water and coiled the rope. Asbjorn had woken the crew.

"Raise the sail! Siggi, keep a good watch to larboard. There lies the Land of the Wolf and I would not wreck our snekke there."

There were still no stars. The anchor should have pointed us south but only dawn would tell me if that was true. If we were heading in the right direction then the sun would come from my left. I kept glancing to the left and, finally, I was rewarded by the thin glow which was false dawn. I did not mind that it was not the real dawn. We were sailing south. Now that I knew where we were, I was more confident and I adjusted the steering board to sail due south.

When the sun came up I saw that the mountains of the Land of the Wolf loomed up to the east of us. They grew the further south and east we went. I saw, in the distance, the mountain after which the land was named, Úlfarrberg. At least I assumed it was the mountain of the wolf. I had an uneasy prickle at the back of my neck. I wondered if the witch was weaving a spell. Would she drag me and my snekke into her lair? I had heard terrible stories about witches and their power. Even the greatest warriors feared them and Ylva was the most powerful of witches.

I closed my eyes and intoned to myself, "Allfather, save me from the witch. We have much to do and we cannot serve you if we are prisoners in the Land of the Wolf."

Asbjorn's hand shook me. He thought I was sleeping, "I will have Olaf relieve you. You were asleep at the helm."

I shook my head, "I was not but I do need some sleep." We waved Olaf forward. I took out the crude chart. "If that is Úlfarrberg," I pointed east, "then we are roughly here." Olaf nodded. "The bay with the treacherous sands is here." I pointed again. "If we have not found my father by then wake me."

"I can sail!"

"I know Olaf, but this is our snekke and I know her. You are older and, probably, a better sailor but *'Jötnar'* knows me. She has kept us safe has she not?" he nodded, "Then wake me when we reach the bay." I did not know where I had found the confidence. When I had been a ship's boy just a couple of years earlier, I had been in awe of Olaf. The Norns were spinning.

Chapter 10

I heard the seabirds crying before Arne shook me awake. The birds were the spirits of men who had died without a sword in their hand. They were to be pitied. "Here, brother, ale and salted meat."

I looked to the east. The mountains had gone and were replaced by rolling hills. I saw sands stretching to the east to meet the hills. I swallowed some ale and as I looked at the sky saw that it was noon. I chewed on the meat. "Is there any sign of the drekar?"

"Siggi thought he saw a sail but as we did not catch it then it must have been a drekar heading south and west. Olaf has sailed due south since you fell asleep."

I went to the steering board and took the helm. Olaf stood and stretched. "My back and shoulders ache. If you need relief again then speak."

I pointed to the land, "If those are the sands then the River Loyne lies just a couple of hours away." He nodded.

Asbjorn was asleep. The others sat by the mast. Siggi and Arne were with the goats. There would be mess at the prow. The goats should have been landed. It could not be helped. It was easier to clean a snekke than bring the dead back to life. We had escaped a trap and helped to save the snekke. I moved the steering board over. We had a shallow draught. *'Jötnar'* would warn me of danger.

As the sun passed its zenith, I edged us close to the shore, "Siggi, climb the mast. See if you can see the estuary."

He quickly shinned up the mast. The ship's boy who had appeared so clumsy just a couple of years earlier now reached the spar in a few heart beats. "Aye, Erik." He pointed south and east. It is a wide river. The sands are to the east of us." He slithered down.

Asbjorn rose and looked east. "There is no sign of the drekar and there are still sands. I will head due south and then sail due east. We will have to use oars for I do not know these waters."

Asbjorn nodded, "We are all well rested." He made water and then after eating and drinking, like the others, he took an oar and sat on his bench. Only Olaf and Leif remained standing. They would have to lower the sail and secure the mast.

Our course south and east meant that I could see where the river met the sea. The water bubbled. Even as I prepared to turn, I noticed the bluffs above the river. They had trees upon them. On the north side of the river, there appeared to be a ruined stone building. It was a good marker. "Down sail, out oars!"

As soon as the sail came down, I began to put the steering board over. The movement made us bob up and down and the goats bleated plaintively. I heard Siggi sing to them and they calmed. Asbjorn shouted, "Pull! One, two, pull, one two!" It took a few pulls on the oars as Olaf and Leif had to get into the rhythm but once they did then the motion became easier and we began to move closer. I put my hand in the sea. The tide was on the turn. The gods were with us and we drew closer to the shore. I kept my eye on the ruined building. I saw a cross. It was a church. I spied no smoke. That meant there were no houses close by and that was a good thing. I had to be helmsman and lookout. I saw that the river turned ahead. It seemed to go from due east to directly north. The estuary was wide but the sands to the north made me cautious. I would keep to the centre of the river. *'Jötnar'* responded well to the oars, her keel was weed free and she slid through the water like a knife in warm butter.

I was not sure what lay ahead and so I said, "Asbjorn, slow the stroke. There is a turn ahead." As we left the sea and entered the river the motion became easier. "Siggi and Arne, I need a lookout ahead." There was no point in one remaining at the oars and so they both put their oars on the mast fish. They both stood at *'Jötnar's'* prow. I saw Arne help Siggi to sit atop the giant's head. Suddenly he slipped down and said, "Stop rowing. The drekar is ahead and she is being attacked!"

"Which bank?"

"The far bank!"

"Larboard oars keep rowing." I put the steering board over and headed for the southern bank although as it turned sharply it would soon be the east bank. The bank was lined with willows and bushes. I spied a patch of sand no bigger than a small house and I aimed for it. Arne and Siggi leapt ashore with the ropes. They tethered the snekke to two trees. Asbjorn and Gandálfr grabbed their weapons and ran upstream. Arne, Siggi, Olaf, Leif, Ragnar and Harald began to don helmets and take their shields from the side. Asbjorn and Gandálfr had just taken their bows with them. I put on my sea boots and slipped one dagger, the Saxon one, in the top. The other I put in my belt. I took Petr's shield. It did not have my design on it yet but it was a bigger shield.

I said to Siggi, "How did you know they were being attacked?"

"I saw arrows in the mast."

"Then they could have been captured."

Arne shook his head, "I think not brother." He tapped his chest. "Our family lives. I feel it here."

Harald pointed to the river, "Look!"

A body floated downstream. It was a Viking but not one of our people. It seemed an age but it must have been moments only before Asbjorn and Gandálfr appeared. We handed them their helmets and shields. "There is a band of warriors attacking the drekar. Our men have made a shield wall but there are dead there. We will go to their aid. The four of us with bows will send arrows into their backs. Olaf, you lead Siggi, Arne and Erik to attack them." He must have seen the doubt on our faces. "The clan is in danger. If we are to be sacrificed to save it then it is meant to be."

We nodded and ran up the path to the top of the ridge. I could hear the sounds of battle as swords and spears clashed on metal and wood. Asbjorn waved us towards some trees. As we reached them, I saw that, forty paces from us, there were thirty or more warriors battling my father and his men. I saw that Reimund and his son lay in pools of blood. Others were being tended on the drekar by the women. This was not going well.

Asbjorn said, "We have no time to lose. When we have loosed five flights of arrows then we will join you. May the Allfather be with you."

I nodded to Arne and pulled my shield up. Drawing my sword, I ran after Olaf. There was too much noise for us to be heard. Normally we would have shouted to put fear into our foes but until the arrows fell and they were alerted we would remain silent. The arrows fell before we had cleared the bushes. I saw my father look up as the ones at the back of the enemy line were hit. At first the warriors appeared confused. I hoped that we would not be hit by a misplaced arrow from one of our own.

I had to hurdle two writhing bodies which had been hit by arrows to reach the enemy. The first warrior to turn faced me and I was committed to the strike even before he was turning. He turned to his left and was swinging his sword at me. The weight of his shield opened his middle and I hacked my sword into him. He had a padded kyrtle which did not stop my sword. His eyes widened as he felt my blade slice across his ribs and into his body. My momentum made me crash into him. All around me I heard shouts, screams, the clash of weapons as our tiny band sought to relieve our families.

From the corner of my eye, I caught sight of a sword which slashed down towards me. I lifted Petr's shield. This was the first time I had used it and it let me down. I know not if it had been weakened or was badly made but it split and the wood shattered leaving me with the boss in my hand. Even as the warrior grinned, I lunged with my sword at his head. He tried to move away but merely exposed his neck. As my blade sawed across it, blood spurted. He turned and, clutching his neck, tried to flee. Others were emulating him for they did not know how many we were. Such was the ferocity of our attack that we had ripped the heart from them.

A Viking voice I did not recognise shouted, "Fall back!"

Eighteen Vikings fled leaving twelve of their own dead or dying. I looked around for any who might be feigning but the bodies now lay still. My father shouted, "Watch where they go. Take the wounded aboard the drekar!" He sheathed his sword and grasped Arne by the shoulders. Arne's byrnie was blood spattered but he was whole, "Never was I more pleased to see my sons! You came just in time. Another few minutes and we would have been broken." He waved a hand and I saw that as well as Reimund and his son there were another three dead warriors. All had come late to our home and I did not even know their names. We would honour them for they had died for the clan.

Snorri asked, "Is the snekke safe?"

I nodded, "It is downstream. I will go and fetch it. Arne, Siggi, come with me."

My father laughed, "Are you the captain now that you give orders?"

Siggi said, seriously, "He is our captain, jarl and a good one. He showed us how to defeat two drekar!"

My uncle's eyes widened, "Two drekar? Here is a tale worth hearing!"

My father shook his head, "First we move to the north bank. Our enemies came from the south and east."

I pointed, "There is a deserted church on the headland. We could defend that!"

My father nodded, "I thought to hide from enemies. It seems I chose wrong. Take your snekke and scout it out for us. If there is danger, wave us off."

My mother came to the gunwale of the drekar. She was beaming, "God has answered my prayers. My sons are safe."

Sheathing my sword, we hurried back to the snekke. I still had the shield boss in my hand. I would melt it down. It might make me a mail hood! When we reached the snekke I saw that the goats had fouled it again. We would have some serious cleaning. While Siggi and Arne untied us, I went to the steering board.

They threw the ropes aboard and I shouted, "Push us off!" I turned the steering board so that their push and the current took us away from the bank. "Take an oar each to give us more control." They rowed just to keep us straight. As we neared the other bank, I could not see any sign of humans but we would take no chances. I grounded the snekke just a hundred paces below and upstream from the deserted church. Siggi and Arne tied us to a tree. "We had better tether the goats and let them graze or we will have no milk." While the goats were being landed, I took my smaller shield and waited at the bottom of the hill. I let Arne lead us. We crouched as we ascended the grassy slope. Bushes and shrubs, as well as young trees, were trying to colonise the hillside. The men who had built the church must have cleared the land.

As we neared the top, I saw the mounds, lumps and bumps which showed where buildings had been. This had been destroyed many years ago. Arne waved me to the right and Siggi to the left. We went around the church while Arne disappeared through the open doorway. Siggi and I met up at the door.

Arne came out, "It is empty. Part of the roof has fallen in and I found runes on the walls. Vikings have been here."

It was safe and so we headed back to the river to let my father know that it was uninhabited. Siggi looked unhappy, "We have fled one foe to find another."

Arne laughed, "Cuz, for a land to be empty it must be worthless. My father knew we would have to fight for the land. I just hope that the warriors we fought were not the Clan of the Wolf."

I shook my head, "I think they were Danes. The Viking voice I heard sounded like a Dane I had seen when we visited Dyflin."

We had reached the river and I took a pail to collect river water. I would begin to clean the goats' mess from the snekke.

"What makes you think so?" Arne broke a branch off the tree to improvise a brush.

"One had a Danish axe and the leader who spoke did not sound Norse." I sluiced the dung and urine to the side. Arne's branch helped to channel it. I took another pail.

Siggi began to empty the snekke. "The Danes are as bad are they not?"

"They live mainly in the east. They will be like us. They will have come for a new land without a king."

Arne shouted, "Here is the drekar." The snekke was not totally clean but it would have to do. We began to offload the chests. Siggi had taken the smaller gear but the chests took two hands. By the time '*'Njörðr'*' had tied up the snekke was empty.

Snorri landed first, "Is it safe? Can our people disembark? They have had a difficult time."

Arne nodded, "There is no sign that anyone has been there for some time."

Snorri waved to my father, "We can unload!" He turned to us, "Come we will take your chest up the hill and you can tell me all."

Our story did not take long. There was little point in making it overly dramatic. Arne insisted on giving all the details of how I sailed the snekke before the drekar and then how they collided. The rest was simplified.

"You have all done well. Your father was confident that you would be able to deal with the drekar. We landed on a beach and had cold fare. We found this river and all seemed well. We were still worried that the two drekar might pursue us and so we hid the drekar up the river. The church made us think that the north shore might be inhabited and so we landed on the south. I can see now that it was a mistake. We were unlucky."

Siggi said, "Or the Norns were spinning!"

We all clutched our hammers. Snorri nodded, "There was a ford upstream and I think that this warband was heading north to raid. When they saw us unloading the drekar they attacked without warning. That was when Reimund and his son died. Your father had sent them to scout and they died without drawing their weapons. We were not mailed and had to fight with swords and shields. Your father learned a hard lesson."

Arne pointed to the ruined church. "Here is a place for a stronghold. You can see where the holy men had their buildings. We can dig them out and use the foundations for ours. We build a palisade." He pointed west. There was a wood."

"But ships from Mann can see us."

Arne laughed, "Uncle, you do not think that we will be invisible here, do you? Already Vikings know where we are. Suppose these Danes are allies of the pirates? We cannot run forever. This is an easier place to defend than our farms. Here we can see folk coming. We have water, timber, clear line of sight and the sea. We make this our home!"

He nodded approvingly, "I am persuaded and the three of you are changed. You are no longer boys. The voyage has moulded you into men." He pointed at the gear which Leif and Olaf had just deposited." Come, let us take our wood axes and fetch some timber."

The four of us headed west, along the river. We had our weapons but not our shields. I was unsure how my father would react to our leaving but Snorri was correct. We had to make a stronghold sooner rather than later. The Vikings who had fled would return.

The wood which had seemed so close was more than a Roman mile away. We stripped to the waist and, using the four axes, began to cut down the trees to make the palisade. When we had felled eight trees, we began to trim the branches. All the time we kept an eye and an ear out for danger. We had just finished trimming the last tree when my father and the rest of the men arrived. He cocked an eye at his younger brother. Snorri shrugged, "We will need a wall. We thought to make a start."

My father's face broke into a smile. "And you have done well but I have another task. I have made mistakes this day which has cost us men. I will not risk another who is not of my blood. We will take over here. I would have you four follow those Danes and discover if their camp is close."

None of us hesitated. Snorri said, "Erik, we will use the snekke to cross the river. If we head upstream, we might cut their trail."

This time, after we had crossed the river and sailed upstream, we armed. We slung our shields over our backs and hung our helmets from our swords. We took an ale skin with us and headed due south and east. We had landed a mile upstream and we spread out in a long line to pick up the trail. The afternoon was wearing on but the sun would not set for some time. There was plenty of cover and we used it. The brown cloak I had taken from the warrior on Mann was a dirty brown and effectively hid me. We entered a wood about two miles from the river when we picked up a blood trail. It came from the west. Had there been any hunters then it might have been an animal. We had seen no sign of hunters. It was one of those wounded in the battle.

My uncle drew his sword and put his finger to his lips. We drew our swords and I swung my shield around. Snorri waved us left and right. He and Siggi followed the trail. Siggi held up his hand and pointed. I peered through the undergrowth. A Dane with a bloody kirtle sat with his back to a tree. He held his sword in his hand. Snorri waved for Arne and me to go around and beyond him. Where there was one Dane, there might be more. We moved silently. No leaves lay on the hard ground and it was easy to avoid the foliage. I gradually headed to my left. When I met Arne and he shook his head I knew that the others had gone. We headed back to Snorri and Siggi.

As we neared them, I heard, "You are dying, Ivar Guthrumsson. We will give you a warrior's death. All we need to know is where the rest of your band lives."

"It is a dishonourable way to die. I will wait for my death."

We reached the tree and I saw that the Dane's guts could be seen. Snorri, who was squatting before the Dane, nodded, "Then we can leave. We can see the way you were headed. Your line of blood leads like an arrow to your camp and it cannot be far. We will leave you here. You will last until night fall. The foxes and rats will smell your blood. Perhaps you will slay many of them before you die."

Siggi nodded. He was clever, "Of course if one chews off your hand or you drop the sword then you will not go to Valhalla. I will watch for the gull with the sad eyes. That shall be you."

Snorri rose, "Let us see if we can pick up the trail."

"Wait!" The shout made the Dane wince. He lowered his voice, "Promise me that after you have given me the warrior's death you will kill my sword."

"I will but you know that if you do not speak true then you will spend eternity with Hel."

"I know." He took his bloody hand from his guts and clutched his hammer of Thor. "Our camp is on the Ribble. We came from Jorvik. Our leader, Halfdan Ivarsson, should not have left me. I would not have told you otherwise. I shall hold him to account when we meet in the Otherworld. That is all that I will tell you. Either give me the warrior's death as you promised or let me take my chances with the rats and foxes."

Snorri leaned forward and his sword entered the Dane's eye. His head fell to the side. "Go to the Allfather. Your honour is intact." He sheathed his own sword and taking the Dane's he put it between two thick branches and pulled. It was a good sword but it bent. My uncle did not break it. He then bent the blade around to form a circle. He placed it back in the warrior's hand. "Come we will return to your father, we have learned much."

As we headed back Arne asked, "What have we learned?"

"That they are Danes. They have no ship and they have a leader who is losing the respect of his men."

"What do you mean?"

"Simple, Erik, he left one to die. He ordered his men to flee a battle. Just one of those might have still given him the loyalty of his men but doing both there will be doubts. The Dane's words told us that. Most importantly though, they have no ship. They came from Jorvik and they marched. They have a raiding camp which means that they have no women."

Snorri was very clever. I knew that he was not as reckless as my father which made them a good combination for the clan.

We reached the church after dark. We dragged the snekke above the high-water mark. I could smell the food which was cooking. I realised that I had not eaten all day. Before we could eat, however, we would need to speak to my father. As we neared the church, I saw that beyond it, the bodies of our dead were laid out. It was too late to bury them this night but we would honour them the next day. They were the first of my father's band to die and I knew, from his face, that he had taken it badly.

He was with Butar, Galmr, Finn and Asbjorn. They were still the closest of his men. "Well?" My uncle told him all. "Thank you. I am relieved. If they have no ship then we have time to build a palisade and if they are a raiding party, we might be able to hold them off. We need to have the walls and halls built within the month."

Finn the Scar stroked his beard, "We need to raid too. We have few animals and no crops. The hunting and the fishing will not feed us. We need grain and that means raiding."

My father frowned. He was not finding this independence as easy as he might have expected. Galmr suggested, "We need to make the walls have but one entrance. That way we can leave a smaller number to guard our families. I know they are Vikings, jarl, but we are in an unknown land and we do not want to lose our loved ones. Perhaps the land of ice and fire might have been better."

"Perhaps but we would not have had enough provisions for that journey. From what I have been told it could take a month. No, we have thrown the bones and, for good or ill, we must live with my decision." He rubbed his hands, "Come let us eat. We rise early and cut down more trees. Erik, you can take out the young boys in the snekke and fish."

I did not want to. I wanted to cut down trees with the other men. I wanted to build our walls but I was the son of the jarl and I nodded, "Of course Jarl Lars."

We had fishing nets and after I had eaten and quenched my thirst, I gathered the six boys who would be sailing with me. I knew that they had all helped to sail the drekar. They were not novices. "We rise before dawn for that is when the fish bite the best. Our task is to catch as many fish as we can for our people. I know you are young but you must become men."

They grinned at me for they were excited. What are your names?"

"Sven Fámrsson."

"Stig Folkmarsson."

They were cousins. That would help.

"Eidel Eidelsson." He was the smallest and, possibly the youngest.

"Rek Rethersson."

"Halsten Haakensson."

"Dreng Ebbisson."

I did not know it then but the Norns were spinning. Those six would sail with me and become part of my crew but on that late summer evening, I was just worrying about how to keep them alive.

The weather was mercifully benign. We left in the dark. I positioned them on either side of the snekke and I gave them precise instructions about which rope to pull. I would not use Ulf's method and clip them. They were keen and wanted to be with me. I would use that. I kept to the line of the estuary. I had never fished from a boat before. I decided to use a mixture of hooks and a net. Two of the boys, Dreng and Rek, used lines. I had the sail lowered and threw out the net. I allowed the current to pull us along and we gathered fish. The first pass yielded just ten fish.

Dawn had broken and the next few passes were so poor that the two fishermen using lines were catching more. Then Halsten spotted some sea birds just fifty paces from us. "Perhaps there will be fish, captain."

"You may be right. Haul in the net and hoist the sail, Dreng and Rek keep your lines out."

The birds scattered when we arrived. The first net brought us over fifty fish. They were the shiny herring. They were a tasty fish. After ten passes we had exhausted the fish there and the well of the snekke was full. It took time to throw out the net and then haul it in. Emptying seemed to take an age so that it was noon by the time we had finished. They were tired and so we headed back to shore. We were a couple of miles out; the current had made us drift. I had the boys gut the fish as we headed east. It would save their mothers and sisters the task. The sea birds returned as the boys threw the guts in the air for them to catch. The boys, generally, were young enough for it to be a game and there was giggling and squealing. Ulf would have shouted at them. I did not. Their smiles made up for the din.

We did not manage to carry all of the fish up until the middle of the afternoon. By then the two posts for the gate were in position and the other main timbers laid out in a circle around the church. Snorri greeted me, "You have done well! I did not know you were such a good fisherman!"

I shrugged, "Neither did I. But I would not do this every day. I wish to help with the walls or watching for our foes!" I had seen Arne and Leif on the headland as they watched for the Danes.

"Do not worry, nephew. Your catch means that tomorrow you and your crew can help put up the palisade. Your father hopes to have the walls in place within six days. Then we can start the ditch."

"And then the halls." I pointed up to the skies which had become threatening and filled with rain. "We need shelter!"

"One thing at a time. Now go and have some ale. You have earned it."

It was only as I poured my first horn of ale that I realised my uncle had spoken to me as an equal. I was now a man.

Chapter 11

Seven days later and the perimeter of palisade was almost complete. We still had a gate to build and a ditch to dig but we were stronger than we had been. The rains which had come had dampened spirits and made the camp a quagmire but the last day had seen the return of the sun and the ground had started to dry out. Men had been hunting too and they had found deer. On the fourth day, as some of us began to dig the ditch, the hunters brought unwelcome news. Asbjorn shook his head, "The Danes are coming. We were about to begin hunting when we spied them across the river. They were heading for the ford upstream."

"How many were there?"

"More than forty."

"Quickly put the spoil from the ditch behind the palisade to make a fighting platform. Get all the animals and women and children inside."

Snorri asked, "And the drekar and snekke?"

Even I knew that if they were damaged, destroyed or stolen then we were in trouble. "Erik, take your fisher boys, Arne, Siggi, Leif and Olaf. Moor the drekar and the snekke in the river. Use your stones and arrows to support us."

"Are you sure? There are five of us who can fight." Arne did not want to sit idly by while the clan fought.

"Do not worry, my son. You will be fighting. Go, we have no time to lose. They will be here by noon!"

I gathered my crew. While Arne attached the snekke to the drekar the rest of us boarded. We had only two bows but we all had a sling and a large quantity of river stones. From what I had seen of the Danes they had little mail. If my father and his men could hold them in the gateway then we stood a chance.

I had only had the helm of *'Njörðr'* once. My father was showing great confidence in me. I allowed the current to take us, rather than using the sail and I had the older boys use the oars to scull us around. We threw out four woollen anchors to steady us. We faced upstream and if we had to, we could rejoin our men and help them fight the Danes.

The Danes appeared along the river. My uncle had been correct to suggest moving the ships. They were after them. They were now thwarted. However, to get to the walls they had to pass within fifty paces of us. Arne took charge, "On my command let us see how many we can hurt."

The two archers nocked their best arrow. We lined the larboard side and whirled our slings.

The Danes appeared along the river. They must have seen the two ships but dismissed them. Their leader glanced at the ships and then pointed up the bank. They began to climb the path. It made them into a single line and a better target.

Arne shouted, "Now!"

The rattle and cracks of stones and arrows as they struck sounded like hailstone on a drekar's decks. They were punctuated by the sound of cries as our missiles hit men. I saw one man fall with an arrow to the thigh. A second was struck in the arm. Four were laid out by stones. I saw one Dane clutch a broken arm as Arne's stone smashed into it. They raised their shields and ran up the slope. As they did so my father ordered the remaining archers to send arrows at them. They could defend either against us or the arrows but not both. None were killed but more than ten were hurt.

And then all were beyond the range of our weapons. We could not see the gate from the river but we heard the clash as the two shield walls met. We had done what my father intended. The drekar was safe and I could not sit idly by. I strapped on my sword. Arne turned to look at me. I said, "I say we pull back to the shore and tie her up to the bank. We can help our warriors. Father put you in command. It is your decision but I back you, brother.

Siggi, Leif and Olaf shouted, "And we do."

He nodded, "Then we go. Ship's boys, you are to guard the drekar. Know that we five did so when we were little older than you."

Sven Fámrsson raised his seax, "We will defend it!"

We pulled in the anchors and sculled the drekar back to the shore. We tied her up and then donned helmets and held shields. We would use the two bows we had but the other three would use swords. We had fought the Danes once and won. We would do so again.

We raced up the slope. The sounds of battle were growing louder. When we reached the top of the bank, we saw that the Danes had a wedge and my father had filled the empty gateway with his best warriors. Four of them had mail. The bodies which lay before us was testament to the accuracy of the arrows and stones the clan had already used. The two lines had clashed. I saw that the Danes' leader, Halfdan Ivarsson, was not in the front rank. He had to be the warrior in the centre with the good helmet and fine mail byrnie.

We had to step over bodies. There were also wounded men. Mercilessly we slew them as we passed them. Then we were just twenty paces from the rear rank of the wedge. We were a pathetically small threat. There were five youths and ahead of us were men who had fought battles such as this many times but we did not flinch. Olaf and Leif sent their arrows into the backs of two warriors and even as they slipped and fell to their deaths another two were struck. The other six in the rear rank turned and tried to bring their shields around. In that heartbeat of a moment, Leif and Olaf sent their last two arrows into their faces. Five of us faced four men but their age and experience did not daunt us. We rushed at them. I ran with Siggi at the warrior in the centre. His eyes flickered from Siggi to me and that was his mistake. He should have chosen one of us to strike but the hesitation gave us the chance. I struck his shield with my sword. I put all of my anger into it and he reeled. Siggi surprised him with a backhand stroke and it drove the Dane's own sword towards his face. He stepped back and I brought my sword towards his head. His shield blocked it but Siggi rammed his sword into the Dane's middle. He twisted the blade as he did so. The Dane fell writhing to the ground trying to hold in the nest of bloody snakes Siggi had unleashed.

I heard a shout from my right. The Dane fighting Arne had hit his shield so hard that the leather strap had broken. The Dane raised his sword to kill my brother and I lunged at his thigh. The blade scraped off the bone and passed through. Arne needed no bidding. He took his sword in two hands and swung it across the Dane's neck. He half severed it and the huge warrior fell to the ground.

"Shield wall!" A Danish voice, I assumed the jarl, commanded and they stepped back as one. The Danes had made a circle of shields. Our sudden attack had unnerved them. Leif and Olaf had managed to kill their enemies although Leif's leg was bleeding. An eerie silence descended.

I saw my father step forward and shout, "Halfdan Ivarsson, enough of your men have died. Come from behind your warriors and face me, Lars Larsson, man to man."

The Dane might have refused but his men stepped aside so that the two faced each other. The Dane had not fought. The Danish axe he held was not dulled by combat. Save for holding his shield above his head to protect himself from arrows he was fresh. My father was fighting to claw a toehold on this land. His shield and byrnie were spattered with blood. His helmet had a dent from a recent blow.

We did not sheathe our swords. If my father lost then we would fight on regardless. I was already eyeing the young Dane that I would fight. The young warrior was less than four paces from the place where the two would fight and I was two places to his left. Arne was next to me. We might yet have to fight. Our deaths might be necessary to save the clan.

The Dane suddenly launched himself at my father and his axe struck the shield so hard that my father recoiled. The Dane took encouragement and punched with his shield. It caught my father's hand. The Danish axe came below my father's shield and although my father danced away the tip of the axe tore through his breeks and I saw blood. The axe had a sharp edge and the wound would be deep. The watching Danes cheered and banged their shields. The women in the palisade wailed.

The wound seemed to spur on my father. Anticipating that the Dane would come again with his axe my father spun around on his good leg. The war axe came down on empty air and my father swung his sword to hack into the back of the mail of the Dane. The mail held and the padded kyrtle limited the effect of the blow but Halfdan Ivarsson was hurt. Perhaps my father had damaged bones beneath the skin. His back arced and with blood dripping down his left leg my father hacked at the Dane's knee. Unprotected, my father's sword tore through the breeks and flesh. When blood spurted then honours were even. Both were wounded. They stepped away from each other. The fight had taken much out of both of them already. Each blow which was struck was intended to kill.

When the next axe strike came Halfdan Ivarsson reverted to his original attack. He hacked at my father's shield and this time, to my horror, the axe hacked through the two layers of board and into my father's arm. There was nothing to stop the axe head from slicing through. The flesh was torn and blood spurted. Even though he was hurt my father still managed to punch with the boss of the shield. He caught the Dane full on the face. The nasal on the Danish helmet merely drove into the nose. It broke and the Dane stepped back, roaring. My father threw the boss at him and drew his seax. I was not sure that he would be able to hold the weapon. His arm hung down. It looked to be sheer willpower. I saw Snorri looking anxiously at his brother. This was not going well.

Neither man had much mobility. They both had seal skin boots which were filling with blood. The Dane shook his head like a dog and then lurched toward my father, swinging his axe. My father did the only thing that he could. He stepped closer to the Dane. He held his dagger up to block the blow. The dagger had no tip. It was a Saxon seax but it was a long one. Even as the axe came down the seax's edge tore across the back of the Dane's hand. The seax was sharp and intended for tearing. Even though my father was losing strength in the hand the blade still ripped tendon, muscle and bone. The axe head caught the wound the Dane had already inflicted. The seax dropped to the ground. My father's left arm hung uselessly at his side. At the same moment the axe fell from Danish fingers which could no longer grip. My father rammed the tip of his sword up under the chin of the Dane. It came up through the skull and out of the back. The helmet fell and rolled. The shield dropped from lifeless fingers and, as the Dane fell, the body slipped from the sword.

While those in the palisade roared and cheered my uncle ran to support my father. He was badly hurt and could barely keep his feet.

My father, leaning on Snorri, shouted, "This clan of warriors is a mighty band! Fear us, Danes, for we have beaten you!"

I held my sword out. This was not over. Suddenly the Dane I was watching ran, with sword raised. He intended to kill my father.

In two strides I was behind him and my sword was already raised. I sensed Arne to my left. The Dane brought back his sword to avenge his leader. My father was no longer conscious and Snorri was supporting him with two hands. Both were within a swinging blade of death. I hacked down with my sword. I hit as though I was trying to fell a tree. The sword bit into the young Dane's right forearm. It grated from the bone and made my arm shiver. The Dane screamed and dropped his sword. Arne's sword drove through his back and out of his front. As he pulled out his sword the Dane fell dead and Arne and I whirled to face the other Danes. This was a moment filled with tension. There were enough Danes left to make a stand and we had lost men too.

Snorri's voice was filled with authority, "Sheathe your weapons and you shall live. Go. Know that this is the land now of Jarl Lars Ragnarsson. Come north of the river again and you will all be slaughtered."

One Dane stepped forward, "What of our jarl?"

Butar Beer Belly stepped forward and picked up the Danish axe. My uncle looked at him and smiled. Butar swung the axe and took the Dane's head. He held it aloft. "You want the body? Take it, but the head stays here!"

Our men began banging their shields in approval. The Dane nodded and sheathed his sword. The others followed. While six men picked up the body of the jarl the warrior who had spoken picked up the young Dane Arne and I had slain. He turned to head east. I saw that he was of an age with Snorri and wore battle bracelets upon his arms. This was a warrior. He stopped when he saw Arne and I. "Had any taken my son's head then this would have ended with more Vikings dead than left alive. I see your faces and they are etched in my memory. You will both die at my hand. I, Hakon Long Memory, swear it on the body of my son. He and my jarl have been denied Valhalla. You shall have the same destiny!"

He led the survivors of the attack east along the ridge. Snorri shouted, "Arne, take your crew back and protect the drekar!"

As much as we wanted to see to our father we knew that we had to obey orders. We had disobeyed once and we would not do so again. We sheathed our swords and headed down to the drekar.

The boys lined the sides. I saw that they had slipped ashore and taken weapons from the dead Danes. They would do.

Sven shouted, "Have we won?"

I looked at Arne. Neither of us knew if my father would live or die. He had two bad wounds. Olaf shouted, "Aye but the jarl is wounded. Go ashore and fetch any more weapons and treasure that you can find." We boarded the drekar as the six of them scurried up the slope to the bodies which lay there.

Leif said, "There are healers. Your aunt, Gytha, is a volva."

Arne shook his head, "The wound to his arm was a bad one. I saw the bone." Neither of us wanted to say it but his luck had deserted him. In the combat he had fought well but he had been luckless. Was this dream of a home far from Orkneyjar doomed to failure? It felt like it. We had lost men in the battle. Already perilously few in number, we would now have a small crew for our drekar.

We busied ourselves making the drekar secure. The boys returned with the weapons and treasure. Arne, as our leader, divided it equitably. We let the boys keep the weapons. We all had good ones and they deserved them. I went to the steering board with Arne. The small chest with the compass was there. I picked it up and opened it. "If he cannot fight can he still be jarl?"

"Do you know our people so little, Erik? You are a navigator but you do not know people. Our father cares not if he is jarl. He leads our clan whole or not. Snorri is a warrior. When we raid our enemies, his sword will lead us. This is just the work of the Norns."

Siggi had joined us and heard our last words, "Arne is right Erik. We are brothers in blood and our fathers are too. The same bond which binds us binds them. This is a setback, that is all."

It was getting on for dark when we were summoned. As we climbed the slope we saw to the east of us a line of Danish heads on stakes. The bodies were gone. Our dead were laid out under their cloaks. My father was not amongst them. Our first dead had been buried and stones in the shapes of boats laid around them. The ones who had died at the battle of the church would join them. Inside the palisade women were cooking. The dead had been attended to and now we would see to the living. Life went on. I saw bandaged men each look up at Arne and I as we passed. They nodded.

Snorri came to the door of the church and beckoned us. Olaf said, "Give Leif and I your shields and your swords. We will sharpen them for you. We are your oar brothers too."

We nodded as we handed them over. I did not want to speak. It was as though my father was already dead.

Snorri gave me a sad smile, "Come and do not look so glum, your father lives and he would speak with you."

The interior of the church which was now our hall was bathed in the light from the fire. I saw my mother holding my father's right hand. Gytha was stitching his leg. Both women looked up at us and smiled. As we neared him my father said, "You disobeyed an order today."

We both nodded.

"It was the right thing to do. Had you not then we might have lost. I keep underestimating my sons and nephew. I will not do so again." There was hope for he sounded as though he would lead us once more. "My left arm is useless. The axe cut through to the bone and I can neither feel nor move my hand. The gods must have aided my arm when I stabbed him. I could not feel my hand. And my leg?"

Gytha did not look up from her sewing. The stitches were tiny. I could not believe that my father was able to endure the pain. My aunt said, "You will limp that is all, jarl."

My father snorted, "Jarl? No left arm and a left leg which limps. Perhaps I am Lars the Lame!"

Snorri said, "This is *wyrd*. The Norns have done this to you. We spoke before the Danes even came of how we would defend our walls. There are four of you hurt and no longer able to fight. We saved the clan from the Danes and the Norns sent us four of you to stand on our walls. You can stand on a wall and fight, brother."

"But I cannot raid!"

Arne knelt and put his hand on that of my mother and my father, "But we can. We are your blood. We have cast the bones and Erik and I will see that the dream is not lost."

My mother smiled proudly at Arne. He was her favourite. "And you are in God's house, my husband. You will heal. It was a miracle that you had the strength to stab the Dane. Do not give up."

My father laughed, "Your mother means the Allfather!"

She said nothing but I knew what she meant.

Snorri said, "We had men follow the Danes. They have fled south of the river. They are hurt. They may return but not before the new grass. Tomorrow, we finish the outside walls and the ditch. We hunt and we fish. We build long houses. In seven days' time, we raid. We go to the land of Mercia and we take the grain we shall need for winter. Larswick will be our home until our jarl decides where next we go."

My uncle had lived in the shadow of his brother for so long that he had been almost invisible but that night he grew and became my father. He took charge and ruled for my father while the jarl of our clan healed.

Later, when darkness had descended and a watch set, we sat and drank the last of the ale we had brought. Finn the Scar said, "We have no name yet for this clan! The jarl called us a clan of warriors. A clan needs a name. What should it be?"

My uncle had joined those who were closest to my father and he stroked his golden beard. "I would say wolf for we are like the wolf. We look after our own but we are too close to the Land of the Wolf for that and I would not risk the wrath of the witch queen!"

Siggi said, "Then why not the fox? The fox is tenacious. It will fight a wolf to protect its young even though it might die. It can live where there is just ice and snow and its fur is the same colour as the hair of my father and uncle."

Finn the Scar said, "That is *wyrd*. We are the Clan of the Fox!" In that moment we were born as a clan. It did not change the way we fought but it changed the way we thought of ourselves. When newcomers came they joined a clan and that clan had a name.

As my father could no longer either work or supervise much fell on my uncle's shoulders. Arne, Siggi and I also took charge of the younger warriors and boys. I took the snekke out to fish while Arne and Siggi had the young warriors dig a deep ditch. By the time we returned from the sea the gates were in place and the ditch half finished. Over the next days the work continued from dawn until dusk. The women dug turf so that when the gates and ditch were finished, we began to build the two halls we would need. As we had had such a productive two days of fishing Arne and I began to build a wooden quay. I wanted the drekar and knarr to be secure.

By the end of ten hard and long days, my father took his first tentative steps and we had one hall already finished. He had a staff and walked without any other support. He nodded approvingly. When he had finished and returned to the heart of Larswick he nodded, "It seems you have done many things without me. We had a new name for our clan. We have walls finished and we have a quay. Perhaps I am not needed."

"No brother, this was done for you. Tomorrow we take '*Njörðr*' and we raid for grain. You will command here." He pointed to the ship's boys I had been training. "We take half of these with us as ship's boys but the others have shown that they can fight. Erik has trained them well." He turned to me, "And we would have your son helm the drekar."

My father turned to me, "That is not a command, Erik. Can you handle, '*Njörðr*'? Can you stand in my stead? You have a beard and you have killed many times. You can sail the snekke but are you ready for the drekar? Only you and your heart know this."

"I barely have a beard!"

Snorri laughed, "You do not sail a ship with your beard. My son has told me how you outwitted the drekar. You are a navigator. You are a sailor. The question is, are you ready for this?"

I looked at my father and then my brother. "Aye, uncle, I am ready."

"Then, Erik the Fearless, go and prepare your drekar!"

Chapter 12

We had the three elder boys as ship's boys. Sven Fámrsson, Stig Folkmarsson and Eidel Eidelsson, had all shown that they could be relied upon. We only had twenty warriors aboard and that would include me. My father would have eight men to protect Larswick for some had not yet recovered from their wounds. Snorri seemed confident that we would be able to manage. All were better armed thanks to the Danish attack. The Danish jarl's byrnie was now worn by Butar. We had their spears. I had taken the best of the shields we had found and painted a fox upon it. I hoped it would be luckier than Petr's had been. We were not sailing far. The Maeresea was a few hours south of us. We would sail up it until we found a settlement and raid it. This was not the way my uncle and father had planned it but the Norns had spun and we had to adapt. When I took back the hourglass from my father, I felt complete again.

My leather byrnie was now studded with even more pieces of metal. I brought my spear. I would have to go ashore. Every warrior would be needed and we would have to leave the drekar under the care of three boys. It was not ideal. We only took ale with us. Any food which we needed would be taken from the Saxons. My uncle stood next to me, along with Siggi and Arne. It was not to ensure that I did things right it was for moral support. We sailed down the coast and that made navigation easier. We left at noon which meant we would arrive at the estuary well before dark. The men would have to row upstream. We had the advantage that we could lower the sail and keep it on the mast fish. It would make us harder to spot.

Snorri said, "Your father is strong you know. He will learn to adapt to an arm and hand which are useless. He is clever. He believes in what he is doing. He should have been jarl on Orkneyjar. The King of Norway would not have taken it over then!"

"I know you believe I can do this but I have never sailed these waters."

"None of us have, Erik. Your father believes, we all believe, that you have a gift given to you by the gods. You are young and yet you seem to be part of the drekar. Ask Olaf. His grandfather sailed for many years but he did not handle a drekar like you do. We have been at sea a short time and yet you have not made a single mistake. The sails have not flapped and you have barely had to move the steering board. That is truly a gift. Trust in this gift. The gods guide your hand."

Sven's voice came from the mast head, "Sands to the larboard side."

I glanced to my left and saw that although the trees were many miles away it was sand which lay between us and not the sea. I had a piece of wood I was using to mark the coast. I had copied one of my father's charts with charcoal and by using the hourglass and the compass was marking the rough position of features as I saw them. This was an important one for if the tide covered those sands then they could be deadly shallows for other drekar.

Arne laughed, "See, little brother. If I had the steering board, I would have looked at the sand and then forgotten it!"

Ahead I could see sea birds. That meant either a shoal of fish or an estuary. I said, "This may be the estuary, Snorri."

He nodded, "Warriors, prepare for war and take an oar. We earn our berth now!"

I was pleased that I had been right and I saw the wide mouth of the river a short time later. It felt strange to be giving orders to warriors. "Oars out!"

I did not trust myself to steer one handed and so I stamped my sealskin boot on the drekar's deck to give them the beat. I put the steerboard over. The river was wide and there was no obstacle I needed to avoid. I saw that there were people living on the bluff overlooking the river. They could not hurt us. We would be faster than any man running to warn them along the river. A signal tower might have worked but there were none.

"Lower the sail!"

The three ship's boys were not as strong as we had been and they struggled. Leif and Olaf were close by. They shipped their oars and ran to help. I should have thought of that. It was not disastrous. We had time to get upstream. As far as we knew there were no burghs closer than Ceaster. The ship's boys managed to store the mast unaided and Leif and Olaf returned to their bench. Sven and his brother came to me shamefaced as Eidel went to the prow. "I am sorry, Erik."

I shook my head, "It is not your fault it is mine. It needs four men to lower the sail and I sent three boys. When we have raided, I will have the warriors raise the sail. Now go and help Eidel to watch. I need all the information you can give me."

The sun was lowering in the sky behind us. I kept turning the hourglass and I had an idea that we had enjoyed ten hours of daylight. At this time of year, we could have thirteen or more. Stig came running back, "There is a sharp turn to larboard ahead and the river narrows."

"The three of you need to form a line to direct me."

"Aye Erik!"

"Snorri, slow the beat. The river narrows."

"Aye Erik."

We had no chant. We wanted no noise to alert those nearby. Once we spied a large enough settlement then we would land and raid.

Stig was by the mast fish and he pointed to larboard. I put the steering board over until he raised his hand. Then I straightened it. As I did, I spied three huts on the south bank. They were not worth raiding. I had just looked up when Stig pointed to steerboard. I put the steering board over and a short time later he held up his arm. I was sweating. It was not hard work it was just nerve wracking. The sun had been steadily setting. As Stig waved his arm to steerboard and I turned a little towards the south bank the rays of the setting sun disappeared behind the bluff we had just passed. The land before us was plunged into darkness. The river was narrowing rapidly. Just before the light had disappeared, I estimated it to be no more than forty paces wide. In the end, the darkness helped us. We saw in the darkness ahead the glow from a house. Someone had opened a door and the light had flared out.

I said, "Snorri, there is a light ahead and the river narrows. I would not wreck my father's ship."

He nodded, "You are right. Put us over. Larboard oars in."

I put the steering board over to take us to the north bank. The ship's boys were ready and they leapt ashore and fastened us to two huge willows which overhung the drekar. If the mast had not been on the mast fish it might have been damaged. I opened my chest and took out my helmet liner and then my helmet. I donned them. I took my shield from the side and my sword. By the time I had done so the drekar was empty and Snorri was leading the warband up the river bank. I knew I would regret not turning the drekar but I comforted myself that the river was still thirty odd paces wide. Our drekar's hull was just twelve paces long. We could turn.

"Sven, I leave your brother and Eidel with you to guard the drekar. You have weapons?"

"Aye, Erik."

"When I was but a little older than you, I had to defend a larger drekar. I killed my first warrior, a Walhaz on that day. If Saxons come do not hesitate."

"We will not."

As I clambered over the side, I could smell man. The fields nearby had been tilled. There were animals. I could hear them. I could smell their dung and I could also smell wood smoke. I hurried into the dark after the others. Galmr was at the rear of the line of warriors. He turned as I approached. He just nodded. We would make no unnecessary noises.

Distance is hard to estimate in the dark. I had been counting my steps. I was half way through my second thousand when we stopped. I could see the silhouette of a building some way ahead. It was a church. I swung my shield around as I waited. Snorri would be sending men to surround the settlement. There were sounds ahead as people spoke in their homes. We were invisible in the darkness to the south. Behind me the river made noises. They would be familiar to those who lived in this village. The line moved forward until there was just Arne, Siggi and Galmr with my uncle and Leif. There was a hedge before us and beyond it, I saw the shapes of dwellings. He pointed to Galmr, me and Arne. He circled his left arm. We were to head to the north. We would encircle the settlement. Galmr nodded and Arne and I followed him.

We moved along the hedge. I guessed that the Mercians had planted it to give some protection from the west winds. Behind us, in the field, I heard the sound of sheep as they moved in the dark. I had counted a hundred steps when Galmr saw a gap and he headed towards it. There was no grass beneath my feet. This was a well-worn path. When we stepped through, I saw that Asbjorn and two others were already there. They crouched behind a crude Saxon hut. It was made of wattle and daub. Smoke spiralled from the opening at the top of the conical shaped roof. I saw sparks within. To the right lay another one and the left, a third. There was nothing behind us.

Galmr gestured for Arne and me to move to his right. As we did so, we drew our swords. My uncle would initiate the attack. He would be attacking from the river side towards the church. We could see it now as it loomed up higher than any other building we could see. It had a wooden cross which rose from its roof. The cry, when it came from the dark, made me jump a little for the silence had been complete. Those in the huts close to us must have been asleep. This was the time of the short nights when darkness meant repose.

The two of us stepped towards the two huts. I went right and Arne went left. The door obligingly opened and a Saxon stood there. He saw me and started to shout something. I lunged and my sword went into his middle. He reeled back into the hut. Women screamed and, in the light of the fire, I saw a woman and two children. We had to eliminate the men. I turned and left. I heard the clash of metal on metal. There were men defending their homes. Screams and shouts now filled the air. I ran to Arne. He had a bloody blade too. We turned and headed towards the church. If there was an eorledman then he would have a hall there. There had been no palisade around the huts. Perhaps this settlement had few warriors.

I heard Snorri's voice, "Clan of the Fox!"

We hurried to the sound of battle. Unlike the raid on Mann here we knew every warrior. We could identify each warrior by his shape, helmet, stance and weapon. Arne and I saw two men with spears running towards the church. They were not our men. As we neared them, they must have smelled us and they turned. Their spears were their undoing. As the one closest to me swung it I hacked down and severed it just behind the spear head. He now had a stick and a shield. As his hand went to his sword, I punched him hard and the boss of my shield hit his hand. I brought my sword over from behind and hit him on his helmet. It made my arm shiver. I cursed my eagerness. I should have used the flat of the blade. I would have taken off the edge. The blow was effective. He must have been bareheaded beneath his metal helmet for he fell to the ground. Arne was pulling his sword from the body of the dead Mercian he had slain as I heard Snorri's voice once more. The Mercians were fighting hard.

Galmr and Asbjorn joined us. We had more than one third of the crew with us. The ten warriors we saw were pushing back my uncle and his men. I saw Siggi lying on the ground. He did not appear to be moving. Galmr shouted, "Clan of the Fox!" And we hurled ourselves into the back of the Saxon line. Our shout made them turn and gave Snorri and the others hope. I blocked the Saxon sword and half dropped to my knee. I was not sure of the edge of my blade but I knew that I had a tip. I lunged up and under the Saxon's round shield. He had pulled back his sword to swing at me again but my move disorientated him and the tip of my sword slid up under his ribs and, as I rose, I drove it deep within his body.

A mailed warrior was fighting Snorri. Around him oathsworn, well-armed and trained, were fighting hard but we now had two men to every one of theirs. Men speak of glory and honour. There had been honour when we had fought the Danes. We had allowed their leader and ours to fight to the death. These were Saxons; these were victims. While I engaged a warrior with a byrnie and a helmet with a mask, Arne sank his sword into his back. Snorri's sword ended the resistance when he drove his sword under the chin of the eorledman.

As much as my uncle wished to see to his son we had a settlement to secure. "Asbjorn take two men and get to the church before the priests take their treasure. Finn and Butar, come with me and we will search the hall. Gandálfr take any men who are left and search the rest of the buildings." He turned to me, "Erik, see to my son!"

As they hurried off, I knelt next to Siggi's body. I put my hand to his neck and I could feel a beat. He lived still. I took off his helmet. There was a large dent in it and my hand came away bloody. He had been struck on the helmet. His head protector had not been thick enough. There was a hut behind me. I stepped over the body of the Mercian man who lay there, gutted. The hut was empty. His family had fled. I grabbed a skin. It would either have ale or water within it. I also picked up the end of a burning log and carried it outside. I laid it close to Siggi's head and poured the liquid on his scalp. It was ale. I put some to his lips. I saw that his head had been cut and his skull cracked. This was for a healer and not me. I suspected that leaving him lying on the ground might be the best thing. I wrapped his cloak around him.

I was just standing when the Saxon whose helmet I had struck lurched towards me. His helmet had gone and his face was covered in blood. The blow had hurt him but he had seen me by the light of the brand. I easily stepped away from the swashing blow. I did not want to kill him for I now saw that he was even younger than I was. I said in Saxon, "If you attack me, I will kill you. I give you a life. Go!" In answer he lunged at my middle. It was a clumsy blow and I pirouetted out of the way and struck him in the back with the flat of my blade. "The next one will be with the edge and you will die!"

He glared at me and shouted, "I am not afraid of you!" Then he ran, leaving his helmet, shield and spear behind.

My uncle, with Arne and Leif, came towards me. "My son?"

"He lives but he has a wound to the head. I am not a healer. I washed the wound with ale and gave him some to drink."

I saw the relief on his face. "The three of you carry him to the drekar. He will be safer there and bring '*Njörðr*' up river to here. We have captured great quantities of grain and treasure." He pointed to the body of Tafæistr. "We have lost warriors."

I nodded. Arne and Leif placed Siggi's shield beneath his head and back. His lower body and feet hung over the edge but his head would not move. I led them back to the hedgerow and then along the river bank. I did not want to move quickly for fear of worsening the wound. It seemed to take an age before I smelled our drekar. She was well hidden.

Stig appeared from the undergrowth. He held my spear. "We heard you coming and I was ready."

I smiled, "Good, now prepare the ship to move. When my cousin is aboard, we will sail upstream."

By the time we had managed to get Siggi aboard and lay him, covered by a cloak and fur, by the prow where *'Njörðr'* could protect him, the boys had untied us and we had drifted out into the middle of the river and we were heading downstream. I took off my helmet and put the steering board in the centre. We were clear of any trees. "Raise the sail. Eidel, lookout!" Fuelled by the need to get to the clan they managed to raise the sail and we moved against the current.

The river headed north by north east. The wind came from the north and west. *'Njörðr'* was a forgiving ship and I managed to make us move towards the settlement. We would not make rapid progress. I shouted, "Arne, how is Siggi?"

"He breathes, brother."

The wind was not a strong one but the river was straight. As we edged up it, I saw the first lightening of the sky. The short summer night was coming to an end. What would we find? Stig shouted, "Erik, I see the houses and there looks to be a quay."

"We will sail beyond it and turn. Leif, have the boys ready to tie us up." It was still too dark to see much as we sailed beyond the houses but I saw Butar Beer Belly. He waved as we passed and then turned to head up to the church which could now be seen on the skyline. By the time we had turned the sky was light enough to see that we had attacked a village which was bigger than we might have expected. The lack of palisade had made us think it was small enough to be taken by twenty men! "Lower the sail." I let the current and the momentum of the drekar bump us next to the quay.

The boys tied us up and Leif and Arne, after putting out the gangplanks, went ashore. As much as I wanted to join them, I was the navigator. I had to be ready to leave. We had not touched the women and the children. They had fled. I knew not what lay to the north and east. "Sven, leave Stig with Siggi. You and Eidel lift the deck and then go ashore and help to load the drekar."

"Aye, Erik."

I took my wooden board and marked the village with a cross. I put in the river turns as I could remember them. When we headed back to the sea, I would have Stig correct any mistakes. If we came back to this river I would sail better.

The sun had risen fully by the time that our men began to bring back the treasure. There were sacks of grain. We had wheat, oats and barley. If we had nothing else then the raid had already been a success. Asbjorn came aboard with the first of the grain sacks. He looked at Siggi and then came down the drekar to speak with me. "How is he?"

"He lives. We need to get him home. His mother is a volva. She can heal him. Do we have much treasure?"

He smiled, "The Norns were, indeed, spinning. We found a thrall hall. There were eight Vikings within. They were from Ljoðhús and they raided last year. They were unlucky for King Ceolwulf had been visiting the church. This is the church of St. Elphin and the King of Mercia was endowing it. The warriors who attacked lost half of their crew. These eight are the only survivors. Others were killed or died. They are in a bad way but they have already sworn to join the Clan of the Fox."

I nodded, "*Wyrd.*"

"Aye, just so. We know that there are none others close by. Snorri has sent men to fetch in as many animals as we can find. We will load what we can and slaughter the rest." He turned to leave.

"Asbjorn, I would not sail a heavily laden drekar down this river at night. We used up all of our luck last night."

"Aye, you did well. I will tell Snorri."

It was noon by the time the hold was full. As well as the grain we had treasures from the church and many weapons. The Saxons had good swords. We had two mail byrnie and the helmets could be melted down. With the deck replaced I had the barrels of ale and salted meat stored along the sides. I heard the sound of cattle and sheep as they were driven towards us.

My uncle appeared. "We have two cows in calf. We take those first."

The two animals were led up and I had them tethered by the mast fish. They were in the centre of the drekar and the widest part. There they could do the least damage. We then boarded a ram and ten ewes. The ewes were all young. They would be close to me at the steering board. It could not be helped. We had to leave room for the rowers. We still had room and so we loaded a boar and two sows. I had those tethered at the prow. The wounded were brought on board. Only Úlfgeirr would not be able to row. He had a gashed arm. Then our men began to slaughter as many animals as they could. The eight thralls came aboard. Asbjorn had told me that they had been dressed in rags. The dead had been stripped and now they were better dressed. Their life would begin anew.

They looked in surprise as they saw the youth at the steering board. One, I later learned that his name was Æimundr Loud Voice said, "Do you not have an older navigator?"

My brother was close by and he snarled, "Insult my brother again and you will not need to worry about being taken by Saxons for I will feed your carcass to the fishes."

An older warrior smiled, "I am sorry for Æimundr Loud Voice. We are used to him. He gives voice to thoughts when others keep them hidden. Forgive him. I am Kalman Peacemaker and I am the one who leads these warriors you have rescued."

Mollified Arne said, "Where do you want them, brother?"

"We will wait until I see which oars are empty."

It was just two hours after noon when we had finished loading the drekar. The bloody carcasses, hides and skins were just laid on the deck. We put them close to the pigs. The other animals would be unsettled by the smell of death.

We made the open sea an hour before the sun set. I had marked as much on my map as I could. I had seen where the Saxons looked to have begun work on a palisade. It was in the south bank of the river just a mile or so from the mouth. I was not sure if we would raid here but it had been productive. Arne, who had helped to collect the animals, told me of a bull he had seen in a field. Too dangerous to take on a ship this land was close enough to make a raid over land and take the animals. First, we would have to deal with the Danes who had begun to raid there too.

The wind was against us for the first part of the voyage home. We could tack but we were anxious to get Siggi to the volva. We rowed and Snorri gave us our first chant.

The Clan of the Fox has no king
We will not bow nor kiss a ring
We fled our home to start anew
We are strong in heart though we are few

Lars the jarl fears no foe
He sailed the ship from Finehair's woe
Drekar came to end our quest

Erik the Navigator proved the best
When Danes appeared to thwart our start
The Clan of the Fox showed their heart
While we healed the sad and the sick
We built our home, Larswick

The Clan of the Fox has no king
We will not bow nor kiss a ring
We fled our home to start anew
We are strong in heart though we are few

When Halfdan came with warriors armed
The Clan of the Fox was not alarmed
We had our jarl, a mighty man
But the Norns they spun they had a plan
When the jarl slew Halfdan the Dane
His last few blows caused great pain
With heart and arm he raised his hand
'The Clan of the Fox is a mighty band!'

The Clan of the Fox has no king
We will not bow nor kiss a ring
We fled our home to start anew
We are strong in heart though we are few

I was touched that I was mentioned. The men at the oars sang it for an hour. It helped to bond the new men. After an hour I shouted, "In oars! I will take the wind!" I put the steering boar over to let the wind from the west take us towards the coast. By tacking a little we could sail all the way to the Loyne and the men could rest. I looked up at the sky and thanked the Allfather. I had sailed on my first raid and the drekar and the crew were safe. I was a navigator!

Chapter 13

We reached the river after dark. There were brands burning at the quay and the tide was on the turn. I thanked the Allfather. We had made it safely home. I would be glad to get the animals from the drekar. They had become distressed the further north we went. As a result, it would be many hours before the ship's boys and me would be able to head to the stad. Snorri came aft as the deck was lifted and men brought out the grain. He clasped my arm, "Erik, you have done more than any could have expected. You are due a larger share than those who rowed."

I shook my head, "I am one of the crew and I was lucky. I would not tempt the Norns by talking more credit than I am due. I am learning and I will continue to learn for many years to come."

When the sacks had been removed, I had the decking laid on the side of the river. With pails of river water, we cleansed them. While they dried, I had the three ship's boys help me to wash down the gunwale and remove the salt from the prow. By the time we had replaced the deck poor Eidel was asleep on his feet. I picked up my chest, "Come you have done enough. I doubt that we will raid again for a while. It will just be fishing from the snekke for you."

As we headed up to the stronghold, I wondered how Siggi had fared. He had not woken during the voyage but he appeared to be at peace. I know that Snorri had worried about his son. The gate was still open when we reached it. I saw that there were now warriors watching it.

Finn the Scar closed it and barred it behind us, "Your father has made new rules. We close the gates at dusk. We were just waiting for you."

I pointed to the animals which were now penned on the far side of the church. "Were it not for those beasts then we would have been back sooner!"

He laughed, "They have stayed food for you." He pointed, "Here is your brother to fetch you." He turned to close the gate.

Arne put an arm around my shoulder. I asked, "How is Siggi?"

"His eyes are open and he can speak but he remembers nothing of the voyage or the battle." He shook his head. "I am going to add more padding to my helmet."

On the way north, I had thought of the raid and what we had seen and left behind. "You know that if we wanted that bull, we could get it. We could raid across the land. It is only forty or so miles."

"But the Danes!"

"The Danes will be back in Jorvik over the winter. Remember what Snorri said; they have no women."

Although he said nothing, I saw that I had planted a seed in his head. We did not go to see Siggi. Gytha was working her magic. She and the other volvas were weaving spells to go with the medicine they had tried. We entered the church. It was now a hall. Mother had persuaded my father to leave the cross on the top. He had acceded to her request.

As I entered Edmund held out his hands, "If you give me your chest, lord, I will dry your clothes and clean your weapons." I nodded. He would not sharpen them. A warrior sharpened his own weapons.

I washed my hands in the pail by the door. I had rinsed them after cleansing the drekar but mother had infused this water with rosemary and thyme. The sweet smell would take away the stink of pig muck. I really needed to change my clothes too but my stomach told me I needed to eat.

Father beamed at me, "I hear from Arne that you and I have our own song!"

"It was your song, father. I was just honoured to be mentioned."

My mother ladled food into my bowl and then she kissed me on the side of the head, "And you let a young warrior live."

I was aware of my father's angry glower. I shook my head, "He was like the small fish we throw back when they are caught in our nets." I tried to make light of it.

"Unlike the fish, my son, when the Saxon grows, he may well hurt us. Better to kill all their men."

My mother surreptitiously clutched her cross. I ate and concentrated on my food. Arne managed to distract my father. "We found a good bull by St. Elphin's burgh. Erik thinks we could go to fetch it once the leaves have fallen. We could go across the land. We have the cows. If we had the bull then our herd would grow."

He smiled, "You are too kind for your own good Erik but you are clever. I will speak with your uncle. How many men would you need?"

"No more than ten or so."

He nodded, "First we finish our defences and our building. Now that you have the grain, we can build an oven and a brewhouse."

Arne picked up a pig bone which still had meat upon it. As he began to gnaw it, he said, "We need a smithy. Siggi's helmet and the other damaged helmets will have to be repaired. The new men need shields and that means metal."

My father leaned back. I saw that he had to lift his left arm with his right and rest it on his lap. "The tree trunk is not a problem but the anvil is something else."

Arne suddenly leapt to his feet as though he had been stung, "When we raid for the bull, we could raid a smithy! A bull could carry an anvil!"

My father's smile was from ear to ear, "You are both clever. I hope that Fótr grows into such a clever warrior. The three of you could conquer the world." His arm slipped down and, as he picked it up again to rest on his lap his face darkened, "Sadly, I will not be able to come with you when you take this bull and anvil. My days of adventuring are gone."

My mother came to his side, kissed him on the cheek and put her arm around him. "I will make a leather sling for this. It will be more comfortable. You have done well and it is only a small inconvenience."

He shook his head, "There speaks a Saxon and a woman. I know you mean well but I am now half the man I was."

In a short time, our world had changed beyond all recognition. Now Snorri led the clan and Arne and I were the future. Where would it end?

For the next months, right until the end of Gormánuður, we worked to make our home secure and to gather as much food as we could. This part of Mercia was empty. When hunting parties went north, they discovered the graves and deserted homes of other Vikings. The roofs had gone and the turf walls fallen but we knew that they were Viking. My father recalled that in the glory days of the Dragonheart his people had colonised it. They were gone and it was now a debated land. We sent scouts to look for the Danes. They found deserted camps less then fifteen miles from us but there were no signs of them. We made the most of the time we had. The new men fitted in well and a couple married the widows of men we had lost. The men had lost almost a year of their lives as slaves and were keen to make up for it while the women liked the security of a warrior. Siggi recovered although he was sometimes a little vague and had trouble remembering things. His mother said he would recover. She was with child again and, that too was a good thing.

We held a Thing at the start of Ýlir. We had had our bone fire. Although we had had fewer animals to cull we still had the bones of many animals we had hunted. We had made salt on the sands just north of us and preserved meat and fish for the winter. Gytha believed that the winter would not be as harsh this far south but it would be as long. With a new bread oven and brewery, we felt as though we were here to stay and that was why we held a Thing. If any other than my father and Snorri had led the clan then there might have been a bid for another to be a jarl. That was not the case and, as the men gathered in the hall, we had freshly brewed ale and pickled fish to eat. Once the women had provided the ale and food they disappeared to Snorri's hall where Gytha had laid on a feast for them.

My father stood and spoke. He was now more comfortable with his leather sling, "We have been here at Larswick for half a year. We have lost warriors and some of us have lost..." he smiled and shrugged. "The gods spared my life and I should be grateful. They still have a purpose for me and that is good. We have to decide if we wish to stay here." He sat. It was a sign that another could stand and speak. Finn the Scar and Butar Beer Belly both stood. Butar looked at Finn, grinned and sat down. He poured himself more ale.

Finn said, "I like it in this land. Life is easier here than it was in Orkneyjar and I would not bow a knee to a king. The Norns may spin and send enemies here. Until then we stay."

152

Kalman Peacemaker stood. He had been thin and emaciated when he had come. He had married Reimund's widow and she was a good cook. He smiled, "We are honoured that you allow us incomers to speak at your Thing. I speak for all of us when I say that we are more than happy to be part of the Clan of the Fox. You have not yet asked us to but we would all swear an oath to Jarl Lars."

My father shook his head and smiled. None of the clan had sworn an oath. We stayed because we wished to and not because we were bound by an oath. Kalman sat and my father nodded to Snorri. He stood. "When we raided Mercia, we were successful but there are still shortages. We need horses and a bull. We need an anvil. My nephew, Arne, has suggested a raid to fetch back those items. This would be a raid across the land which is claimed by the Danes. Our scouts say that there are no Danes but this is still a risk. Is it worth it?"

As my father had expected this caused debate. When Snorri sat men spoke with their neighbours. Arne and I just drank. If any objected then we had arguments we would use. Gradually the chattering stopped. Snorri stood again, "There are no objections?" Men shook their heads. "Then Arne and Erik will lead the raid. It was their idea and I think that they are ready for it. This does not need mailed men who can fight in a shield wall. This needs clever young minds and quick feet."

Asbjorn stood, "I would go with them. I am not too old."

Men laughed and Arne stood, "Any can come but we take but ten men including Erik and me. We would not leave our home undefended and we need to be able to hide."

He was still standing when Butar Beer Belly burped and burst out, "You will find it hard to hide a bull and a pair of horses." He thought he was being funny but no one laughed and everyone glowered at him. He had not obeyed the rules of the Thing. "Sorry."

Arne smiled and sat. Snorri said, "Then it is decided. The Thing is over!"

Over the next days, we chose our men and prepared to head through unknown lands to the land of the Saxons. It was as we were preparing to go that we realised we needed horses more than the bull. Horses would have meant it would have taken us just a day to ride far to the south, make the raid and be half way home. The journey would take a day, perhaps longer for we would have to try to stay hidden. We took ale skins, rope, salted meat and two cloaks. The cloaks would act as blankets. It was becoming cold although not as cold as it would have been in Orkneyjar.

A Viking farewell is brief. My mother was a Saxon and it was she who wept. The men just waved us off. Siggi was at the gate. He had wished to come. His mother had not been willing to sanction it and we were not happy to take him. We had few enough men and they had to be the best. Asbjorn was the oldest and the only one with a mail byrnie. He had taken one on our Saxon raid. As we began to run towards the ford I wondered if his mail might slow him down.

I had my compass with me. I had no hour glass and there was little sun but when the sun did shine then I would be able to estimate our position. For that reason, I led. My helmet hung from my shield. A scout used all of his senses. Without the sun I was forced to use the landscape to help me. The high ground was to the east. We knew that from our voyages down the coast. The high ground had always been visible to the east. So long as we kept parallel to it then we were heading roughly south. I was also aware of the streams. We passed many which flowed north, towards the Loyne. Then we found others which headed in the opposite direction. They had to feed the Ribble. We halted at the Ribble. We were half way to our destination. It was just after noon and we had seen few people. We drank from the river to save our ale skins. The beer would help us sleep! We ate from our salted meat and I took out the hare skin which had been dried and cured. I used charcoal to mark our route. It was crude but by putting marks indicating how long it took us to reach a point we could use it on our return to estimate distance.

Olaf chewed on the salted meat and looked around him. "This is good land to farm. I am no farmer but look at the trees and bushes which grow here. Yet we have only passed one deserted farm and one village."

Asbjorn said, "Men have fought over this land. It is far from the heart of Mercia and the Land of the Wolf is to the north of us. The Danes from the east now begin to pick over the bones of this land. It will take Vikings to settle it."

As we moved south the land became flatter. We saw one or two villages but they were small and we needed one with a blacksmith. Nor had we seen any bulls or horses. The raid had shown us that we had managed to find somewhere which was relatively well off. We passed through a wood and there was a spring in the middle. We rested there and ate. It was a brief rest and then we headed south once more. We found a greenway. They were the paths used by ancient people. They were not Roman and had no stone upon which we would tread. The grass upon them was easier on unshod animals and the trees gave shade in summer. In winter they made for shelter and a little more warmth than in the open.

The Norns had been weaving. Nine miles or so south of the wood where we had rested, we began to climb a little as the setting sun showed us where the west lay. Arne had just said that we should find a camp when I heard the sound of cattle. We were not on a road. It was a greenway. I looked and saw signs of cattle. There was dung and hoof prints. I waved my hand to stop the others and took my shield and helmet from around my back. The greenway obviously led to a farm of some description. Asbjorn and Arne joined me. I pointed to the dung and cupped my ear. A few moments later we heard the lowing of cattle demanding to be milked. Then I heard the sound of a bell. There was a church nearby. It was not dark yet. Perhaps the church had some service. I did not understand the religion of my mother.

Arne pointed down the greenway. He gestured that we should be cautious. This time he and Olaf led. Asbjorn brought up the rear. The sound of the bell grew closer as did the sound of the cattle. Then I smelled the smoke of a home. The ground was still rising as the trees lining the greenway ended. I saw a movement ahead and dived to the bottom of the trees. I heard voices to my left. They were Saxon. The land rose there and I could smell cattle. The sound appeared to be coming from inside a building. Arne hissed and pointed. He wanted me to investigate. I dropped my shield, helmet and spare cloak. I drew my dagger and crawled around the side of the hedge. The sun was almost setting. It was low in the sky and was the thin sun which gave no warmth. I crawled towards the building which I knew was to my left. There was a small orchard and I crawled into it. The fruit and leaves had gone but the branches broke up my outline and I was able to move through it easier. It was a farm. The path which led to it was muddy. I saw that it was rutted and covered in the marks of animals. The ground was already hardening as the frost set in.

I saw two thralls. Their heads were down and they had yokes about their necks. They were not Viking and did not look like Saxons. I wondered if they were of the Walhaz. One headed into what looked like a barn. The other carried two wooden pails into the farm house. It looked substantial. This was a Saxon lord or perhaps a thegn. I took a chance and ran back through the orchard to the track which led to the farm. There was a mound covered in thin saplings on the other side and I crawled up it. I saw, to the south, a village. There was a church. It stood on another mound. Both mounds looked to be man-made. The church had a cemetery and an arch of yew leading to it. I saw a house close by the church and I heard the whinny of an animal. The priest had a horse. There were five houses and I saw a glow from one of them. It was a smithy. I had seen enough. I turned and made my way back to the others. Picking up my shield, helmet and cloak I gestured for them to go back up the greenway so that we could talk.

I told them what I had seen. When I had finished, I said. "I do not know that there is a bull but I believe there must be one. There is a smithy."

"What are you saying, brother?"

"I am saying that the Norns led us here. We do not need to go further south. We wait until dark and steal the anvil. We go back to the farm. It is a big one and look for horses and a bull."

Asbjorn said, "You make it sound simple. What if there are armed men here?"

"This is smaller than St. Elphin and its burg. We would have to fight further south too. We might have to fight for what we take but we might have to do that further south with a longer journey back."

"The clan appointed me to lead and I will. I like Erik's plan. When it is dark and all are asleep, we crawl back and take the anvil. We go to the farm and we find horses and, if they have one, a bull. If we have to, we fight. Make water, eat and drink. When the moon has risen, we go."

We were lucky that it was almost winter. No one came down the greenway. We heard Saxon voices in the distance as the people left the church. Arne looked up into the clear sky. The moon had risen. He rose to his feet. I slipped my shield over my back and Arne and I led the small band down the greenway towards the village. The air was so cold that our breath could be seen in the air before us. Not a creature stirred. Doors were shut and fires were banked. People slept. This was winter. Candles were expensive. This was the time to make babies. While we had waited Arne had suggested that Leif and I see if there was any treasure in the church. When we reached the village Leif and I headed to the church while the rest went to the blacksmiths' workshop.

The door of the church was not locked. I had seen a house attached to it. That would belong to the priest. We opened it silently. It was pitch black and so I opened the door wide and used the light from the moon to illuminate the interior. The altar was simple but there were good candles in candlesticks. They stood on a good piece of linen. Leif picked up the candlesticks and I made a bag from the linen. He put the treasure inside and I gave it to him. When we went outside, I pointed to the smithy and I strode to the yew trees. I selected a branch which was as long as I was and I used my dagger to saw it off. I would strip the leaves from it later. I had my bow stave. The Norns had sent me here!

The workshop was simply a shelter over the forge. The anvil embedded in the tree trunk was to one side. When I reached it, I saw that Arne and most of the men were ready with weapons while Gandálfr and Faramir, who had secured ropes underneath it, were lifting it. They nodded. They could take the weight. Arne nodded and they moved towards the greenway. The village slept. The hard part would be to take the animals. We headed up to the farm. I stepped in the frozen ruts but Sigismund stepped on a raised piece of mud. It crunched and cracked. Arne held up his hand and we stopped. Our frozen breath rose before us but there was no other sound. We had not been heard. Arne waved his hand and we moved on.

Arne reached the barn. He waved for Asbjorn and Sigismund to follow him and he pointed to the door of the barn and me. I nodded and put my shield, helmet and yew stave on the ground. The door was closed but not barred. I slowly opened it. I hoped that it would not creak. It did not. A wall of warm air hit us as we slipped inside. I heard the animals within as they moved. There were stalls to separate them. Then, as I sniffed, I smelled humans. There were men in the barn. I waited until my eyes adjusted to the dark. I saw two forms which lay close together in the straw. They were the thralls. There was no way we could move any animals without waking them. I took out my dagger. It was the Saxon one. I tapped Leif on the shoulder and pointed to the animals. I tapped Olaf and pointed to the two slaves.

We moved closer to the two men. I looked at Olaf and nodded. In one motion we had our hands over their mouths and a dagger above their eyes. As they opened them and stared in terror I said, in Saxon, "We will not harm you. Do you understand?" I moved my hand away.

The one I held croaked, "Yes master."

I stood, "Then rise but make no sound or you will die." They stood. I saw that they were a little older than me and were very thin. I could see better now. I saw that there were two horses. Neither were particularly big but they were horses. "Leif, fit reins to them."

"Aye, Erik."

"We are going to take the horses. Is there a bull?"

The one I had spoken to said, "Yes, master, Peter. He is in the stall at the end."

I was relieved, "Would you two like to be freed?"

Their eyes lit up. "Yes, master, but we come from the land of Hibernia. How would we get home?"

I had not thought of that but I did so then. "Come with us to our home and when the new grass comes and we trade with Dyflin, we will take you there."

"Then we will come. You will need our help anyway. Peter does not take to strangers. He does not even like the master."

I went to their thrall yokes and freed the two of them. I made more noise than I wished and Arne put his head in the door. He hissed, "What are you doing? We do not want to wake the house."

"We have the animals and two thralls I had freed. We need them for the bull."

He looked relieved, "Good!"

I said, "Olaf, Leif, put blankets and saddles on the horses and lead them out." I turned to the two men. "What are your names?"

The one who had spoken to me the most said, "Padraig."

The other said, "Aed!"

"Then fetch the bull." While they went, I looked around the barn and saw two large sacks. I opened them and smelled them. One was barley and one was oats. They were heavy but I tied a piece of halter rope to join them and slung them over my shoulders. I saw a coil of rope on the ground and I picked it up. The two former slaves had the bull. They had a rope through its nose. It was not the largest bull I had ever seen but it was big enough. I did not risk putting the sacks over the bull. I would use the horses.

Once we were outside, I saw that Olaf and Leif had led their horses to the greenway. Arne saw me with the sacks and he picked up my shield, helmet and yew stave. With Sigismund and Asbjorn watching the hall we followed the lumbering bull towards the greenway. The bull crunched on the frozen ruts but it could not be helped. I hoped that those in the hall were sound sleepers. When we reached the horses, the anvil and our men, I slung the sacks over one horse and gave the rope to Gandálfr and Faramir. We had a problem. If they tied the anvil and tree trunk to one horse then it would unbalance it.

Faramir said, "If we sling the anvil between the two horses then we can tie the sacks on the other side of each horse to balance it."

Arne nodded, "Then do it. This bull will slow us down."

"Then while you load the horses, I will take the bull and Leif. We will head down the greenways and you can catch us up."

"Aye."

"Padraig, let us go." As they started down the greenway, I saw that the two slaves had wooden clogs upon their feet and just a shift. They shivered. I took my spare cloak and gave it to Padraig. Leif saw what I did and gave his to Aed as we walked. Time was of the essence. By the time they were cloaked we had moved four hundred paces from the others. The bull was now moving a little faster than I had expected.

Padraig shook his head, "Are you Vikings?"

"We are."

"Then why do you care if we freeze or not?"

I pointed the yew stave at the bull. "We want the bull and the bull needs you. Besides, I have two cloaks and I can wear but one."

I realised why the bull was moving more quickly. We were travelling down a slope. In my head I began to work out the problems we would encounter on our way north. We would need to rest and I remembered that there was a wood some ten miles north of us. I looked at the moon. We would be lucky to reach the wood by dawn. Folk might not be out at night but they would be up to make the most of the short days. We would have to stay on the greenway as long as possible. I had not heard the horses and that was a good thing. I glanced behind us and saw, four hundred paces or so behind us, the tell-tale breath of the animals and the rest of our men.

I said, "What is your tale?"

Padraig shrugged, "The tale of many of our people. We lived in the west where the seas stretch as far as the eye can see and we fished. The chief from the next village raided our home. They killed our fathers and took us and our families."

I asked, "When was this?"

He looked up at the sky as though calculating. "I had seen six summers. That was twelve years ago. We were sold to the Vikings at the place you call Veisafjǫrðr. They took us to the slave market at Dyflin and we were bought by a Mercian. He was the reeve who worked for the eorledman, Ethelred."

"You can speak Norse?"

He shook his head, "I understood some of the words you said but it has been twelve years since we spoke it."

"Aed does not say much."

Padraig smiled sadly, "Our master used to beat him. What little joy he had from his life has gone."

"You were not beaten?"

"I found I had a way with animals. I was too valuable. Ethelred is a cruel man. He will come after us. If he does, we will fight him with our bare hands. We will not be enslaved again."

I nodded, "If they come then we will give you weapons. How many men does he have? Men who can fight?"

"There are six house warriors. He also has six men who work the farm. They are not slaves and they have weapons. Ethelred is lord of the place you found us, St. Oswald. That is the church built by the saint. The lord can command the fyrd. There would be a hundred of them but they would take time to catch us. The six men he commands ensure that the taxes are paid and the land free from raiders such as you."

I laughed, "They have not done a very good job then have they?"

"You have fooled them by coming in winter. That is clever."

Leif asked, as we heard Arne bringing the horses and the others behind, "What did he say?"

I told him. He nodded, "Then we may have a fight on our hands."

When Arne joined us, we dropped to the rear and I told him what I had learned. He said, "You are the navigator. You have a course charted?"

I nodded, "Do you remember the wood with the spring?" He nodded. "It is off the greenway. We stop there to rest. If we can we disguise where we leave the greenway so that we are hard to follow. But if they do come after us then the wood will be a better place to fight them. There could be thirteen men but only seven will be warriors. Aed and Padraig will fight."

"You trust slaves?"

"It is in their interests to fight hard for if they are taken then they may well lose limbs. The Norns sent them. They are fishermen and they know the bull!"

"You are right."

In many ways, it was good that we were walking for the night became colder and the walking kept us warm. I hurried ahead of the column. I was navigator and I would find the wood. It was our prints that told me where we had joined the greenway. There was an open area. When we had joined the greenway, it had been daylight and the ground had not been frozen. I waited for the others and then pointed across the grass to the wood which could be seen in the distance. It was in the east and already I could see the sky becoming lighter. Leif headed across the field along with the bull. They were followed by the horses. I saw, as they passed me, that they were sweating.

"Arne, Olaf and I will try to mask our trail."

"Aye, brother. We will be at the spring. You navigate well, even on land."

When they had gone, I saw that the horses had dropped two piles of steaming dung just thirty paces from the gap. "Come and pick up the dung."

Olaf nodded. We picked it up and I led him two hundred paces beyond the gap. We laid them there. We walked back along the greenway for four hundred paces. The animals had left no other sign. There was no frost on the ground. Our feet had warmed it slightly. "Olaf, walk back and forth across our tracks and then we will walk back to where we laid the dung. We need to make them believe that we carried on. Once they doubt themselves then they may panic. The further north we can take them before they find us the better."

We spent some time walking from the gap to the dung and well beyond. I saw the sky becoming lighter. "Come, we head back to the others." I had left my yew stave, helmet and shield at the gap. I recovered them and we headed across the field. It had been frosty and the prints of the animals and our men could be clearly seen. I had to hope that the thin winter sun would quickly melt the prints. If the Saxons were close behind us then they would easily find us and we would have a fight on our hands. The Norns had spun and we had no choice over the outcome. It was *wyrd*.

Chapter 14

The two slaves were asleep beneath their borrowed cloaks. Arne and Asbjorn were on watch with Leif. Arne nodded and said, "Sleep, brother, you have done well."

I shook my head. "I have a yew bow to trim and besides I am not tired. If we have to fight then it will be you who needs your strength. You are the warrior of the family."

He shook his head and handed me the ale skin, "You underestimate yourself, brother, but I will sleep."

After drinking some ale, I took out my Walhaz dagger and began to trim the small twigs and foliage from the yew stave. I had much work to do when I reached home but the stave would be easier to carry without the foliage and twigs. It also helped me to listen. The sun, thin though it was, rose. It would melt our prints. Asbjorn watched me as I worked, "Why do you need a bow?"

"I watched Olaf and Leif when we fought the pirates of Mann. They slew more with their bows than we did with stones. If I can slay my enemies when they are further away then I will live longer."

He nodded, "If you are happy to watch then I will sleep."

As he curled up, I took my stave and walked to the edge of the woods. I peered towards the greenway. To my relief the prints had melted. I knew where we had stepped but I doubted that the Saxons, unless they were supreme trackers, would. I knew that they would follow. We had taken their only horses and their bull. All that we had left them was the pony belonging to the priest. The Mercian, Ethelred, would be angry and want to catch us and hurt us.

I went back to the camp. Leif stretched, "I am tired."

I nodded, "Then wake Olaf, he can watch."

Olaf started as soon as his arm was touched. He nodded, "I will watch with you, Erik."

I gestured behind me. "I would have you watch by the edge of the woods. Let us know if they come."

I ate some salted meat and made water. I walked to the bull. He snorted as I approached. I spoke in Saxon, "Peace Peter. We wish you no harm and take you to a better life." I knew not if he understood me but he no longer snorted.

I had just returned to my stave when Olaf appeared. "I heard them. They are heading down the greenway."

We woke the others. I gave my Walhaz dagger to Padraig, "You and Aed watch the animals."

He nodded, "Aye master."

I smiled, "I am not your master. Call me Erik." Donning my helmet, hefting my shield and drawing my sword, I hurried after the others. They were hiding at the base of the trees and peering through the undergrowth. The sun was behind us and would not reflect from our helmets. We were close enough to hear them. The arching trees which marked the greenway hid them but we heard their voices and their horse. Three figures appeared in the gap we had taken. I saw them studying the prints which lay there. There was no sign of our footprints but, as the sun rose higher, then they would become visible. The lord appeared. He was riding a very small horse. His feet almost touched the ground. He wore a short mail byrnie and had a helmet with a face mask covering his eyes. The three men with him had spears and shields. Saxon shields were smaller than ours. I wondered if our luck had run out and they would head to the woods. From ahead came a call. I saw the lord turn his horse and urge his horse down the greenway. They had taken the bait. We heard their voices for a while and then they faded. We rose and hurried back to the camp. We all looked at Arne. This was his decision. We would all offer him advice but only once he had given us his plan.

He looked at me, "Navigator, how far are we from the Ribble?"

I took out my hare skin map. "It took us half a day to reach here. With the bull it will take a little longer."

He nodded, "Then we head north. The greenway leads north and west. They may think we have a ship on the coast or they may soon discover that we are not ahead of them. Either way, we have time. We are rested," he smiled at me, "almost all of us are rested. We go north. Erik, lead the way!"

As I passed Padraig, he held out the dagger. I shook my head, "Keep it until we reach our home."

"You trust me?"

I pointed to the west, "Ethelred is there. I trust you."

We headed north through land which had been farmed but the wars between Viking and Saxon had left it without those to farm it. We saw wattle and daub huts which were falling down. The paths we followed had been used a generation ago but were now covered in wild weeds and grass. This was a land ready for the taking. The gods had sent us here for a purpose. As the clan grew, we could expand south. Perhaps others would come from Orkneyjar rather than risking a long and dangerous journey to the land of ice and fire. The lack of human touch had allowed trees and bushes to grow unchecked. We were able to use the folds in the land to remain hidden. The three animals had been able to graze and to drink when we had stopped and Padraig did have a way with animals. We made better time than we might have expected.

When we dropped to ford the small stream. I knew that we had just four miles to travel to the Ribble and the ford which would take us almost within touching distance of the Loyne and safety. I was tired. The animals drank and I submerged my face in the icy water to wake me up.

Arne came next to me, "Are you able to continue brother.? You and Leif have had no sleep."

I smiled, "A navigator has to learn to do without sleep. This will be good practice for when we have a long voyage. If you let Olaf come with me then we will scout ahead. The river is just over an hour ahead." I pointed to the sun. It was past its zenith. By holding up our hands we were able to roughly estimate time.

He nodded, "Go, and be careful. I would not lose my lucky little brother!"

I beckoned Olaf and we forded the brook. My shield was at my back and I used the yew stave as a staff. The ground rose a little. The path we trod was better used. It was bare in places. That would make it easier for Arne to follow us and also ensured that we would reach the ford. The path twisted and turned using the folds in the land. It climbed small slopes and dropped into dells. My nose was attuned to the land and I smelled the water. That is, I knew that there was water ahead. I held up my hand to stop Olaf.

Taking off my helmet I crawled along the path to the edge of the ridge. Below me, I saw the river. I waved for Olaf to join me. He too crawled.

I spied the ford. The path led to it and over years animals and humans drinking from it had crushed all vegetation at the river's edge. We not only had Saxons to fear there were also Danes. I looked upstream and saw no one. I looked downstream and there was just a pair of deer drinking. I was going to move when something startled the deer and they fled. I watched and saw two of the Saxons we had seen hours earlier. They were heading for the ford.

As I backed down and stood up, I wondered how they could have travelled so quickly. We ran back to Arne. He knew that we would not have run if we had found nothing. "Saxons at the river. There are two of them."

Arne was quick thinking but he did not know Saxons. He looked at Asbjorn. He had fought the Saxons before. Asbjorn was here as a foster father to give us guidance. Asbjorn said, "They may have realised that they had lost the trail and, finding no sign of it taken the chance of heading for the ford. They may believe we are Danes."

Arne nodded, "That makes sense. And Erik has given us an advantage. We know they are there but they are unaware of us."

Asbjorn said, "You would attack them?"

"Better than waiting to be attacked. We are Vikings. Do you fear the Saxons Asbjorn?" The older warrior shook his head. "And we have the two slaves to watch the animals. If we hit them hard enough then they might flee. I have decided!"

We donned helmets and prepared shields before we started to move the animals up the trail. The dell just before the ridge was protected by trees and we left the two Irish boys there with the single dagger, my yew stave and the animals. We crawled to peer over the top. The two Saxons we had seen were leaning over the water and lapping like dogs. Downstream we could hear the others as they approached. The river was just a hundred or so paces from us. We could hear the Saxons as they lapped. Arne used his quick mind, "Leif and Olaf string your bows. We will attack these two and when the others come then your arrows from ambush will distract them."

We nodded. Arne rose, raised his sword, and we ran down the trail. The two Saxons had helmets, spears and shields but they had laid them down to drink. The Saxon lord and his remaining men saw us before the two kneeling by the water. The lord dug his heels in and his horse charged towards us. The two men looked downstream and, as they rose, Arne and Asbjorn charged into them and hacked their swords across their middles. As they sawed them back the two men fell into the river which became red with their life blood.

Arne was a fighter, a warrior. He had a mind for battle and tactics. He grabbed the two spears and, handing one to me, said, "Shield wall!"

Asbjorn, Sigismund, Faramir and Gandálfr flanked us. The Saxon lord had allowed his anger to get the better of him. It was the wrong thing to do. He still had his men with him. They outnumbered us. The little priest's pony was no war horse and I could see that it was lathered and sweaty. As Arne and I lunged with our spears it whirled to escape the steel tipped ash. The lord was thrown from its back. Arne lunged with his spear at the prostrate Saxon thegn and the head tore into his thigh. The Saxon rolled away as his men ran to defend him. Six were warriors. Their helmets, good weapons and stance all told us that. It was when they were just ten paces from us and as the lord rose that Olaf and Leif timed their attack to perfection. They launched their arrows. The Saxon shields were on the wrong side to defend from arrows. One arrow struck the lord in the shoulder and one of his oathsworn was hit in the neck with an arrow.

"Now!" There were just six of us and we faced eight men who were unwounded but we had surprise and the Saxons were looking over their right shoulders to the ridge. One paid the price when an arrow hit him in the eye and he fell. A second was hit in the arm. Then the arrows had to stop for we hit their line. My spear entered the middle of an oathsworn.

Two of the ones who were not warriors turned and started to flee. The lord shouted, "Help me!" They hesitated and then went to him. Putting their arms around him they lifted him. The delay enabled Leif and Olaf to hit one of them in the leg and the lord in the arm. We had parity of numbers. I pulled back the Saxon spear and thrust it at the Saxon oathsworn. This was no novice and he fended it off with his shield and, as he did so, lunged at my middle with a knife held in his shield arm. Had I not had quick reactions then I might have been wounded. As it was, I turned to my right and hit him in the side of the head with the boss of my shield.

To my left, I heard Olaf and Leif as they charged down the slope shouting, "Clan of the Fox!"

The man I was fighting reeled from my blow and glanced to the right. I pulled back my arm and stabbed down at his foot. I pinned it to the ground. He screamed in pain and as I withdrew it swashed his sword at me and then, limping and with a bleeding foot, fled. Olaf and Leif had made the Saxons think we outnumbered them. As Arne rammed his spear into the middle of his enemy the survivors, all three of them, joined the man I had wounded and they ran after their lord and his men. I think that Arne was considering making the victory complete when he saw that Asbjorn had been wounded. The Saxon spear was still sticking from his right shoulder.

"Erik, fetch the animals. Faramir catch the pony! Sigismund, search the dead!" Sheathing my sword and slinging my shield around my back I ran up the slope. The two slaves looked up in terror as I appeared. Padraig's face creased with relief, "They are gone?"

"They left dead and their lord is badly wounded. They are gone."

By the time we had led the animals down to the river, where they drank for a long time, Asbjorn had had his wound tended. I went to the man I had killed. He had a sword and a seax. I handed the seax to Padraig. "Here is a weapon for you."

He handed me back my dagger and Arne threw a seax to Aed, "And here is one for you. Erik was right, you did not run and you deserve to be rewarded."

We had spears, shields and helmets. We loaded them on to the two horses' saddles. Asbjorn used the pony as a staff. The animal was too exhausted to carry him but it was able to support him. We crossed the river. We left the bodies where they lay. As we climbed up the valley side Arne said, "How far, navigator?"

I did not need to look at the map to give the answer. I said, "Twenty miles. We will not make it home in one march. We will need to camp. The animals are suffering and Asbjorn is wounded. Let us find a wood in which we can shelter."

He nodded, "Good advice."

In the end the gods sent us something better. We found an abandoned Viking farm. Half of the roof had collapsed but there was still a roofless barn and there was water. We found, close by the barn, the bones of the last occupant. He had either been slain or died some years earlier. If we had time, we would bury him. In the house we found a pot which just had a crack close to the top. We could use it to cook with. It would do. Arne showed that he was the leader. "Leif and Erik, you had no sleep last night. You sleep this night."

Faramir said, "Asbjorn needs hot food. We all need hot food."

My brother frowned. I smiled, "Arne, if there are enemies nearby then the Norns do not wish us to get home. If we are to die then let it be with a full belly!"

He laughed, "Aye for they have spun a good web thus far. Hot food it is."

After a hot meal, Leif and I just fell asleep close to the welcoming fire. I was so tired that if I dreamed, I did not remember it. We were not attacked and although Asbjorn's wound ached we were able to finish the march home and we reached there before noon. We were greeted as heroes and our stad was safe for the winter.

The fact that we had horses now made an enormous difference to our lives. We could use them to haul timber from the woods and we had great quantities of timber laid in for the time of the new grass. We had frost and ice that winter but no snow. We saw snow, in the distance in the Land of the Wolf. We had none and by Gói we were able to build more halls. We had a smithy and forge to make weapons but no smith. That did not matter over much. Most of us knew how to shape iron. I spent the long nights shaping my bow. It was not a quick process but when it was finished and it was strung, I knew I had a good weapon. Leif and Olaf showed me how to make arrows. I did not waste metal on the end. I used flint and stone arrows. When the heads broke it did not matter. I became quite proficient. I hunted larger birds and small animals. They added to the pot and improved my skills.

As Gói came and went I approached Padraig and Aed. "You have fulfilled your side of the bargain and now we shall honour our side. I will take you to Dyflin in my snekke."

They looked at each other and Padraig said, "We are happy here. We are free. We have fished in the snekke and our life is good. The roof we have over our heads was built by us and we both like your people. If you would have us, we would join the clan."

I nodded, "For my part I am happy but that must be put to the whole clan at the next Thing. There will be one in the middle of Einmánuður when the days are the same as the nights."

"We are happy for the clan to decide."

The ship's boys enjoyed going out with the two Hibernians. I fished less now. I knew that I needed to improve as a warrior. Arne and I practised each day. We now had more men with mail. Arne and I did not but our leather jerkins were studded with the thin metal we had beaten out on the anvil. I had retrieved the Saxon lord's helmet from the river. It fitted me for I had a smaller head than my brother. He was envious but accepted that the helmet had chosen me.

Two days before the Thing I went out in the snekke with the two Irish men and the ship's boys. If the clan chose not to accept them then this might be my last chance to speak with them and I had enjoyed their company. We had landed a sizeable catch and we were just enjoying the sea. I was loath to head back. We talked of their lives in Hibernia. It seemed similar to our life. The three ship's boys were also rapt. However, we still had one on lookout and it was Stig who shouted, "I see birds and they are flocking around something in the water." He pointed to the north. I stood and looked. It was in the distance but it looked like wreckage. We hoisted the sail and headed for it.

I sent Eidel up to the mast and he shouted, "There are people. They are clinging to the wreckage." He shaded his eyes, "I think that they are our people. They have seal skin capes and boots."

Here was a tale. How had they reached us and were the Norns spinning? From the wreckage it looked like a knarr. There was one man, two women and a child. It was hard to tell if they were dead or alive. I began to call as I neared, "Hello! I am Erik of Larswick. We come to help you." I saw a feeble arm raised. One of the women, at least, was alive. "Stig, Sven, move the catch. We must make space for them. Padraig, secure the wreckage. Aed and Eidel help them aboard."

Eidel said, "And if they are dead?"

"Still bring them aboard. We have a cemetery and they can be buried amongst Norse."

I lowered the sail myself as Padraig grabbed the wreckage and acted as a human grappling hook. Aed and Eidel clambered aboard the wreckage. Even as they did so it began to break up. They passed the children and the two women first. Stig and Sven had created enough room and they made a space for them by the mast fish. The man was the hardest to pull for he had the fur of a bear upon him and his seal skin boots were filled with water. Aed and Eidel had just managed with the help of Padraig to pull him aboard, when the wreckage separated. Another few moments and they would have gone to Ran.

"Raise the sail!" I put the steering board over. I saw Padraig checking them. He raised his thumb and smiled. He took the spare sail and covered them with it. Aed took the ale skin and tried to force some down their throats. They were deathly white and looked more dead than alive. I had seen this once before. When we had lived on Orkneyjar we had seen a knarr founder on some rocks a mile away. In those days we had no snekke and my father and uncle had waited on the beach. When the only three to survive landed they were shivering and could not even speak. It had taken many hours for them to become men again. These people looked to have been at sea for a very long time. There had been little left of the knarr save for the steerboard side and part of the prow.

As we neared the mouth of the river I wondered at this turn of events. The Norns had to have been spinning. Our timing had been critical. We might have turned for home had not the conversation been so enjoyable. We would not have had that conversation if we had not rescued Padraig and Aed. *Wyrd*.

I sent Eidel and Stig to the stad to fetch help. We needed Gytha. Although heavy with child, she would come down the slope and begin to heal them on the quay. My father and uncle came down as well as two other women. While they tended to the four we had rescued Snorri said, "You have landed the biggest catch I have ever seen." He glanced down and said, "I know this man. It is

Wraghi. He moved from Orkneyjar to Ljoðhús for he did not get on with the jarl. That would be his wife and sister but where are his brother and his sons?"

Gytha looked up, "Instead of chattering like a magpie have these carried to the hall. They are close to death, especially the child. Maeve, bank up the fire and take off all their clothes."

Snorri said, "Take off…"

"Do I tell you how to fight battles? No! Then do not tell me how to heal. My baby is due any day and I would not have its birth cursed by the deaths of these four. Erik has saved them from the sea. We must save them from Hel!"

I turned to Sven, "See to the unloading of the fish. Padraig, take the man's feet. Aed, help my uncle take one of the women."

I grabbed the man's shoulders. Gytha smiled, "At least one who has Ragnarsson blood knows how to act!"

When we entered the gate, I saw Olaf and Leif practising with their bows. "Go to the quay. There is a woman there, bring her to the hall."

When I reached our hall, I saw that my mother had, indeed, put more logs on the fire. Padraig and I took off the man's clothes. Water poured from his boots. His breeks and kyrtle were sodden. His pale flesh was icy to the touch. My mother went and found a fur. "Go. When Gytha and her volvas arrive, they will perform their magic. They will be naked when they do so and this is not for the eyes of men."

I shook my head and we left. I later found that this was the volva's magic. By putting their naked bodies next to the four who were near to death they would drag them back from the brink by giving them their warmth and part of their life spirit. Had someone told me then I would have said they had eaten of the mushrooms which make men mad but as the four were all recovered by the next day then all that I can say is that it must be true.

I did not sleep in my father's hall. Arne and I slept in the warrior hall with the unmarried warriors. When we entered the hall, the next morning, Wraghi was dressed and with a red face. He had recovered. He smiled when he saw us, "This must be Erik and Arne. I remember them when they were no bigger than my sea boot. And I understand that I owe you four lives, Erik."

I shook my head, "You owe us nothing. I am glad to have arrived in time."

He clutched his hammer of Thor, "Aye, the Allfather was watching over us." Snorri and Siggi entered, "And I owe your wife and the volvas too, Snorri Long Fingers."

My father said, "Sit, tell them what you told me, Wraghi."

"When we heard, last year, that you had left Orkneyjar we wondered what it meant. We soon discovered what it meant for the King of Norway came to our island. He brought an army. Jarl Eystein was with him and Bjorn, Lord of Mann. They said they had come to save us from a life of hardship. They demanded that we swear an oath to them and that we pay taxes. We told them that we would not and wished to live the life we had always led." He shook his head, "We should have either run, as you did, or fought there and then. The King and his henchmen let the men leave to return to their homes and then sent their warriors to kill their men and take their women. Agnete, here, my brother's wife, was one who escaped. My sons and brother were slain and their wives taken as slaves. When she told us, we saw the cunning of the plan of the King of Norway. We should have stayed together and fought but he ate us piecemeal. We gathered what little we had and we fled in my knarr. We encountered a storm off the coast of the Wolf. I managed to get all aboard the wreckage and then you found us."

I asked, "Who is the boy?"

"He is Naddor, my grandson. He was staying with us. He is but three and does not know yet that his father is dead."

"You are welcome here."

"I am not sure that you will have much longer to enjoy this freedom. He knows where you live. You killed his men and he has sworn to have vengeance upon you. He will come for you, Lars. You know that in your heart."

I saw my father look at his left arm. He was now half a man. He limped and could not hold a shield. He could no longer fight against the King of Norway. Snorri had recently and reluctantly taken over more of the decision making. He said, "Then that leaves us the land of the Northmen in Frankia or the land of ice and fire."

My father shook his head, "I do not wish to run anywhere but as there are few people in the land of ice and fire it strikes me that it might be the best place to build a new life." He shook his head, "But the land here is perfect."

My mother shook her head, "If we have to defend it from so many enemies then it is not perfect and although I fear this land of ice and fire if it can be our home then I would go there."

The Norns were spinning. Their web was both large and powerful. It had dragged folk from across oceans and planted them here on this green and fertile piece of land. We were going to exchange it for an unknown world filled with ice and fire. My choice would be to stay and fight but I was young and had no voice.

The Thing accepted and welcomed all of the new folk into the clan including Padraig and Aed. It was an important moment. As part of the clan they could now have families. They could marry. The Norns were indeed spinning their webs.

Chapter 15

We had almost a year where we prospered. Neither Dane nor Saxon came for us. The King of Norway was busy dealing with islands and lands further north. Four more knarr made it from the islands with more refugees and we grew. We raided Mercia and we raided Ireland. I did not even need to go ashore for when we raided the Irish they were not as well armed as we were and when we raided Mercia, we had more men. Padraig and Aed did not raid. They stayed at home to defend Larswick. We began to believe that King Harold of Norway had forgotten us. He had not. My father was now an important jarl in the King's mind. He had flouted his authority and so long as he remained alive then he would be a reminder that men could fight the King of Norway. His Lord of Mann was having trouble with those who lived on the island closest to us. That was the only reason we had escaped his attention.

I was in the snekke, fishing with Padraig and Aed when we spied a laden drekar. We hauled in our nets. Since our encounter with the two drekar sent to hunt us down I had grown in confidence. "Be ready to use your bows if they attack."

"You are going to speak with them?"

"They have no shields along the side and they are laden. They come from the north and west which means Mann. I will shadow them. If they make for the Loyne then we can beat them to our river and give warning. If they keep heading south, we will see where they go."

I had learned that the snekke was so lively that she could sail with any wind. The drekar, in contrast, was labouring. She was so laden that waves broke over her side as she wallowed towards land. The captain put her helm over to come towards us. It was a mistake for it took her beam on to the waves and one broke over her showering those on board. He wished to speak to us and he was not a good captain. I headed towards him and he resumed his course. I sailed around his stern to keep the wind. Aed and Padraig had two bows already strung if this was some sort of elaborate trap.

I adjusted the sail to slow us down. As we came close to their steering board a Viking leaned over, "Are you from the stad they call Larswick?"

"I am."

"We are fled from Mann. Where is there land we could take to make a new home?"

I knew that my father would not welcome these men from Mann even if they were refugees from Finehair. He did not trust them. I pointed south and east. "There is a river, the Ribble. It is just a few miles south of here. The land on the two banks has no settlers but I should warn you that the Mercians from the south and the Danes from the east may challenge you."

He nodded, "Then we will fight for the new land. We had to fight for that which had been ours for many years on Mann and we still lost. The King of Norway wishes the world and we will not bend the knee. My brother brings the rest." He pointed astern. I saw a sail low down on the horizon. "May the Allfather be with you."

"And may he protect you and your families too." I made us fly down the side of the drekar. She was so low in the water I could see that they were mainly women and children. I was pleased that they had not asked to come to Larswick. The refugees we had had before had come from the islands. They were our kind of people. We knew many of them. Two boat loads could bring trouble. We headed home. That evening, as I told my uncle and father of the events, I could see that they were concerned. Siggi and Arne sat either side of me as I spoke. Both were now men grown with full beards. I knew that we were the future of the clan. The five of us spoke each day. We were of one mind.

"I do not blame them for seeking a land free from the iron hand of a ruthless king but if there are large numbers then they might try to take that which we have."

I knew what he meant. Most of the men now had farms. They were all dotted around the stad and none was further than a mile away but if we had neighbours to the south that might bring us conflict.

Arne was the most belligerent of the three of us who had sworn an oath on the blade. He emptied his horn. "The ford upstream is the place that they would have to cross. It would be simple enough to have those who would be warriors to watch. Erik's ship's boys tire of fishing. They spend most days with Siggi and me. They practise with bow and sword. If they took the pony, they could watch there each day. It would give us warning of any coming here and would be good discipline for them." He turned to me, "What say you, brother?"

I nodded, "Padraig and Aed enjoy the fishing. I only go with them to learn more about sailing. If Snorri is right then one day we will have to leave and the only land for us would be the land of ice and fire. If I had to sail for a moon or more then I would need more skills than I have."

The raid on Dún Lethglaise had given me the chance to sail a long way and I had returned more skilled but I still had shortcomings. I was young. I needed the leathered skin of a navigator who has stood and steered through a winter storm before I could even contemplate a voyage to the land of ice and fire.

Siggi said, "I do not think we will have to go to the land of ice and fire. This is good land. The Allfather guided us here and so far he was watched over us. The people who have come have made us stronger. Even some of the women and girls practise with weapons."

He was right. There were four girls who had come from Beinn na bhFadhla. They were sisters and cousin. They had come with their grandfather for the men had been killed by the King of Norway's men. They had their families' swords and they practised. Freja, the elder was a formidable fighter. She often sparred with Siggi and Arne. From what Arne had told me he found her attractive. Soon he would ask her to be his bride. We both knew that we needed children. I had not seen a woman yet whom I wished to bed. Siggi too had taken to courting Freja's cousin, Gefn.

My father nodded. He was now accustomed to the leather harness he had for his left arm and he was no longer self-conscious about it. He lifted it to the table and said, "Then we watch and we wait. If enemies come then we will fight them. At Haustmánuður we raid the Mercians for their grain. Let us see what the Allfather brings our way."

The grain raid was a great success. We landed on the southern bank of the Maeresea. We had not raided there before. I think that they thought their burgh of Caestre afforded them protection. They were wrong. I was now more familiar with the waters of the Maeresea. I knew where the shoals lay and we sailed in at night on a high tide. While Arne and Snorri led our forty warriors to raid the three settlements which lay between the Dee and the Maeresea, we turned around the drekar. They arrived back before dark with wagons laden with grain. They also had two more ponies and we loaded them too. As we headed north, in the dark, I reflected that I was a good navigator but only in waters with which I was familiar. I really needed to test myself on a longer voyage.

Arne had slain a Saxon thegn. Those who had not been slain told Arne that the Mercian was the nephew of King Ceolwulf and his death would bring destruction to us. Arne had laughed it off for he had a fine mail shirt and helmet to show for the battle. When he returned he and Freja were married. Siggi and Gefn also chose that time to be wed. My mother was delighted. Fótr had been her last child and now she had a daughter, more, she would soon have grandchildren. We built Arne and Siggi two small halls and after the feasting, they retired to their new homes. For the first time since I had been born, I did not share a room with my brother. Fótr would take his bed but he was a child. He was my brother but not my blood brother. He and his cousin, Tostig, were closer.

My father and I sat before the fire. He looked thoughtfully at me, "And have you an eye for a woman, Erik, or does your eye and mind still sail the seas?"

I started for it was as though he was reading my mind. "The last knarr which came spoke of the islands which lay in the middle of the ocean, Føroyar. They said that Naddod, who found the land of ice and fire, was sailing for those islands when he discovered the new land. I would travel there before winter sets in properly."

He frowned, "That strikes me as risky. Do not tempt the Norns, my son."

"I have thought this through, father. What we lack here is seals. We have to trade for oil and seal skin is as expensive as grain. We could hunt seals on the islands north of here but they now belong to the King of Norway. I would take Padraig and Aed. We would sail to Føroyar and find a beach with the grey seal. We could hunt them, make the oil and bring back the skins and oil here."

"A long way to go for oil, my son."

I smiled, "People call me Erik the Navigator. I take it as a compliment but I am not yet a navigator. I have not sailed the empty seas. I need to do so. We both know that one day we might have to sail to the land of ice and fire. I am not yet ready."

"You would be travelling when there is little sun."

"If we have to leave this land and travel to the land of ice and fire then that may be when the days are like nights and we cannot see the stars. Arne has tested himself in battle. He is a great warrior. He has bested a thegn. I am the navigator. I need to test myself."

"I would not lose you. I wish to see you in Valhalla."

I touched my father's leather harness, "The Norns have spun, father. They took your arm and made me the one to sail. It is in my blood. You were the navigator and the warrior. Arne is the warrior…"

He nodded, "Your mother will be unhappy."

I shook my head, "No she will not for she has a new daughter and Arne will spill his seed soon enough." I smiled, "He may have done so already!"

We sailed at Gormánuður. Both Arne and Siggi tried to dissuade me but I was determined. "Do you not trust me to return?"

"The sea is wide and this is the season of storms."

"Then if I do not return then watch for the sea bird who swoops to spoil your mail!"

He laughed, "Brother, we three swore an oath!"

"And I will keep that oath. I did not chastise you for fighting a thegn. This will be my battle. I will be gone but a moon, perhaps more. By then Freja should be larger eh?"

He grinned, "Perhaps!"

I asked Padraig and Aed if they wished to sail with me. I would force no man to follow my dream. To my delight they were happy. "We have heard of those islands. Our grandfather told us tales of the old days when the prince of our land took men to settle there. I would be interested to see them."

179

We made barrels to take for the seal oil and we took hunting spears and bows. I left my shield in the hall. I would not need it. I did not take my helmet. We slipped away during the night. I did not want a great fuss to be made of me. I had my charts and I had my compass and hourglass. We had a barrel of ale and salted meat. We would fish as we sailed north. Until we reached Ljoðhús we would spend each night on land. There were many islands which were uninhabited. We would land and sleep ashore. After Ljoðhús we had a voyage due north. I had been told that there was nothing between Ljoðhús and Føroyar. We would have to make that leg in one voyage. None had done the journey but piecing together what I had learned I estimated that it would take a whole day and part of the night. If we left Ljoðhús while it was still night then we might sight the islands during daylight. We had a spare sail. Gytha and her volva had woven it for me. My hair and that of my mother were in the weave. Gytha told me that the spell would protect me. She was the only one who was confident that we would return. She had healed Siggi and I believed her.

In many ways the first six days were the hardest and the most nerve wracking. We sailed the waters which were now claimed by the King of Norway. Every drekar and knarr we saw was a danger. It kept us alert. We chose the most remote of beaches for our camps but we lit a fire each night. Winter was coming and the nights were cold. Food in our bellies would fight off the cold during the day. The three of us got on well. Aed had always been the quiet one but the voyage made him speak more. I learned that he hoped that he might marry the daughter of Finn the Scar. To be truthful Maren was a plain little thing but I had seen her flirting with Aed. It would be good for both of them. As we made our last camp on Ljoðhús Padraig surprised both Aed and me.

"Tomorrow we sail into the unknown. Before we sail, Erik the Navigator, I would have you know that, like Aed, I have set my eyes upon a wife."

"That is good."

He paused, "It is Helga, your cousin." I was silent. "Would your uncle approve?"

I rubbed my chin, feeling the salt in my beard, "My uncle is a fair man but what of Helga? I know that Maren Finnsdotter likes Aed, but Helga?"

He smiled shyly, "We have spoken. She likes the way I sing." Padraig had a good voice. When we sat around the fires and sang our songs, he often gave us those from Ireland. We did not understand the words but they evoked thoughts which our sagas did not.

I nodded, "Then that is good. When we return, I will speak with my uncle if you wish."

He had been right to speak before we sailed. It cleared the air. There were no secrets between us as we headed towards the unknown. As we headed north with rain coming from the east it was like stepping off a cliff. You knew the bottom would come but you knew not when. Sleet and then snow flecked the rain. I had my seal skin cape but Aed and Padraig were soon soaked for their cloaks did not keep out the wet.

"Take out the spare sail and shelter beneath it. I am content to sail north." In many ways I was sailing blind but the wind had been from the east and even without the sun I could estimate north. When daylight came the snow was falling even heavier than it had been the night before. *'Jötnar'* did not seem to mind. We had cleaned the weed from her hull and sealed her with pine tar before we had left and she cared not that the snow fell and lay upon her thwarts. I guessed it was noon, for I had been turning my hourglass and estimated that the sun would be at its zenith, when the snow stopped. The Allfather must have taken sympathy on me for the clouds cleared and I was able to see the sun. It was behind me. I saw a thin shadow on the mast fish. We were heading north. It confirmed that the wind, which had been from the east, was now blowing from the north east. I would have to adjust our course accordingly. The clouds came back but not the snow.

Aed and Padraig rolled up the sail and laid their cloaks to dry. They pulled in the hooks and took off the six shiny fish they had caught. They gutted them and we ate. No sea birds swooped for the waste. We were not near land. Padraig took the steering board while I made water and checked the ropes. We had spares but we had fitted newly made ones before we had left. They needed adjustment. All new ropes did. I returned to the steering board and we ploughed north. The black seas were empty. I had to trust my compass and the chart which I was now building in my head.

It was coming on to dark and I wondered if I had missed the islands when Aed shouted, "Sea birds! There!"

I followed his finger. He pointed to the steerboard side. Sea birds meant land and it was to the north east of us. We were sailing into the wind. We had to tack back and forth and zig zag towards them. Darkness came and the sea birds disappeared. Clouds hid the stars and we were sailing blind. I was tired beyond words but I knew this was a test. If I could find land after what must have been two hundred miles across open water then I was a navigator. Aed and Padraig hung over the prow looking for the tell-tale foam of rocks.

"I see land! It is dead ahead!"

The Allfather had not made it easy for us. We had to negotiate some rocks which would have torn the hull from *'Njörðr'* but we made it through and saw a beach. As we ground onto the sand, I clutched my hammer of Thor and said, "Thank you Allfather!"

After lowering and storing the mast on the mast fish we dragged her up beyond the weed which marked the high-water mark. We needed a fire but I did not relish searching for wood on an island we did not know. Instead we had some ale, ate some salted meat and wrapped ourselves in our blankets. I was asleep in moments.

When I awoke it was to a grey damp day. Padraig and Aed slept on. I stood and wrapped my seal skin cape around my shoulders. As I looked south, I saw another island. We had missed that one. Looking to the north I saw a rocky beach. On it lay basking grey seals. We would not have to go far to hunt. Taking my spear, I climbed up the slope to get a look at the island. There were no paths. As far as I could tell the island was uninhabited. My joy at that evaporated when I saw that there were no trees either on this island or the island to the south. We would have to use the shrubs and leaves for kindling. I saw puffins and other birds nesting in the heather. We would not starve. Having established that we would not be disturbed I returned to the beach collecting as much dead and dried vegetation as I could. Padraig and Aed had woken.

"There are sea birds and their eggs up yonder," I pointed, "but little wood. I will scavenge for wood. We will need a fire if we are to render down the oil. You two hunt for breakfast."

I wandered along the beach. I found wood which had been washed ashore. There was more than I had expected. I made a pile of it by the snekke. I kept going further and further north until I was almost at the grey seal colony. The two sentries raised themselves up and barked at me. I guessed they had seen few men and would assume I was a strange looking seal. By the time I had collected the wood as far as the seals, Aed and Padraig had collected a few eggs and two puffins. I had eaten puffin before and quite enjoyed the taste. We would have to cook it.

"Padraig, fetch the pot. Aed, prepare the birds."

I set to making the fire. I had seen more wood but it was close to the seals. We would cook our meal and then hunt. I used my flint. We had some dried wool I had brought and I used that to start the fire. The warmth made me feel human again. We had been chilled to the bone for the last two days and nights. I did not know how my two companions were coping for my seal skin cape kept the worst of the cold and damp from me. We had brought a metal tripod and the pit hung from that. Once plucked we put the birds in the pot of sea water. We ate the eggs raw. They were delicious.

"While the food cooks we can hunt. The sooner we hunt the sooner you can have a cape and we can render the beasts down." I knew that they were nervous. They had fished and killed quite large fish but a seal was as big as a man. "You two stay behind me. I will do the hunting. Your job is to protect me from any others which try to attack me. If you poke your spears at them then they will back off." They looked dubiously at me. "Trust me."

"We do, Erik, we do." Both men were Christian and I saw them clutch their crosses.

I gave each of them two spears and I took one. I had the Walhaz dagger and a seax in my boots. We headed up the beach. I did not want to waste time and so I headed for the sentry. It would be a male and it would be big. I needed one with layers of fat. He opened his mouth and roared at me. I had sharpened my spear and, when I speared it, the head sank deep into its body. I must have been lucky and struck the heart for blood gushed and it fell dead. I retrieved my spear and headed towards the next sentry which obligingly headed down the beach towards us. This time the seal launched himself at me and his weight and my strike drove the spear so deep that, although he died, the spear was stuck. The seals were heading for the sea. I shouted, "Spear!" Aed handed me one and I ran towards the nearest one. I lunged and speared it in the side. This time I was able to retrieve it. One was just two paces from the water. I pulled back my arm and threw it. The seal did not die immediately. It managed to make it to the shallows before expiring. I was pleased. Four seals were enough for a small barrel of oil. "Let us take them back to the camp where we can butcher them."

By using two spears pushed through each one the three of us could carry all of them back easily. As Aed and Padraig went back for the fourth I saw sea birds swooping to take advantage of the kill.

I set to work to first skin and then remove the fat which we would render. We had brought a specially made render dish. It was metal and shallow. I checked the stew, it was almost ready. I began to remove the fat. I found a large flat rock and used that to cut the fat up as small as I could. The smaller the pieces the quicker it rendered down. The crunchy fat which was left when we had finished could be eaten with salt. It tasted like the skin of the pig and was delicious. By the time Aed and Padraig had reached me I had finished chopping some of the fat off one of the seals.

"Take the pot off the fire." They used a folded piece of cloth to do so. I tied the four pieces of cord to the rendering platter and attached them to the hook. I hooked it to the top of the tripod. The metal platter would prevent the cord from burning. While Padraig ladled the stew into our bowls, I took the barrels we would use for the seal oil and placed them close to the fire. That done we ate. The two-bird stew went quickly. Had we had bread we would have wiped them around the pot.

I showed them how to skin a seal and left them to it. I went to the oil. Using a cloth, I tipped the oil into a barrel. More would come. I put more wood on the fire and added more fat. We developed a routine. There was little talk for it was unnecessary. The animals were quickly skinned the fat removed and then the flesh chopped up. We put it in the pot with plenty of salt water. Aed and Padraig sourced more wood from the now deserted beach. It took most of the day to render down the fat. We emptied the small barrels into the firkin. With all the fat rendered we put the pot back on to cook the seal meat. We ate the residue left over from the cooked fat.

"We keep the fire going all night. We sleep in shifts. Slowly cooked the meat will preserve better."

The next day was a repeat of the first. We crossed the island to find another beach. There we killed four seals and collected more wood. We stored the seal meat in a barrel with brine which we made. We prepared eight seal skins. We painstakingly scraped them clean and then made water on them. We pegged them out with rocks to allow them to air dry.

The weather began to become even colder and dark black clouds threatened on the third day. The gods were telling us that we had spent long enough on the island. By the fourth day, we had enough oil for our barrels and cooked fat was no longer something we looked forward to. The snow came. We would leave the next day. We wrapped up the seal skins and stored them. Aed and Padraig had two big enough to use as capes. When time allowed, they would be able to finish them properly but they would not be as cold going home. We found some eider ducks which we killed and we enjoyed duck meat. The down was saved. That was treasure beyond words! We had great quantities of offal. If we had had more barrels, we might have saved it. As it was the birds gorged as we set sail amidst a snowstorm. We headed south knowing that so long as we did not deviate from our course, we would hit land at some point. I had kept a record on my chart. I would know how to find the two islands again. If we went to the land of ice and fire, we would call at Føroyar first. We would be able to replenish supplies and make any repairs we might need. *'Jötnar'* had been lucky. The drekar might not fare as well.

We pushed off and the wind took us. The snekke had had enough of the beach and the land. She was a creature of the sea.

Chapter 16

We were away for twenty days. It was almost Ýlir when we returned.

While Ade and Padraig, aided by Edmund, emptied the snekke I went to the hall. I could tell that most of the clan had all worried about us. Their faces were all etched with concern. Gytha was the exception. She smiled beatifically as she greeted me, "I knew you would return safely. The spirits spoke to me." My parents, Snorri and my brother, along with Siggi were there. "Føroyar is close enough for the drekar to make the journey in fourteen nights. It could be faster if we did not rest at night. The islands are without trees. We could not repair our ship there and we would need to take kindling but there are many seals and sea birds there."

"Could we live there?"

I looked at my father. He did not wish to lose this home but if he did then he wanted a choice of a new one. I nodded, "Aye but we would have no meat nor would we be able to use wood. If I am honest it would be a place to stop. The ground was covered in heathers. I am unsure what we could grow there."

Arne said, "The same could be true of the land of ice and fire."

I drank from my horn, "I do not wish to leave this land. None of us do but if we are forced to move then where do we go?"

Gytha was nursing Anya, her youngest. "There may be other lands to the west. We do not know. Until this Naddod found the land of ice and fire we did not know that there was any land to the west. We have a navigator. He has sailed further from land than any of us, you included, Lars Ragnarsson. The Norns have spun. I agree with Erik, I do not wish to leave here but none of us wish to be ruled by a Norwegian king!"

She had spoken and there was no argument. We would continue to live in this beautifully green land and we would prosper. If the Allfather wished us to move then he would send a sign. On the way back Aed and Padraig had been persuaded by me to ask for the hands of Helga and Maren sooner rather than later. Neither father would be happy about the two newest members of the clan sneaking around behind their backs. Surprisingly both fathers agreed to the marriages. The two Irishmen had shown themselves to be hard working and willing to fight for the clan. That was enough. They were married at the winter solstice. Both Finn and Snorri had insisted that we follow the old ways. We had no priest in any case. Gytha joined them as husband and wife.

As we broached a fresh barrel of ale Arne and Siggi teased me for I was still without a wife. I laughed it off. "I am married to the sea!"

Arne had nudged me in the ribs, "Brother the sea is cold and unforgiving. Freja is warm and comfortable. These long nights are bearable with a woman in your arms. Your duck down is warm and that is all, now a woman…"

I did not mind the teasing. When I found a woman with whom I wished to spend the rest of my life then I would take her. For the moment I needed nothing save my ships.

As we had sailed back, I had thought of ways of helping our ships sail together for long periods and at night. I had Sven, Stig and Eidel make clay pots. Instead of a hole in the top I had them make a hole in the side. They also had two small holes in the side so that they could be suspended from the stern post. They were there to be a light for another ship to follow. If we hung them astern using broken pieces of mail then there would be little or no risk of fire.

When both Gefn and Helga were with child at the start of Þorri then the teasing became worse. I took to riding one of the horses we had taken from the Saxons. It helped me to enjoy this land. I had a feeling that we would be sailing soon. I wanted to enjoy trees and green fields. We had little or no snow in this land we had found. When snow did fall it melted within a short time. I rode south and west first and found another river and a place which would make an even better place to moor ships. We had not seen it before as we normally headed due west to take advantage of the winds. I stored the information and when I returned to the hall, I marked it on my map. When I headed east, I found that the land rose and, in the distance, I saw the high divide. To the east of it lay the land of the Danes. I saw few farms between our stad and the high ground. Finally, I headed south and east. I had intended going north the next day, towards the Land of the Wolf, but the Norns had been spinning. I crossed the Loyne and headed for a rocky knoll which would give me a view of the land to the south of me. The Allfather sent me a fine day. The horse whom we had named Thor in honour of the god had enjoyed being part of the clan. He responded well to my commands and he climbed the animal path to the top of the rock easily. I dismounted and gave him some water from my water skin. I poured it into my helmet. I gave him a handful of oats and then let him graze the scrubby grass. The rock rose above me and, hanging my sword from the saddle, I climbed.

As I stood, I felt the wind pushing against me. I looked back, towards Larswick. The smoke told me where it was. I could not see the drekar for the mast was stepped but I saw the palisade. I turned and saw the new river I had found and then I looked south. The Allfather sent a shaft of sunlight. It glinted off something metal. I shaded my eyes. The flash came again. As I stared, I realised what I could see. More than ten miles away was an army and it was heading north. I almost panicked and went to my horse. Then I realised it would take hours for them to come close to our river. Once I had identified it as an army, I tried to identify it. When I saw that the shields were smaller than those used by the Danes, I knew that they were Saxons. King Ceolwulf had had enough of our raids and had sent men to punish us.

I went to my horse and rode hard back to Larswick. We had an enemy and we would have to fight. I rode quickly for if the Saxons were coming north then it was for us. I passed men who were already preparing fields for the animals to be born in the spring. Hurdles were made from the willows which grew by the river. I shouted, as I passed, "The Saxons are coming. Get to the stronghold!"

As I neared the river, I saw the drekar and the snekke. If the Saxons burned them, we would be stuck. We would have no means of escape. I galloped through the gates and hurled myself to the ground. My galloping hooves brought my father and the other warriors from their halls. Arne said, "What is it, brother?"

I said the bare minimum, "The Saxons are coming. They have an army! I estimate them to be three hours away."

My father nodded, "Then we had best send for those with farms beyond the walls."

"I have told those to the east."

"Good. Arne, warn the others. Erik, the drekar…"

I nodded. "I will moor them in the river. Padraig, Aed!" The two now had wives and their own huts. They appeared from within. "Get your weapons. War has come!" They just nodded. They kissed their wives and, grabbing their swords and bows followed me. "Sven, fetch the ship's boys!"

Already the stronghold was a hive of activity. There was no panic. Men donned mail, helmets and fetched weapons. Those women who fought also took weapons. The ones such as Gytha and my mother began to shepherd the younger children into our hall. The boys took their slings and stone pouches and ran to the fighting platform. Since the Danes had attacked, we had built a fighting platform and there were ladders for men to use to ascend. We had yet to build a tower. That would come.

We hurried down the path to the boats. "Sven Fámrsson, tie the snekke and the two knarr to the stern of the drekar. Eidel Eidelsson and Rek Rethersson, you guard the snekke. Stig help your cousin. Halsten and Dreng, you two watch the knarr. Stay aboard until I tell you otherwise. The eight of you will defend the boats."

"You will not be with us?"

I shook my head, "I was not at my father's side the last time we fought and he almost died. You eight will be sufficient to keep the drekar and snekke safe."

None of the vessels had their masts in place. They rested on the mast fish. My plan was to let the tide take them to the mouth of the estuary. There the water would be too deep for the Saxons to ford. I stripped off my clothes and, after putting them on the ground, I boarded the drekar. The ship's boys had tied the snekke to the stern. I shouted, "Cast off and board." As soon as the last rope was loosened the drekar began to drift towards the mouth of the river. We now had a metal anchor. We had used old swords and made our own crude anchor. This would be the first time we had used it. "Padraig and Aed go to the anchor. When I give the command then let it fly. Stig and Eidel, have the drogue anchors ready too." We were moving very quickly now. I had to judge this right. When I saw the water change colour I shouted, "Now!" As the anchors were thrown out, I shouted, "Sven, lower the drogue anchors on the snekke and knarr." The four ships almost jerked to a halt. I looked over the steering board. "Sven, climb aboard the drekar." He clambered hand over hand to the ship. I pointed to the shore. "You will all see the battle from here. I hope that we win but, if we do not and there are no survivors, then I leave the four ships to you."

Stig said, "But you must survive!"

"And I hope I do but there are no certainties in war. May the Allfather be with you." I stood on the stern rail and dived into the water. The current was strong but I was stronger. Eventually, I reached the quay and clambered up. I dried myself with my kyrtle and then ran up the path. The gates were already closed. Arne had them opened and I ran to the hall to prepare for war. I dressed in my leather jerkin. It was now studded with a great deal of metal. It would take a lucky blow to find somewhere unprotected by iron. I donned my good boots, head protector and then my helmet, I strapped on my sword, picked up my bow, shield and spear and headed for the walls.

Arne shouted, "You take the river wall! That way you can keep an eye on your precious ships!"

I laughed, "Those ships will be our only way out if our defences fail!"

"Then we are safe for I helped to build them! The Saxons will blunt their blades on our walls."

When I reached the wall, I saw that Leif and Olaf were amongst the warriors there. Siggi would fight alongside Arne. They always did. With the enemy coming from the south and east then those were the two walls we would defend. The women and wounded warriors would watch the north wall. The west wall backed to the sea. I laid down my shield and spear on the fighting platform and strung my bow. It was hard to do and that boded well for it meant it was still powerful. Faramir and Farman were on my wall as were Sigismund and Gandálfr. I had fought with all of them.

Olaf asked, "How many were there?"

"They were too far away to count. I saw they had the priests carrying their cross and men carrying banners." I sensed nervousness. I tried to calm their fears, "Our walls are strong and they have marched. If they camp then we can raid them this night.

The day will be short and they will have a cold night. We have fire and hot food. All of our animals are within the walls. I have never attacked a stronghold and I would not like to."

Gandálfr said, "This was to be expected. We have raided them three times already. When we defeat them then they will let us be."

I hoped that he was right. Someone on the gate wall had good eyes for a shout went up, "They come!"

I leaned over the side and saw their banners as they crested the bluff. They had men banging drums and I could hear chanting. That would be their priests. They were not using the path which was close to the river. They must have known that the ground was quite marshy there. Instead, they were spreading out in a long line. I found it hard to see.

It soon became apparent that they were not doing what we expected. Arne shouted, "Erik, they are spreading to attack the north wall too. Leave three men there and take the others to join the women and boys."

"Aye, brother!"

"Olaf, Leif, Faramir, Sigismund, Farman and Gandálfr come with me. You three stay here!" We descended the ladder and ran across the interior of the stronghold. Whoever led them knew how few we were. They were going to attack us at many points.

I saw that my cousin, Helga, was there. She wore a helmet and carried a sword and shield. She grinned at me, "If the Saxons come here, they are in for a shock. They have never seen women fight!"

I now saw what Arne meant. There looked to be two hundred warriors. They had with them fifty or so men of the fyrd. We would be outnumbered in warriors by five to one. The women and boys we had would decrease those odds. Had I not put eight on the fleet then we would have more men to fight. Had I made a mistake? The priests turned their back on us and began to chant. I took an arrow and nocked it. The Saxons were less than a hundred and twenty paces from us. Standing on the fighting platform increased my range. I pulled back and released. The priest had no mail or leather to protect him. The arrow struck him in the back and knocked him to his knees. As the women and men on my wall cheered Olaf and Leif sent two more arrows into another two of the priests.

It unleashed the Mercian beast. Without waiting for orders the warriors and the fyrd ran at us. We began nocking and releasing arrows as fast as we could. The slingers sent a veritable stone storm at them. Men fell for, in their anger, they had forgotten to hoist their shields. I only saw those charging our wall but fifteen men fell including three warriors wearing either leather or mail. They were nearing the wall now and I urged those alongside me, "Keep it up! We must stop them reaching the walls!"

There was a shout from my side. The Saxons also had archers. Sigismund had been hit in the cheek. He was lucky that it was a hunting arrow and not a war arrow. He snapped it off and threw it back over the wall. I saw an archer pull back on his bow. My arrow was nocked and I released it. It smacked into his chest. I nocked another arrow. I had but two war arrows left. I saw a thegn urging his men on. He was thirty paces from me. As he turned, I released and my arrow hit him just below his nose. He fell backwards. We had not seeded the ditch with traps but it was slippery. I sent my last arrow into the shoulder of a warrior and then picked up a throwing spear. It was one I had used on the seal hunt. The Saxons ran to the shelter of the wall where the stones could do little damage. More than half of the men who had started the attack now lay either dead or wounded. We were still outnumbered. I pulled back my arm as the first Saxons tried to make a human ladder. A warrior stood with his back to the wall. I hurled my spear and it went through his shoulder.

Helga shouted, "They have made the gate!"

Our weak point was the gate and they had men with axes. I saw that Arne and Siggi had organised men to brace the gate.

"Then we beat these and go to help Arne."

I picked another throwing spear and threw it into the arm of a Saxon who had placed his foot in the hands of a comrade. Sigismund picked up a rock. He dropped it on to the helmet of the warrior who braced his back against the palisade. He wore a helmet but the rock was a big one. The helmet and skull were crushed. The attack was broken. The survivors ran the gauntlet of slingers as they raced back across the ditch.

"Helga and the women watch here. Warriors with me! My brother needs us."

I picked up the Saxon thrusting spear and my shield. I ran down the ladder just as the gate burst open. I saw my father and Snorri lead the men from the wall to go to the aid of Arne and Siggi. The two stood together with four warriors who had wounds. I screamed, "Clan of the Fox!" My legs moved quicker than I had ever known and as Arne and Siggi used their shields to block the swords of the first Saxons I rammed my spear into the side of the warrior on the far left of the line. I pulled it out and thrust at the arm of the next Mercian. Then a spear came at me. I instinctively flicked up my shield and blocked the blow. I swung the spear around and it clattered into the warrior's helmet. As he reeled, I pulled my arm back and skewered his left leg. He shouted and arched his back. I lifted my shield and brought it down across his throat. He died!

The gate was open and the Saxons rushed in. It became a confused battle for more of our men ran from the walls to join in. I heard the clank of stones as they hit Saxon helmets and mail. The boys on the walls were still fighting for the clan. I heard a scream as Helga led the six women with weapons. I lunged at a Saxon who was trying to stab my father with his sword. My spear stuck in his right side. He hacked down with his sword and the spear was cut in two. My father was safe for the moment but I was not. Even as I tried to draw my sword he swung at my head. I barely managed to block the blow with my shield. He was wounded but sought to finish me first. He punched with his shield and I tried to dance out of his way. I bumped into someone behind me. I dared not turn to see if it was friend or foe. His shield caught my shoulder. My sword freed, I went on the attack although I expected a blade in the back at any time. The Saxon pulled back his arm for another strike. I did the unexpected, I lunged at his thigh and my blade ripped through his breeks and into his leg. I twisted the blade. It fought against muscle and sinew. When I pulled it out blood spurted. I punched him in the face with my shield and he fell writhing to the ground. His hands went to his leg but it was a mortal wound. I had no time to celebrate for the gateway was a maelstrom of swords, bodies and shields.

Even as I looked for my next Saxon, I saw a Mercian encased in mail ram his sword into my father's shoulder. My father should never have had to fight. His shield was attached to his harness but he could neither raise nor lower it. I pushed aside the Saxon who was fighting Siggi and ran towards my father. He bravely tried to block the next blow with his sword but he did not have the strength. The Saxon sword came down and hacked through my father's hand at the wrist. Still he did not fall but he was defenceless. I hurled myself at the Saxon lord as he raised his sword to end the combat. It was a clumsy attack but I managed to knock the Saxon to the ground. I landed on him and he spat at me and cursed me. I brought my knee up hard between his legs and he squealed in pain. I wrestled my sword arm free and drove it up and under his byrnie deep into his body. Warm fluids told me that he was finished but I made certain by ripping it out sideways. His body was still and I stood.

Arne shouted, "Clan of the Fox! On me"

He and my uncle stood together with Siggi. They were a metal barrier between the Saxons and my father. I joined Siggi as others obeyed the call. We had six of us and more were joining when Arne raised his sword and shouted, "Charge!" The Norns had been spinning or this might have been part of the Allfather's plan for the Mercians who stood in the gateway had neither mail nor leader. As we ran at them, they turned and fled. My brother stopped in the gateway and then turned. Inside our stronghold there were, perhaps, ten Saxons left standing.

"Helga, have the women bar the gate! We end this now."

The ten Mercians suddenly realised that they were trapped. The desertion by their comrades had left them trapped. Every blade and spear in Larswick headed to them. Three dropped their weapons to beg for mercy. With my father lying on the ground, being tended to by Gytha, there was little likelihood of that. They were butchered and the others stood back to back. They did not last long. Arne and my uncle were like men possessed and soon the only Saxons left in Larswick were the dead.

Arne and I ran to my father. Gytha gave the slightest shake of the head. He was dying and he had no right hand. The bloody stump was testimony to his fate. His eyes opened. He smiled, "My sons you cannot know how proud I am of you. With you and my brother, I know that the clan is in good hands."

I turned to find his sword. It lay just a pace away. I took it as Snorri held his brother's head in his hands, "I swear I will watch over your family for you brother." As my father closed his eyes and nodded, I undid the leather harness and threw away the shield. I prised open the fingers which had not been of any use since the fight with the Danes. I forced them around the handle.

He opened his eyes and smiled. "Arne and Erik, you are like two sides of me. Arne, you are the warrior and Erik, you are the navigator. Erik, lead the people to a home where they will be safe. Swear that the two of you will find a land untouched by our enemies." He closed his eyes and I thought he was dead.

I said, "We swear!"

Arne shouted, "Father do not leave us! We have much to tell each other before then!"

My father opened his eyes, "And I fear that I have been given no time. Perhaps I truly am Lars the Luckless. When you sleep watch for me in your dreams for…" His eyes glazed over.

Gytha stood above us with her eyes closed. "He is gone. Already he ascends to Valhalla where they will welcome a great warrior."

From the walls Finn the Scar shouted, "The Saxons are fleeing!"

Arne stood and said, grimly, "Come, brother. Let us take the horses and wreak vengeance on these Saxons."

My uncle said, "Your father would want you to stay here and care for the clan."

Arne's voice was both cold and commanding. He sounded like my father, "When the foxes feast on their dead bones then my brother and I will return." I ran to the stable. I did not bother with saddles. I just put halters on the two horses and led them back to Arne. I picked up a spear and slipped on the back. I would not need a shield.

Siggi shouted, "And I will come with my brothers of the blade!" He ran for the pony.

"Open the gates!" Arne and I dug in our heels and we galloped from the stronghold. The Saxons were not in sight. Their dead littered the ground but those who lived had fled. They had to run upstream to the ford and we knew the land better than they did. I heard hooves behind and saw that Siggi and Asbjorn had mounted two ponies and were coming after us. I knew that if I struck too hard with the spear I carried then I would fall from the horse. I would look for flesh. The Saxons were keeping to the top of the bank for the riverside was both muddy and treacherous. Gripping with my feet I rode towards the two Saxons who were the closest to me. They glanced over their shoulders. Had they been Vikings they would have turned to face me. They would have fought me knowing that if they had died with their swords in their hands they would go to Valhalla. As one turned, he slipped and tumbled down to the river. I sliced my spear across the neck of the other. The spear had been sharpened and I must have cut his throat. His body tumbled down the bank. Arne was also skewering the fleeing Saxons. We rode like avenging Valkyrie. Our spears rose and fell. The Saxons died. We only stopped when darkness came. The ford had been the undoing of many for the tide had come in and the river was deeper than when they had crossed. We saw bodies floating in the shallows. The four of us led our animals back to Larswick.

Arne looked at me, "I do not want to leave Larswick, brother."

I nodded, "Nor do I but it seems that every hand is turned against us. The Danes may return."

Siggi said, "You both forget our most dangerous enemy, King Harald! He will not forget us and Bjorn Bjornson is Lord of Mann."

Arne looked at my cousin, "You think we should leave? We should go to the land of ice and fire?"

Siggi was ever the most thoughtful of the three of us. "I think that we should be ready to leave. From what Erik said, while there might be a lack of enemies there is also a lack of trees. We need to hew lumber and that takes time. The new grass is not yet here. We have time. The wood will come to no harm as it seasons. It may be that the Norns spin and we can stay here but your father's words tell us all what he thought and my uncle was the head of the clan. We should give his words the respect they deserve."

The walls were manned when we returned. My father's body lay in our hall. Gytha and my mother had cleaned it and dressed him for burial. My uncle greeted us at the door. "They are gone?"

Arne nodded, "Those few who survive will not return. They have a long journey home and their bodies lie like autumn leaves."

"The clan wish to bury your father this night." He pointed up to the sky. "It is a wolf moon this night. It is a good omen."

I had seen the moon as we had ridden back. I had noticed it for it was red. It looked to be covered in blood. *Wyrd.*

As we carried my father to his grave, I reflected that, had we had time, we might have buried him in *'Jötnar'*. That would have been fitting. The drekar and snekke still floated in the estuary. We laid my father in his grave with his shield, sword and helmet. He was placed on his right side with his knees towards his chest. Before he had been born that was how he had lain in his mother's womb and now his body would return to the womb of mother earth. We put his compass with him. He was a warrior and a navigator. Every warrior helped to pile the soil on his body. We shaped it like the upturned hull of a drekar. Then we laid stones around the outside. In years to come, all would see the grave of Lars, first jarl of the Clan of the Fox.

Chapter 17

Two days later we held a Thing. We had many things to decide. The first was the choice of jarl. Arne and I suggested Snorri. My uncle shook his head. "I am not meant to be jarl. That was my brother. He knew who would follow him. Arne, you should be jarl and if you are then I will be your foster father. I will be there to guide you as you lead the clan to the future."

Arne looked surprised when the whole assembly approved. He nodded his acceptance and said, "My brother, Erik, will be the navigator. If we must leave this land then it will be he who leads us to the land of ice and fire."

Butar Beer Belly said, "Is there no other choice? Can we not stay here?"

My brother waved an arm, "Outside the cemetery is filled with the warriors who have died already. We are not a large clan. When the Danes return, we might well defeat them but we will lose warriors and then there is the King of Norway." I saw Butar nod. "We have a choice, we fight him or we bend the knee. Would you bend the knee?"

Butar Beer Belly stood a little taller and shook his head, "And I would have my sons have a life. You are right."

I saw all eyes look to me. My father's death had suddenly thrust Arne and me to the head of the clan. We had decisions to make. I was a man. I had a beard but I had expected to have more years to learn how to lead. My father had left us too early.

Arne said, "My brother and our cousin have spoken of this. The land of ice and fire is many days hence. We need to prepare. If we are to leave then we must take as much as we can. We need timber and we need animals. We also need to watch for enemies. I hear the Norns spinning."

The clan, now that they had decided, threw themselves into the preparations. We had already left one home and people knew what was important and what was not. I was luckier than most. I had my chest and my world, save for my mother and brothers, lay within it. All else I would leave behind.

My brother was right. I had ships to prepare. There were two knarr as well as the snekke and drekar. Padraig would sail the snekke with his family, Aed and Aed's family. The knarr would be sailed by the men who had brought them: Pridbjørn and Sighwarth. I gathered the three of them and the six ship's boys, Sven Fámrsson, Stig Folkmarsson, Eidel Eidelsson, Rek Rethersson, Halsten Haakensson and Dreng Ebbisson. "The journey will take up to half a moon. Once we leave these waters then there will be no opportunity to find spars, ropes and sails. There will be no pine tar and little wool. Your ships must carry all that they might need. Haul them from the water and see that they are weed free and their hulls are sound. My brother would sail at Sólmánuður when the days are at their longest and the weather less hostile. My six ships boys are here to help you."

Sighwarth was an older Viking. He stroked his grey flecked beard, "You are young for this, Erik Larsson."

Padraig shook his head, "Have you sailed beyond sight of land? Have you found a tiny speck of an island after days at sea?" Sighwarth shook his head. "He has for I was with him. I would follow Erik beyond the edge of the world for he is a navigator."

I smiled at the Irishman. "Thank you for those words but I do not know all and travelling with others is hard. Your knarr wallow and you do not have the luxury of oars. It may be that we become separated. You will need charts. I have made a copy of the journey to Føroyar but all I know of the land of ice and fire is that it lies west of Føroyar. Some say that the journey can be made in two days with a favourable wind while others say a knarr might take a week. The ocean is wide and we will need more than a little luck to find it."

Sighwarth smiled, "I can see that you know what you are about. I am content." I told them of my journey to Føroyar. They were seamen but they would be travelling with women and children. They had to be prepared.

Each night Arne and I sat with Snorri and Siggi. We spoke of what we would leave and what we would take. The knarr could carry more cargo. We would load the two of them with as much as we could. The animals would be spread out in the four ships. We would not be taking the pigs. We would take the bull and the cow as well as a ram and three ewes. We would need the bull for our new life. We would have to be careful. The rest would be slaughtered. Although I was reluctant, we decided not to take the horses and ponies. We were loath to lose them and so it was decided that Siggi and I would take them to Úlfarrston where we would trade them. It was a risk for the Land of the Wolf was no longer the most welcoming of places. I would take '*Njörðr*' and a small crew. Siggi, Olaf and Leif, as well as Padraig and Aed would come with me. They had pine in the Land of the Wolf and we needed spare masts and spars. If we could trade then our new lives might be better.

Arne was worried about leaving me to face the warriors of the wolf. I smiled, "Should we take all of our warriors and be ready to fight them?" He shook his head, "You are right, we would lose. Better this way. I do not believe that this trading expedition will end in disaster. Since our father died, he has come to me in my dreams. He has smiled at me. Thus far there are no words but I have been planning this voyage in my head and he has not stopped smiling. He will watch over me."

One advantage of '*Njörðr*' was the fact that she could be rowed by as few as ten men. We took ten to row and the six ship's boys. It was a short journey north. We could have travelled over land and been quicker but we had no means to bring back that which we needed. We sailed. We had no shields along the side and we did not wear our helmets. We were trading. Whale Island was where the clan had a stronghold. I would not head for there. Instead I headed for Úlfarrston. This was an older port. It was smaller than Whale Island and the people who lived there were a mixture of Norse and those who had lived in this land when the Romans had lived here. The ships which had recently joined us knew the story and they had told us. There were just three knarr tied up and there was room for us. While the ship's boys tied us up and Padraig and Aed prepared the animals for landing I stepped ashore with Siggi. We walked towards the palisade. It was just forty paces from the quay and I saw that they had a bridge over the ditch. The gates were open and there were no sentries.

A grey-haired man walked over to meet us. He had with him two younger men who wore sealskin boots and had good swords. I could not work out if they were his guards or his family. He held out his hand, "I am Coel ap Pasgen. I am the headman here. Welcome."

It was formal but he spoke our language well. "I am Erik Larsson from the Clan of the Fox. This is my cousin Siggi Deck Crusher. We have a stronghold along the Loyne. We are here to trade." I gestured behind me. "We have horses to trade and we have coin." We had decided that we would be unlikely to need coin in the land of ice and fire. I had with me a chest filled with coins and a list of items which we needed.

"And what is it you wish to buy?"

"We need pine for our masts and spars, arrows and arrow heads if you have them. We need good cooking pots which we could take to sea."

He smiled and looked relieved, "We have many of those here. The pine which you need for a mast we do not have. We can have two masts for you by the morrow."

"One for a drekar will suffice and three for knarr."

"Then bring your animals within the walls and we will discuss the price for that which you need."

I was relieved. I had been worried that the Land of the Wolf would not trade. I was wrong. I headed back to the drekar. "We can trade. Leave a deck watch. Siggi, go and ask Olaf and Leif to bring the animals and we will speak with the headman."

As we headed back to the palisade, I saw one of the two warriors who had been with Coel ap Pasgen. He was mounted and he rode west. I frowned. Was there some deception? Were they luring us into the walls to trap us? We had our swords and if we had to then we would fight our way out. Coel ap Pasgen was either a supreme actor or he was totally innocent for he made us more than welcome. He agreed a good price for the horses and we the pine and then took us to meet the merchants and traders who had the other items we needed.

Siggi was suspicious, "And if the quality of the pine is not worth the price?"

He smiled, "It will be but I will let you decide. We know timber. The shipyard of Bagsecg Bollison is just upstream and the Clan of the Wolf use our wood for their drekar." He smiled. "They are twice the size of yours. I think you will be satisfied but if you are not then we will refund whatever you think fair. We are not bandits."

Siggi seemed satisfied and we spent the rest of our coin to satisfy those back at Larswick. While the cargo was loaded Coel invited Siggi and myself to eat with him. Now that we had the drekar crewed I was less anxious.

"Did you find any problems with the Mercians?"

I drank some of the ale. It tasted different to ours. That must have been the result of the water they used, "Only as a result of us raiding them. We had two battles with the Danes."

His face darkened, "The Danes are the real enemy. We have to watch our borders for they raid us and try to eat into our lands."

"And who is the jarl now?"

"Sámr Ship Killer, the Dragonheart's great grandson. He will be here soon."

"Here?"

He smiled, "When strangers come into the Land of the Wolf then he wishes to meet them. In the past we greeted all with warmth and we were betrayed. Now the jarl greets all. It is said he has inherited some of the powers of his aunt and cousin. He can look into a man's eyes and know what he thinks. Some say he can smell if someone has a bad heart." He shrugged. "I know not but he will be here before dark. Judge for yourselves. You are both welcome to stay here in my hall or, if you prefer, sleep on your drekar."

If we slept in the drekar then the jarl might deem it an insult but if we stayed in the hall then we risked worse. The Norns were spinning. "We will take advantage of your hospitality and stay in the hall."

I looked around the hall and saw that everyone looked healthy and well fed. They had good quality clothes and appeared content. Even the slaves looked happy. We had heard that the Land of the Wolf was a troubled place. What was the truth? Perhaps it was a spell woven by the witch and intended to frighten everyone away. It made sense to me. We enjoyed a pleasant conversation with the headman. He appeared to be genuinely good hearted. I detected no guile in him.

A servant appeared and whispered in the headman's ear. The headman smiled, "The jarl is come."

We stood as the doors were opened and the jarl walked in. He had grey in his beard and his hair but his eyes were bright. Behind him walked two warriors who had to be his sons. They showed what he might have been like twenty years ago. He smiled and held his hand out for me to clasp it. "I am Sámr Ship Killer."

"And I am Erik Larsson. This is my cousin Siggi. We come from the land of the Loyne."

He gestured, "Sit. We have heard of you. These are my sons Ragnar and Haaken."

"I am flattered, lord, but how have you heard of us? We have done nothing of merit."

He smiled, "You stood up to Harald Finehair when many others did not. You have fought against Mercians and Danes even though you were outnumbered. You have sailed beyond the northern sea. You have done much for a clan so young and a navigator who has not had a beard for long."

I was not insulted. "I am sorry, lord, but how do you know such things?"

He leaned forward. "Ylva is the daughter of the great volva, Kara, and the galdramenn, Aiden. She has great power. She sees all that goes on around the Land of the Wolf. She dreams and she has seen you and your people."

I wondered why they did not come to our assistance but I said nothing.

"So what brings you here?"

"We are trading for pine. We need masts."

"You are building drekar or preparing for repairs?"

"Preparing for repairs."

"Good." He drank his ale and stared at me. I got the impression that he was trying to read my mind. "There is danger for you."

"The witch?"

"Ylva did not tell me this. We trade with Dyflin and they know not to antagonise us. The King of Norway has them cowed but a war with the wolf warriors is not to be contemplated lightly. The Lord of Mann is gathering drekar to attack you. We believe they are almost ready. Even now they may be preparing to sail. If you are planning to protect yourselves then do so sooner rather than later."

I glanced at Siggi. Did I dare to trust this jarl? He seemed to know much. I closed my eyes and I thought I heard my father's voice. Perhaps it was wishful thinking but the voice said, '*Speak.*' I put my hands on the table, "The truth is, jarl, that we are too few to defend our land. We are going to go to the land of ice and fire."

He nodded, "Then you truly have courage for even I might baulk at such an undertaking." I saw him studying me as though he was debating what to do. "You can always ask for our protection."

I nodded and smiled, "That is something we did not know. That may change the mind of the folk who live in Larswick."

"I offer this as solution but Ylva has told me that she has dreamed your future and it is not in the land of ice and fire."

"It is here?"

"No Erik. It is in a place where the land turns red before the leaves fall; where mighty waters crash into rivers as wide as oceans." He saw my look of confusion. "Ylva told me. She knows not where this place is except that it is west of here. She has dreamed it and she has seen you there. When she spoke to me, she sounded almost envious of you. She has never envied any that I know of. You are honoured. If any of your people seek sanctuary then they can have it but I fear that you will never settle here. You will only be happy on the sea. That is your destiny." My face must have shown that I was confused. The jarl smiled, "The Dragonheart had a destiny. His was to make the Land of the Wolf a stronghold for the old people of this land and us. Yours is to find a new land. I envy you. I am destined to cling on to this land in the face of enemies from the east, the west and the north. My future will not be glorious. None will sing of my deeds in the future but if you succeed then all will know your name. We will watch the seas for you. Perhaps we can help but we do not have the numbers we once did. *Wyrd.*"

We ate with the jarl and Coel ap Pasgen. It was like being transported to a different time. I wondered what it would be like to speak with Ylva. She was the witch queen of this land. Even as the thought came into my head, I dismissed it. I did, however, have the uncomfortable feeling that her spirit was in the hall watching me. I felt the hairs on the back of my neck stand on end. I learned much as I spoke with the two of them. The jarl told me that they had many mighty drekar. They still raided but did so judiciously. They were well off and did not need much. They both told all that they knew of the land of ice and fire. The visitors who landed brought the stories of the new land.

"My drekar, *'Dragonheart'*, was built to honour my grandsire. She has twenty oars on each side and a red wolf for the sail. When men see her, the battle is half won for the warrior who wielded the sword touched by the gods still inspires fear."

"You have the sword?" I would dearly have liked to touch the legendary blade.

Enigmatically he said, "The sword sleeps until it is needed again!"

"And do you make war on the men of Mann?"

"We have in the past and, if we have to, then we will do so again. We will put to sea in the next day or so and sail to Mann. The new Lord of Mann needs to know who rules these waters and it is not the King of Norway."

I enjoyed the meal although Siggi and I said little. We answered questions which were asked of us and we told them of our battles. We had the greatest compliment we could have when Sámr Ship Killer said, "You are truly Vikings. When you sail from this land may the Allfather be with you."

By the time we rose the jarl and his sons had left. Coel told me that he would ride to the cave beneath the Lough Rigg where he would speak with the witch. I almost said that she should know all that we spoke when I realised what a nonsense that was. The witch lived in a world of spirits. Sámr was her connection to our world.

We set sail with all that we had been sent to acquire. The Allfather sent a powerful wind to help us and we reached our river as quickly as if we had flown. The pine was aboard the drekar and we would leave it there. I left the others to secure the drekar and I hurried, with Siggi, to the hall. We burst in and Snorri and Arne looked startled, "What is amiss, brother? Did they not trade?"

"The Jarl of the Clan of the Wolf was more than helpful. He gave us news. The Lord of Mann has a fleet and they are come to destroy us."

"When?

"He did not know but soon." Arne turned and I said, "One more thing. He is willing to give shelter to all who wish it. We do not need to go to the land of ice and fire."

Arne gave me a sad smile, "We do, brother, for we promised our father. I will summon the clan. We will prepare for departure. If the others do not wish to come then so be it."

"Come Siggi. We will tell our mothers. They will need time to prepare."

Gytha was philosophical about the impending flight but my mother was upset. Edmund comforted her as she said, "My husband's body lies here. How can I desert him?"

Gytha put her arm around her and waved us away, "You are not deserting him. He is there in your three sons. His spirit is in the Otherworld. You leave his body only. If you stay here then when the enemy come you will join him. Would you have that?" She shook her head and put her hand out for Edmund to grasp it.

Siggi and I left. I understood my mother but Gytha was right. We had the living to think of. The horn had sounded and men rushed from the fields, their halls and their homes. I ran down the path to the river and I said to my crew, "My brother is calling the clan. He is offering the chance to go to the land of the Wolf to any who choose it. You may go and listen if you wish."

They grinned, "We are your men Erik Larsson. We go with you."

I looked at the six ship's boys. "It may mean leaving your families."

Dreng nodded, "We decided while you were speaking with the jarl. We are Vikings and we would go with you."

"Then, Eidel and Dreng, you will sail on *'Jötnar'* with Padraig, Aed and their families. You will lead the knarr if they choose to sail." I pointed west, "It may be that the Lord of Mann and his fleet come for us. If they do then I will fight them and allow you to lead the knarr to Ljoðhús. You will wait seven days and if we have not joined you then it means we are dead and the clan is gone."

"We could stay with you!"

"If we fight drekar then a snekke and two knarr will be a liability. Let *'Njörðr'* do that for which she was built by my father, let her fight."

We had much to do. I had the decks lifted so that we could store all that the people would wish to take. We were starting a new life and there would be nothing where we went. While the clan spoke, we loaded the ships. The knarr would only be loaded if their captains chose to come with us.

It was dark by the time that Arne descended to the river. "It is decided. There are eight families who wish to join the Clan of the Wolf. The two knarr come with us. They will carry the animals. When we leave on the morrow then the families who are travelling north will fire Larswick. If the Danes or the Norwegians come, they will have to start anew."

"Good. Padraig and Arne will lead the knarr in case we are attacked. I hope we will not but it is good to have a plan. We sail for Ljoðhús. There is an island there without folk and we can rest for a day before we head to Føroyar."

He clasped my arm. "This is it, brother. We begin the great adventure. I leave the ship to you. I will organize all else."

I dragged my chest close to the steering board. I attached the two ropes from the cleats to the rings on the chest. It was secured. Inside were all that I owned save for my weapons. I had old sea clothes as well as better ones for when we feasted. I had my better seal skin boots and my seal skin cape. My compass and hour glass were protected above and below by my clothes. I had spent every coin I possessed. I had bought arrows in the Land of the Wolf. I could make arrows but the Clan of the Wolf were renowned as archers. It was worth paying for the best. I had bought two spare knives and four bow strings. I needed nothing else. I placed my sword and Saxon dagger inside the chest. If it came to war, I could take them out quickly. I had bought a fur hat in Úlfarrston. When we had sailed north to the seal island, I had needed one. Going further north would guarantee that I would get good use from it. I laid my fur and sleeping blanket on the top before closing and securing the lid. I had had holes drilled in the thwarts to take spears and my bow. This was my drekar now and I would make it suit me. It was not normal to have a shield at the stern but I had my original small shield there. My other one was on the side with those of the rest of the crew. We would be undermanned.

I then walked the drekar as the cargo was loaded. We put the sacks of grain in the hold. They were well tied and protected by barrels. We put some of the ale there too. I heard men grunting and looked as the anvil and blacksmith's tools were brought as well as the scrap iron we would use. I had had some of the ballast taken from around the base of the mast and these heavy items were placed there. It would give her better balance. I did not discard the stones. They would be used to balance the boat better.

Leif came from the hall. He had a bowl of steaming food. "Your brother said to eat! He knows what you are like."

I laughed, "I am hungry and no mistake."

Leif had brought his own food and he wolfed his down too. When we had finished, I pointed to a new chest at the prow. "That is the chest for bowls, spoons and horns. This will be our home for up to a moon. We need to be organised."

While the crew continued to load the hold, the items we would have on deck were stacked on the quay. They would be loaded once the deck was replaced. I had the spare masts and yards laid in the hold too; as well as the spare sail, pine tar and lanolin to grease the sails.

"Captain, the hold is full!"

"Right Sven. Replace the deck and then we can load the barrels of ale and food." As well as meat and pickled fish we had dried beans, fruit and vegetables. The fruit and the vegetables would soon go off but we would consume them before that happened. When they were secured to the sides of the drekar I sent a message to Arne that the passengers could board before dawn. I knew that many would like some sleep on land before we set sail. For myself, I curled up in a ball by my chest and I slept. It was not a deep sleep but I still dreamed.

It was a silent dream.

A beautiful white-haired old woman floated down from the top of my mast. She stroked my head and woke me. I was sailing through seas filled with large lumps of ice which were bigger than my drekar. I was terrified but the old woman just smiled and touched my hand. I wondered why and then I saw that she was helping me to steer the ship. A bank of fog loomed up. I went to lower the sail but she restrained me. As we sailed through a wall of mist, I feared we would strike a ship of ice. Then the mist cleared and I saw trees higher than any I had seen rising from the white sandy beach. When I turned to thank the lady, she was gone. I woke.

It was dark but I heard the sound of voices as Arne led the women down to the drekar. It was time and I had slept longer than

I had expected. Arne grinned as I stood and held my shoulders. "This is the great adventure brother. We will do what no other warrior from Orkneyjar has ever done."

"And I am glad to have you at my side." I saw that Fótr clung on to my mother's hand. he was almost five. "And by the time he is five we will have a new home and a new life!"

Chapter 18

As the last of the men came aboard, I could smell fresh bread. Gytha smiled as she and Snorri climbed aboard. She handed me a basket. "Here Erik. This is the last bread we will have for some time. Enjoy."

"Thank you, lady."

"And where is our home to be?"

"The boys are rigging a shelter for you by the mast fish. It is the widest part of the drekar."

"Thoughtful as ever. You should be married!"

I shook my head as a sudden flaring could be seen on the headland. Snorri said, "We are giving Larswick a Viking funeral. Already the women and children march north. When the walls are afire the men will join them. We have burned our old home. Let us hope we can find a new one!"

I carried the weight of the clan on my shoulders. Cupping my hands, I shouted, "Padraig, are the knarr ready?"

"Aye, captain."

"Then follow us out." It was dark but it was high tide and the thin grey behind us promised sun soon. I hoped for an empty sea. "Hoist the sail!" As the red and white striped sail was raised everyone cheered. "Cast off!" When the sail was tied off the ropes securing us to the land were untied and Halsten and Rek leapt aboard. We left the land and headed down the estuary to the sea. "Sven, prow. Stig, masthead! Halsten, and Rek man the stays!" The four ship's boys scurried off. I braced myself with my feet apart. Once we left the land and entered the sea then there would be movement. We now knew the waters well. It was high tide now and the sands to the north of us would be hidden. They were, as we knew well, perilously close to the surface. We would head due west before heading north and west.

I glanced astern and saw the snekke leading the two laden knarr. The knarr would determine our speed. Like our drekar, they were shallow draughted but they were both wider to accommodate cargo. Padraig was a good length behind us and the two a further length back. I could see the flames flickering as the fire consumed Larswick.

By the time we reached the sea, I saw the sky beginning to lighten in the east. The breeze was coming from the south and west. The smoke from Larswick headed back across the land. The wind would aid us as we headed north. The seas were black ahead of us but becoming lighter by the minute. I had my compass and hour glass already on my chest. When the sun shone, I would begin the hour glass. It was laid on its side and was as though time had stood still. There was power in turning the glass. It was as though I controlled time. I knew I did not but I enjoyed the feeling. The sun suddenly broke the land behind us.

Stig shouted, "There is a sail to the north and west." I looked up and saw him pointing to confirm.

Arne came aft with Siggi and Snorri. My face told Arne that I was concerned but we seemed to know each other's thoughts anyway. "You are the navigator. Can we outrun him?"

"If he is alone, we need not outrun him. With the snekke snapping at him we could defeat him but he may not be. I would have the warriors arm themselves and tell the others to take shelter. The Jarl of the Land of the Wolf warned us of danger. We would be foolish to ignore it."

"Aye! Come, warriors. Let us prepare for battle!"

I turned and looked astern, "Padraig, there is a drekar. Lead the knarr to stay to the steerboard of us but keep well astern of us for I may need the sea room."

He waved his acknowledgment. I saw him and Aed don their helmets. Helga did so too. She might be with child but she was a warrior and she would fight. I opened my chest. I would not need the compass and hourglass for a while. I put them inside and, one handed while I steered, took out my sword and helmet. I saw the Saxon dagger. It drew my fingers to it and I picked it up and slipped it inside my sea boot. I closed the lid of the chest. Using my weight to hold the steering board in place I donned my helmet and strapped on my sword. There was a piece of rope ready to fix the steering board to the gunwale. I could fight while *'Njörðr'* steered herself. I saw that the warriors were armed. We had fewer of them than we might have hoped. Others were on the knarr.

"Captain, it is more than one drekar. They are travelling in line astern. Look!"

I peered ahead and saw a line of drekar gradually filling the horizon. They were spreading out like hunters to encircle their prey. I looked at the sky and the pennant. The breeze would bring them quickly to us. I counted six ships already. I had said we could beat one in a straight fight but not six. I kept heading towards them. We had only one chance. I turned astern and shouted, "Padraig, bring the knarr land side of us. There are at least six drekar. We turn to steerboard soon. We will use the sands. Watch for my signal."

This time he cupped his hands and called, "Aye, Erik!"

A seventh and an eighth ship appeared. They were rapidly approaching us. Arne came to the steering board. "You cannot do as you did with the snekke, brother. They will ram us and grapple."

"I know. I am using the sands." I pointed to the deceivingly calm waters which covered the shellfish sands. "We will have more speed and, unless I miss my guess, Bjorn Bjornson will have brought his largest drekar filled with as many men as he could pack into them. We are shallower draughted. Trust the drekar."

He nodded and patted my shoulder, "I do but I trust you more."

When they were less than a mile or so away, I waved my arm and then put the steering board over to sail due north. It was as though we were a horse pricked with a spur and we leapt forward. The snekke was as fast but the knarr took longer to move. The snekke was almost level with our stern but the two knarr were strung out. It could not be helped. The line of ships immediately turned. They would be travelling even faster now for they would have the advantage of the wind behind. Four of them turned north and east as they tried to cut us off. The others continued on their original course. We had not a scrap of weed on our hull and we had sealed her well. She flew. It was though she did not sail through the water but on it. I now began to fear for the knarr. They were three lengths adrift of us and becoming detached. The last four drekar could take them.

I tied the steering board to the cleat. We would sail north now until we hit the coast of the Land of the Wolf. By then the battle would be over and I would either untie the rope or I would be in Valhalla explaining to my father how I managed to destroy the Clan of the Fox. I knew that we were sailing over the sands. I could see them below the stern but we were shallow draughted. I would have to turn soon or the tide would catch us out. My plan was working. The bigger drekar had run out oars and used them, along with the sail, to head north. The four which were further south now adjusted their course so that when we turned, they would be able to pick us off from behind. I shaded my eyes from the sun. I did not recognise any of the drekar. The Lord of Mann had new ships. They were all too far away for me to see them. When I saw a warrior with a metal raven on his helmet then I knew that would be Bjorn. He liked to show off.

I could see that we would collide soon enough for the drekar ahead had almost cut us off. I untied the rope. The first drekar suddenly hit the sands. The mast seemed to judder and then the stays broke. The mast came down and the drekar slewed around. The others were travelling too quickly. A voice in my head told me to turn. It was the voice of a woman and was melodious. As I put the steering board over to sail north and west, I saw the other two grind to a halt on the sands. The tide was receding slightly. I felt a subtle bump beneath our hull. We had almost struck the sands but the Norns had spun and I had turned at the right time. I thought the last drekar must escape too when it suddenly stopped as the receding tide trapped it on the sinking sands.

We now had clear water but the knarr were still strung out. We could escape the four drekar but the knarr would not. Already the sands had gripped the hulls of the four drekar which had grounded. The snekke and the knarr would pass within four lengths of them but their crews would be impotent. Their only chance was to wait for the next high tide and have other ships drag them off.

"Captain, one of the drekar has changed course. She sails due north."

"Watch her!"

I glanced to larboard. The disaster which had struck their four consorts had made the three drekar which lay astern of us more cautious. They did not wish to risk the sands. The two knarr were like a sea anchor. The snekke and the drekar could fly away but not so the knarr. The three drekar would catch them and we would have to fight the single drekar which now sailed obliquely across our bows to cut us off. We could not turn to steerboard for fear of striking the sands and if we turned to larboard then we would be attacked by three drekar.

"Captain, there are four more drekar approaching from the west!"

My heart sank. The Norns had, indeed, been spinning. Eight drekar to one doomed us. Surrender was out of the question. We would sail and fight until we died. Suddenly the three drekar closest to us changed course and began to sail parallel to us. The drekar ahead was just eight lengths away and on the same course. Whichever way we turned she would cut us off but I did not understand the manoeuvre of the other three drekar. I could see the new drekar which were arriving. There was something about the one which led them. "Stig, describe the largest drekar now approaching from the west."

There was a pause, "She is large and has a red wolf on her sail."

I shouted, "It is the *'Dragonheart'*! Sámr Ship Killer comes to our aid as he promised!" Arne turned to look at me. I pointed ahead, "We fight that drekar and we are free."

Arne nodded, "Get your bows!" He came aft. "Brother let me use yours!"

I laughed, "Aye, it is hard to steer and to loose arrows."

He took my bow and opened my chest to take out ten arrows. He went to the larboard side with the other bowmen and slingers. Glancing to the land I saw that the tide was racing out and the drekar were stuck in the mud. I saw some men floundering in the treacherous sands. The land and the sea were fighting them. To larboard I saw that the Clan of the Wolf were attacking the three drekar. Sámr Ship Killer would destroy them; of that, I had no doubt. The men of Mann would learn of the power of the land made by the Dragonheart.

I saw that the drekar ahead was turning. If she continued on her course, she risked being caught by the drekar of the wolf. She was going to attack us. I tied off the steering board and shaded my eyes. I saw that by the stern was a warrior with a raven topped helmet. "Arne, it is Bjorn Bjornson!"

I heard his voice, "Then we shall avenge our father!"

"Stig, Sven, by the steering board! Halsten and Rek guard the women." I knew that the enemy would try to take control of the steering board. If they could kill me and capture the stern then the drekar would be theirs. The battle to the south and west of us would rage on. Our own battle would be settled long before that one was concluded. The enemy drekar put his steering board over to sail parallel to us. The ship then began to ease over. They were putting distance between themselves and the Clan of the Wolf and closing with us. They were bigger than we were and would be able to board us.

Arne shouted, "Loose!" Arrows and stones began to thud into the shields and bodies of the crew.

Stig and Sven joined me. They both had short swords. I took my small shield from the stern. "We defend the steering board with our lives. Here the fighting will be the fiercest."

"Do we not lower the sail?"

"No, Sven, we let *'Njörðr'* join the fight. They will lower their sail and our drekar will drag them." I pointed to the two hand axes. "If they use ropes to grapple us then sever them. We fight for our lives. We take no prisoners. Strike to kill!"

Their stern was now just half a length away and I saw Karl the Lame. He was on his father's ship. He pointed his sword at me. I drew my own sword and pointed it at him. We would end here what was begun on *'Moon Dragon'*.

Four of the men of Mann were a little eager and clambered to cling to the stays. Arrows struck them and they plunged to the sea. We had women aboard and these pirates saw them as plunder. I saw Gytha and the other women had armed themselves. If the pirates tried to take them, they would see that our women had teeth!

I heard Bjorn Bjornson shout, "Lower the sail and put the steering board over!"

As the drekar closed with us I saw ropes and grappling hooks snake across the black waters. Even as they were thrown those throwing them were hit by stones and arrows. Arne and the others would use their bows and slings until the last moment. It was better to kill the enemy on their ship than ours. It meant that the three of us would be alone for the first moments of the battle. Then I saw my uncle, Snorri, lead Finn the Scar and Butar Beer Belly. They ran to the steering board just as the drekar's stern struck ours. My uncle and his two oar brothers stood between me and the pirates. I sheathed my sword and took a spear from the rail. I hurled it at the warrior who tried to leap aboard. I hit him in the chest while he was in the air. He landed in a heap on the deck. Sven ran and took the spear from the body. As the next pirates jumped aboard, he held the spear above him. A huge warrior landed on the spear. His body covered Sven's and then the battle started.

I drew my sword and stood next to Butar. A half-naked warrior wearing a full-face helmet and wielding a long sword ran at me. The drekar came to my aid as the sail pulled us around and he lost his footing. I slashed across his middle. My blade bit into his flesh but he continued to swing his sword. I took the blow on my small shield and my arm shivered. His own blood was making the deck slippery. I kept my feet as I brought my sword over to strike his shield. He slipped to the deck as he fell and his blade embedded itself in the gunwale. I hacked across his throat.

Bjorn Bjornson and his oathsworn leapt aboard and headed for us. I saw Karl the Lame clamber awkwardly across the two drekar. He would come for me. The only men I recognised, of those that boarded us, were Karl, his father and his father's oathsworn. Apart from those eight, the rest were just the sweepings of Mann.

I shouted, "Arne!"

There were just four warriors facing eight. If we could defeat these eight then we stood a chance for the rest might decide that discretion was the better part of valour and flee. I saw a warrior lunge at Butar Beer Belly's unprotected side. I brought my sword down on the hearth weru's right arm. He had quick reactions and managed to turn and block the blow. Butar's side was safe and he continued to fight two other warriors. Arne and Siggi led men to come to the aid of Snorri and the others. The oathsworn I had attacked tried to turn. As he was still off balance, I punched him in the side of the head with my small shield. As he reeled, I punched him again. He fell backwards into the advancing Karl the Lame. I brought my sword backhand across his unprotected neck and he fell to the deck in a pool of his own blood.

Karl the Lame swung at my shield with his war axe. It hit it so hard that it dented the boss and cracked the wood. "I will have my vengeance for my wound. I will not kill you. I will maim you and we will take you back to Mann to be a slave used by all. You will beg for a death but it will not come!"

"Fight, for your words are empty air." I swung at his head but he brought up his shield to block the blow. The fighting was intense all around us but, behind Karl the Lame, I saw Eidel climbing up the steering board of the enemy drekar. There was no one there. In his hand he carried a small axe. He was going to sever the steering board withy! Eidel was a ship's boy but he had heart. Even though Karl was bigger and better armed than I was I drew hope from Eidel's brave act.

Karl the Lame hit my shield again and all that held it together was the leather strap. I stepped back and he took it as a sign of weakness. I was making him move away from the larboard side and towards a pool of blood. In his eagerness to close with me he was too quick and his good foot slipped on the blood. Instead of slashing at him I lunged and my sword struck the lower part of his mail byrnie. As he twisted the tip caught in the links and the sword was pulled from my hand! I was almost defenceless. I saw the joy on his face as he drew his axe back to swing at my leg. He was going to cripple me. I did the only thing I could. I threw my broken shield at his head and when he pulled up his axe to block it, I dived at him and knocked him to the ground. He was bigger and stronger than me but he wore mail and had a bad leg. Both would make it hard for him to rise. I drew the Saxon dagger I had taken from him. Even as he tried to push me off, I rammed it under his armpit. It grated off his shoulder blade and he screamed. I put my left knee on his right arm, and held the dagger above him. "Remember this? It will be the last thing you see!" I drove it through his right eye and into his skull. I quickly stood and recovered my sword. I was just in time to see Arne and Snorri drive their swords through Bjorn Bjornson at the same time. With his oathsworn all dead the other pirates jumped back aboard their own ship. Stig and Sven had managed to cut the ropes binding us. As the wounded aboard *'Njörðr'* were despatched I sheathed my sword and ran to untie the steering board.

The drekar of Mann lay almost dead in the water. Her sail was furled and she had no rudder. I glanced to the south east and saw that Sámr Ship Killer's drekar was heading towards the pirates. Eidel had not only saved us he had doomed the pirates. I put the steering board over to sail around the drifting drekar towards the north and west. The wind took us.

I saw that Butar was wounded. Gytha was tending to him. There were other dead warriors too but the bulk of the dead were the men of Mann. Arne came up to me, "What happened to the enemy ship?"

I laughed, "I trained the ship's boys well. Eidel climbed the steering board and hacked through the withy! Thanks to the Clan of the Wolf and Eidel's quick thinking, we have a chance!"

As we sailed towards the open sea, I clutched my hammer of Thor and I thanked both my father and Ylva the witch. I knew that both had aided me. The spirits were with us and I finally believed that we might make it to the land of ice and fire.

Epilogue

We stopped for the night on the beach of an uninhabited island south of Dyrøy. We would be safe and we could strip the dead and dispose of their bodies in the sea. I also wished to check the hull. The drekar had struck us hard. While food was prepared and the bodies of the men of Mann thrown into the sea, I took some pine tar to check for damage. One of the strakes, thankfully above the water line, had sprung. While Sven packed it with wool and feathers, I liberally coated it in pine tar. I was grateful that the collision had not cost us more. When I reached the fire, my brother had saved a place between him and Siggi.

"You were right about Sámr Ship Killer. I had wondered if he was playing a game with us."

I frowned, "Arne, I looked into his eyes and I saw that he spoke the truth. Was it me you did not believe? Did you think I made up the story?"

"No, brother, but you are too trusting. You believe the best in people. I see the worst. Now we are free from the curse of Mann and we have a new future."

I nodded as I ate the stew. "And we have had the easiest part of the voyage. From now on pirates and drekar will be the least of our worries."

"The sea will be that bad?"

"The sea will be unknown. If there is the sun and the stars then this will be a voyage as easy as sailing to Norway. If there is cloud, or fog or both then who knows?"

That night I put away my sword and helmet. I had taken Karl the Lame's byrnie. That, too, went into my chest. I was not sure I would ever wear it but it was a reminder of how close I had come to death. I took out my compass and hourglass. I took Stig and Sven to one side and explained to them how the compass worked. "When we sail one of you will be at my side. You will turn the hourglass and hand me the compass and charcoal. I will mark our position. This compass is the only way we will find the land of ice and fire. Halsten and Rek can be lookout and tend to the passengers."

"Aye, Captain."

The waters through which we first sailed were familiar to most of those aboard. We spied small settlements and fishing boats but the drekar of the King of Norway were not to be seen. The wind continued to aid us. The long days helped us and at the end of the third day out of Dyrøy we saw the seabirds and the islands of Føroyar. They would be our home for seven days or so. We would hunt seals and collect shellfish. I hoped to make the journey to the land of ice and fire in less than seven days but if we did not manage that then we would need food and water. The ale was almost gone. We had had no showers and so we would have to collect water from the island. Gytha insisted that we boil it before we barrelled it. She did not say why but she was a volva and we trusted her.

I landed us at the beach I had used with Padraig and Aed. We made a bigger camp this time and while the men hunted the women and children prepared the cauldrons of water we would use to cook and salt the meat. I sat with Padraig and the two knarr captains, Pridbjørn and Sighwarth. I took out the hare skin map I had made. "From what I have learned at both Orkneyjar and Úlfarrston this land of ice and fire appears to be much bigger than this group of islands. It is between four and ten days from here."

Sighwarth asked, "And what if we do not find it?"

"The witch, Ylva, believed that we would find it. I trust in her. We will find it." He nodded. We trusted our volvas and witches. "Padraig you will be the sheepdog. From now on the knarr sail close behind us. You will watch their stern. I have pots we can fill with burning coals. If we feed the fire then it will burn and be a beacon for you to follow. The nights are short and we do not have to burn them for long but we cannot lose sight of one another."

Pridbjørn asked, "And fog?"

"I have no answer for that save that we use a horn to signal our position." I shrugged, "There are no certainties. We are in the hands of the Allfather and we hope that the spell the Norns have spun is one which brings us safe."

The seal hunt was a great success. With the whole clan helping, we filled three large barrels with the oil. Four other barrels contained their flesh and we had plenty of bones. We would make bone arrows and bone spears. If we were lucky then we might find iron but none who had been to the island had found any. We could not guarantee it.

Snorri advised Arne to make a blót. We sacrificed one of the chickens. As we had captured and caged twelve or so ducks then we would have eggs on the voyage but a chicken was a worthy sacrifice. We left in daylight on a day when the sun shone. This was not a time for taking chances.

The wind had veered and now came from the north west. It was a cold wind for it came from the north and the land of ice. It meant that we did not travel as fast as we might have hoped but the sun helped me to keep track of our position and we ploughed on steadily west. The lights were used at night time. We had kindling and we had wood. I kept glancing astern to ensure that the knarr were close. I slept in two-hour stints. I was spelled by Snorri, Olaf and Arne. They found the experience harder than I did. I was now comfortable at the steering board. *'Njörðr'* had forgiven me for sailing in *'Jötnar'* and responded well to every touch.

I had heard that a captain called Floki had used ravens to help him find the island. We had no such aid but Coel had spoken to one of his crew. He said that the fire on the island came from below the ground and filled the air with the smell of cooked eggs which were bad. More than that, he said that the few harbours they had found were often wreathed in smoke which resembled mist. The best harbour was called, 'Smoky Bay'. It lay on the south of the island. There was a thriving colony there. We did not mind neighbours but the clan wanted somewhere without other people. I intended to sail until our noses told us we were close. The gods had sent this wind to aid us. So long as it blew from the north and west then it would bring the smell of the island to us. We just had to find it.

The hardest thing for most of the passengers was the emptiness of the ocean. There was nothing to be seen. We had seen no sea birds since a day after leaving Føroyar. We had seen whales and seals. We had spied dolphins and sharks. That boded well for we could go to sea and hunt them. What we needed was the sight of a bird which nested on land. The passengers huddled by the mast. The exception was Gytha. One night as I sat alone at the steering board, she came to sit with me. She had made, while we were on Føroyar, some honeyed beer. She put some in a pot and placed it on the clay light pot to warm. When it was ready, she handed me the warmed drink.

"Here, nephew, is a treat. I hope there are bees in this land of ice and fire. If there are then we shall make mead."

"I know not what there will be."

She smiled and put her hand on my knee. "It is a stop along our journey. When we were in the battle with the pirates, I felt the mind and thoughts of Ylva. She is the most powerful of witches. She told me that there is a home waiting for those with the courage to step into the unknown. Your brother is a great warrior but you are the one with the greatest courage for you pit yourself against the sea and the Norns. Never doubt what you do." She took the empty pot from me. "Your mother, I fear, will never recover from the death of your father. She is still a Saxon at heart and she almost stayed at Larswick. If you need a crutch then use me. I will always listen."

That conversation changed me. Knowing that Ylva believed in me gave me great confidence. When the fog came two days later I did not panic. I blew the horn to warn the others and then shouted for the other ships to close up on our stern. The wind had almost stopped and so I had the oars run out. Lines were passed to the knarr and snekke. One advantage of fog was that while there was little wind the sea would be relatively calm and so we sailed on through the mist. Sven hung over the prow and Stig sat on the spar. Halsten and Rek peered into the murk. Snorri sang our song and those on the knarr and the snekke joined in. It was eerie as we sailed in a grey and chilled world.

The Clan of the Fox has no king
We never bow or kiss a ring
We fled our home to start anew
We are strong in heart though we are few

Lars the jarl fears no foe
He sailed the ship from Finehair's woe

Drekar came to end our quest
Erik the navigator proved the best
When Danes appeared to thwart our start
The Clan of the Fox showed their heart
While we healed the sad and the sick
We built our home, Larswick

The Clan of the Fox has no king
We never bow or kiss a ring
We fled our home to start anew
We are strong in heart though we are few

When Halfdan came with warriors armed
The Clan of the Fox was not alarmed
We had our jarl, a mighty man
But the Norns they spun they had a plan
When the jarl slew Halfdan the Dane
His last few blows caused great pain
With heart and arm he raised his hand
'The Clan of the Fox is a mighty band!'

The Clan of the Fox has no king
We never bow or kiss a ring
We fled our home to start anew
We are strong in heart though we are few

Suddenly Stig silenced the song as he shouted, "Ware steerboard, Captain!"

I trusted my crew and I put the board hard to larboard. Out of the fog a wall of ice which seemed to reach to the sky loomed out of the sea. I had never seen such a large piece of ice. I watched the hour glass half empty and we still had not passed it. I wondered if this was one of the ships of ice Coel ap Pasgen had told me of or was it the island? When the ice disappeared, I risked putting the board to steerboard. I trusted Stig and Sven to keep us safe. We still saw nothing.

Arne shouted, "Brother, the men tire. Can we not rest?"

The woman's voice in my head told me to sail on. I said nothing. I peered ahead. I saw shadows and then as I sniffed, I smelled rotten eggs. "Stig, what is to steerboard?"

"Nothing, Captain I... I see birds! The mist is clearing! I see land. Captain, you have found it!"

Almost as though by magic the fog parted and I saw the treeless rock that was the island of ice and fire. Sven shouted, "There is a beach! I see seals!"

I put the steering board over and, as the mist evaporated, I saw, ahead, our new home. As a flock of seabirds took flight and seals dived from rocks into the sea, I knew that the first part of our journey was over. We had found the land which would keep us safe from King Harald Finehair but my talk with Gytha told me that this would just be a stop on our journey. As the crew and passengers cheered and banged the deck, I clutched my hammer of Thor, "Thank you father and Ylva. Your voices brought us here. Now it is up to me." There were new lands to find and perhaps, even a new world.

The End

Norse Calendar

Gormánuður October 14th - November 13th
Ýlir November 14th - December 13th
Mörsugur December 14th - January 12th
Þorri - January 13th - February 11th
Gói - February 12th - March 13th
Einmánuður - March 14th - April 13th
Harpa April 14th - May 13th
Skerpla - May 14th - June 12th
Sólmánuður - June 13th - July 12th
Heyannir - July 13th - August 14th
Tvímánuður - August 15th - September 14th
Haustmánuður September 15th-October 13th

Glossary

Afen- River Avon

Afon Hafron- River Severn in Welsh

Àird Rosain – Ardrossan (On the Clyde Estuary)

Balley Chashtal -Castleton (Isle of Man)

Bebbanburgh- Bamburgh Castle, Northumbria also known as Din Guardi in the ancient tongue

Beck- a stream

Beinn na bhFadhla- Benbecula in the Outer Hebrides

Blót – a blood sacrifice made by a jarl

Bondi- Viking farmers who fight

Bjarnarøy –Great Bernera (Bear Island)

Byrnie- a mail or leather shirt reaching down to the knees

Càrdainn Ros -Cardross (Argyll)

Chape- the tip of a scabbard

Cyninges-tūn – Coniston. It means the estate of the king (Cumbria)

Dùn Èideann –Edinburgh (Gaelic)

Drekar- a Dragon ship (a Viking warship) pl. drekar

Duboglassio –Douglas, Isle of Man

Dun Holme- Durham

Dún Lethglaise - Downpatrick (Northern Ireland)

Dyrøy –Jura (Inner Hebrides)

Dyflin- Old Norse for Dublin

Eoforwic- Saxon for York

Føroyar- Faroe Islands

Fey- having second sight

Firkin- a barrel containing eight gallons (usually beer)

Fret-a sea mist

Fyrd-the Saxon levy

Gaill- Irish for foreigners

Galdramenn- wizard

Hersey- Isle of Arran

Hersir- a Viking landowner and minor noble. It ranks below a jarl

Hí- Iona (Gaelic)

Hjáp - Shap- Cumbria (Norse for stone circle)

Hoggs or Hogging- when the pressure of the wind causes the stern or the bow to droop

Hrams-a – Ramsey, Isle of Man

Hundred- Saxon military organisation. (One hundred men from an area-led by a thegn or gesith)

Hwitebi - Norse for Whitby, North Yorkshire

Jarl- Norse earl or lord

Joro-goddess of the earth

kjerringa - Old Woman- the solid block in which the mast rested

Knarr- a merchant ship or a coastal vessel

Kyrtle-woven top

Ljoðhús- Lewis

Lochlannach – Irish for Northerners (Vikings)

Lough- Irish lake

Lundenburh/Lundenburgh- the walled burh built around the old Roman fort

Lundenwic - London

Mast fish- two large racks on a ship designed to store the mast when not required

Midden- a place where they dumped human waste

Miklagård - Constantinople

Njoror- God of the sea

Nithing- A man without honour (Saxon)

Odin- The "All Father" God of war, also associated with wisdom, poetry, and magic (The Ruler of the gods).

Orkneyjar-Orkney

Ran- Goddess of the sea

Roof rock- slate

Saami- the people who live in what is now Northern Norway/Sweden

Samhain- a Celtic festival of the dead between 31st October and1st November (Halloween)

Scree- loose rocks in a glacial valley

Seax – short sword

Sennight- seven nights- a week

Sheerstrake- the uppermost strake in the hull

Sheet- a rope fastened to the lower corner of a sail

Shroud- a rope from the masthead to the hull amidships

Skeggox – an axe with a shorter beard on one side of the blade

Skíð -the isle of Skye

Skreið- stock fish (any fish which is preserved)

Smoky Bay- Reykjavik

Snekke- a small warship

Stad- Norse settlement

Stays- ropes running from the mast-head to the bow

Strake- the wood on the side of a drekar

Suðreyjar – Southern Hebrides (Islay)

Syllingar Insula, Syllingar- Scilly Isles

Tarn- small lake (Norse)

The Norns- The three sisters who weave webs of intrigue for men

Thing-Norse for a parliament or a debate (Tynwald in Isle of Man)

Thor's day- Thursday

Threttanessa- a drekar with 13 oars on each side.

Thrall- slave

Trenail- a round wooden peg used to secure strakes

Tynwald- the Parliament on the Isle of Man

Úlfarrberg- Helvellyn

Úlfarrland- Cumbria

Úlfarrston- Ulverston

Ullr-Norse God of Hunting

Ulfheonar-an elite Norse warrior who wore a wolf skin over his armour

Veisafjǫrðr – Wexford (Ireland)

Volva- a witch or healing woman in Norse culture

Waeclinga Straet- Watling Street (A5)

Walhaz -Norse for the Welsh (foreigners)

Waite- a Viking word for farm

Withy- the mechanism connecting the steering board to the ship

Woden's day- Wednesday

Wulfhere-Old English for Wolf Army

Wyddfa-Snowdon

Wykinglo- Wicklow (Ireland)

Wyrd- Fate

Wyrme- Norse for Dragon
Yard- a timber from which the sail is suspended
Ynys Enlli- Bardsey Island
Ynys Môn-Anglesey

Historical Note

The Vikings were a complicated people. Forget movies where they wear horned helmets and spend all their time pillaging. They did pillage and they could be cruel but they were also traders and explorers. The discovery of Iceland and after that Greenland and America has been put down to the attempt by King Harald Finehair to create a Viking Empire. True Vikings never liked kings. Rather than be taxed they sought new lands. Iceland was empty and bare but they made it their home.

http://www.hurstwic.org/history/articles/daily_living/text/Demo graphics.htm is a good website with some interesting stats. In 1000 AD 75% of Vikings were under 50 and under 15s represented half! A boy was considered a fully-grown man by the time he was 16. A man could be a judge at the age of 12. Helgi and Bergr were 10 and 12 when they avenged their father by killing his killer. We cannot imagine their world.

The compass I refer to was used in the Viking times. There is a Timewatch programme made by the BBC in which Robin Knox Johnston uses the compass to sail from Norway to Iceland. He was just half a mile out when he arrived.

St. Elphin is Warrington. The name Warrington is Norse. The nearest Saxon settlement whose name survives is Wilderspool. The same is true of St. Oswald. Its name now is Winwick; once again a Viking name.

This is the first of a trilogy. Erik will get to America. This is a work of fiction. I have no time machine. My time machine is the books I write! Enjoy!

I used the following books for research:

- Vikings- Life and Legends -British Museum
- Saxon, Norman and Viking by Terence Wise (Osprey)
- The Vikings (Osprey) -Ian Heath
- Byzantine Armies 668-1118 (Osprey)-Ian Heath
- Romano-Byzantine Armies 4th-9th Century (Osprey) - David Nicholle

- The Walls of Constantinople AD 324-1453 (Osprey) - Stephen Turnbull
- Viking Longship (Osprey) - Keith Durham
- The Vikings in England Anglo-Danish Project
- Anglo Saxon Thegn AD 449-1066- Mark Harrison (Osprey)
- Viking Hersir- 793-1066 AD - Mark Harrison (Osprey)
- Hadrian's Wall- David Breeze (English Heritage)
- National Geographic- March 2017
- Time Life Seafarers-The Vikings Robert Wernick

Griff Hosker
November 2018

Other books
by
Griff Hosker

If you enjoyed reading this book, then why not read another one by the author?
Ancient History

The Sword of Cartimandua Series (Germania and Britannia 50 A.D. – 128 A.D.)
Ulpius Felix- Roman Warrior (prequel)
Book 1 The Sword of Cartimandua
Book 2 The Horse Warriors
Book 3 Invasion Caledonia
Book 4 Roman Retreat
Book 5 Revolt of the Red Witch
Book 6 Druid's Gold
Book 7 Trajan's Hunters
Book 8 The Last Frontier
Book 9 Hero of Rome
Book 10 Roman Hawk
Book 11 Roman Treachery
Book 12 Roman Wall
Book 13 Roman Courage

The Aelfraed Series
(Britain and Byzantium 1050 A.D. - 1085 A.D.)
Book 1 Housecarl
Book 2 Outlaw
Book 3 Varangian

The Wolf Warrior series
(Britain in the late 6th Century)
Book 1 Saxon Dawn
Book 2 Saxon Revenge
Book 3 Saxon England
Book 4 Saxon Blood

Book 5 Saxon Slayer
Book 6 Saxon Slaughter
Book 7 Saxon Bane
Book 8 Saxon Fall: Rise of the Warlord
Book 9 Saxon Throne
Book 10 Saxon Sword

The Dragon Heart Series
Book 1 Viking Slave
Book 2 Viking Warrior
Book 3 Viking Jarl
Book 4 Viking Kingdom
Book 5 Viking Wolf
Book 6 Viking War
Book 7 Viking Sword
Book 8 Viking Wrath
Book 9 Viking Raid
Book 10 Viking Legend
Book 11 Viking Vengeance
Book 12 Viking Dragon
Book 13 Viking Treasure
Book 14 Viking Enemy
Book 15 Viking Witch
Book 16 Viking Blood
Book 17 Viking Weregeld
Book 18 Viking Storm
Book 19 Viking Warband
Book 20 Viking Shadow
Book 21 Viking Legacy
Book 22 Viking Clan
Book 23 Viking Bravery

The Norman Genesis Series
Hrolf the Viking
Horseman
The Battle for a Home
Revenge of the Franks
The Land of the Northmen
Ragnvald Hrolfsson

Brothers in Blood
Lord of Rouen
Drekar in the Seine
Duke of Normandy
The Duke and the King

New World Series
Blood on the Blade
Across the Seas

**The Anarchy Series England
1120-1180**
English Knight
Knight of the Empress
Northern Knight
Baron of the North
Earl
King Henry's Champion
The King is Dead
Warlord of the North
Enemy at the Gate
The Fallen Crown
Warlord's War
Kingmaker
Henry II
Crusader
The Welsh Marches
Irish War
Poisonous Plots
The Princes' Revolt
Earl Marshal

**Border Knight
1182-1300**
Sword for Hire
Return of the Knight
Baron's War
Magna Carta
Welsh Wars

Henry III
The Bloody Border
Baron's Crusade

Lord Edward's Archer
Lord Edward's Archer

Struggle for a Crown
1360- 1485
Blood on the Crown
To Murder A King
The Throne
King Henry IV

Modern History

The Napoleonic Horseman Series
Book 1 Chasseur a Cheval
Book 2 Napoleon's Guard
Book 3 British Light Dragoon
Book 4 Soldier Spy
Book 5 1808: The Road to Coruña
Book 6 Talavera
Waterloo

The Lucky Jack American Civil War series
Rebel Raiders
Confederate Rangers
The Road to Gettysburg

The British Ace Series
1914
1915 Fokker Scourge
1916 Angels over the Somme
1917 Eagles Fall
1918 We will remember them
From Arctic Snow to Desert Sand
Wings over Persia

Combined Operations series
1940-1945
Commando
Raider
Behind Enemy Lines
Dieppe
Toehold in Europe
Sword Beach
Breakout
The Battle for Antwerp
King Tiger
Beyond the Rhine
Korea
Korean Winter

Other Books
Carnage at Cannes (a thriller)
Great Granny's Ghost (Aimed at 9-14-year-old young people)
Adventure at 63-Backpacking to Istanbul

For more information on all of the books then please visit the author's web site at www.griffhosker.com where there is a link to contact him.